I0685731

THE GREAT BETRAYAL

MICHAEL G. THOMAS

© 2013 Michael G. Thomas

The right of Michael G. Thomas to be identified as the Author of the Work has been asserted by him in accordance with the Copyright, Designs and Patents Act 1988.

First published in the United Kingdom in 2013 by Swordworks Books.

ISBN 978-1-911092-27-8

Typeset by Swordworks Books
Printed and bound in the UK & US
A catalogue record of this book is available from the British Library

Cover design by Swordworks Books
www.swordworks.co.uk

THE GREAT BETRAYAL

MICHAEL G. THOMAS

CHAPTER ONE

The four racial groups of the Helions purported to represent all of their culture. The ANS Conqueror Incident of 360CC, however, revealed a massive underclass known as the Zathee who had been exploited for centuries. These people had fought as cannon fodder in the wars with the Biomechs and now lived as little more than servants.

The Zathee Insurrection, as it soon became known, spread through the entire planet of Helios before igniting slave revolts on other Helion worlds. Within three months, the flames of revolution had spread as far as the empires of the Anicinàbe, Byotai, and even the Khreenk.

History of Slave Labor

The dull blue star sent a shimmering glint of light over the thousands of ruined and smashed ships. The ancient graveyard circled the system's single sterile planet like a cloud of pestilence that betrayed some apocalyptical battle hundreds of years earlier. One capital ship waited while a small group of robotic fighters hurtled through the debris in search of their quarry. A larger shape moved ahead of them, a spacecraft bearing the markings of the old Centauri confederacy.

"Here they come. Let's do this!" shouted Khan.

Spartan nodded and activated the controls that sent a surge of power to the maneuvering thrusters. The obsolete Broadsword class heavy bomber spun about on its axis so that it was facing in the opposite direction. Due to the peculiarities of space travel, the bomber continued on its original trajectory but now faced directly at the group of pursuing Biomech fighters. All of them were forced to travel slower than they were capable of as they moved through the thick debris field. The front of the delta shape spacecraft exposed a plethora of weapons, each one easily capable of tearing apart a fighter.

"Now!" shouted Spartan as he depressed the trigger.

He expected to feel the shudder through the structure as the array of weapons opened fire, but instead there was only a deathly silence and three red indicator lights on his gunnery control panel. He pressed it again and again but was met by nothing more than the click of the trigger.

"Good work, Khan, still no guns!"

He shook his head and hit the thruster controls to bring the vessel back around. A rocket rushed past them on the left of the craft and exploded when it struck one of the many pieces of debris floating about in the polluted zone of space.

"I can get the turrets working, just give me another minute!" called out his friend.

"Yeah, if you say so," Spartan muttered under his breath.

He redirected a burst of emergency power to the dorsal thrusters just in time to move past a large piece of capital ship wreckage.

Bloody hell!

His heart pounded as he half expected the top of the craft to tear open from the impact. As they moved past, he watched the top with his right eye. Luckily, nothing untoward happened, and he was able reset their course without further damage to the aging bomber. He reached out instinctively with his left arm to try and speed things up before remembering the hideous wound caused by the Biomechs. His left arm was now no more than a stump. The thought of what had happened merely increased his zeal. A flashing light above his head caught his eye.

What now?

Glancing at the light, he spotted the fuel-warning marker next to it. For a moment Spartan thought that was it. They were out of fuel; and would soon be dead and adrift in space. The light flickered though and then burst. With no indicator, he was forced to check the management screen on his left. There were three tanks and all showed as being well stocked with fuel.

Must have been a faulty light, he hoped.

The computer system monitored the debris thousands of times a second and brought up potential vectors for them to follow. Unfortunately, the safest routes made them the easiest targets for the fighters. They had also been forced to alter course, and this bought them a few more seconds. Spartan glanced out through the tiny windows on the sides and at the space junk flashing by. Most of it was unrecognizable, but some parts were visibly ship related.

There must have been one hell of a battle here.

He tried to imagine how many ships would have been crippled and torn apart in such a small part of space, but the sight of the robotic fighters brought his attention back.

Concentrate you fool. You have to escape!

The battered and exhausted looking Jötnar shook his head. He'd been pulling on cables and panels for the last five minutes to no avail. The interior of the bomber was hardly conducive to a warrior of his oversized stature, and he continually struck his head or became stuck as he moved about. Since their escape, he'd managed to bring a number of key systems online, including the prized countermeasures. The weapon system had unfortunately so far eluded him.

"We won't make it to the Rift at this rate!" Spartan shouted.

Khan turned from his work and threw an angry stare at him.

"Not helping. Spartan not helping at all. Just keep flying."

The crew area was placed a quarter the way along the twenty-two meter long body of the spacecraft and filled almost half of the interior. The design was very different to those in the commonly used Thunderbolt Heavy Fighter or the much more modern Hammerhead. It was considerably larger and unable to carry an assault team or dogfight in atmospheric flight, but its great strength lay in its range and capacity to sustain damage. Like most vehicles of its time a generation earlier, the heavy bomber was a spacecraft designed for a specific role rather than the universal design now being used. It could travel for weeks, even months at a time to support warship squadrons of the Confederate Navy in battle. At least that was how it might have been used twenty or thirty years earlier.

"Tell me something, Khan; I don't care what, just something!"

Khan shouted at the engineer panel inside the filled the cramped interior, as once more he tried to bring more of the systems back on. Each time he tried to divert power from one place to another, he lost access to an existing system, and it was starting to annoy him. He looked at the last active system with surplus power, the emergency life-support package and moved his hand to alter the power.

It dropped enough for him to divert a small portion to the secondary capacitor and instantly rewarded him with a series of status indicators flashing green.

"Railgun is charging up. We have a gun."

He scanned the figures on the screen before allowing himself to smile.

"Even better, we have power reserves building in the primary and secondary capacitors."

Spartan looked back from his pilot's seat almost eight meters further along the craft. He was jammed into the front of the bomber, and a dozen screens around him fed information from the many complex systems aboard the craft. They bathed him in a mixture of pale blue and red light.

"Which gun?"

Khan nodded with a smile that seemed excessive even for him.

"Just the one, the one down there."

He point at the floor of the craft.

Spartan smiled for the first time in what seemed like months.

"Now that's more like it. Shame about the others."

"Hey, it's a damned big gun; just make sure you hit something with it."

Spartan struck the emergency reverse-thrust button, and the directional cowls on the engines altered shape to direct most of the thrust ahead. Spartan pushed forward in his seat and would have crashed into the controls, if it weren't for the heavily worn, yet extremely sturdy straps. Khan was also strapped in, but the rapid deceleration caught him by surprise. He coughed out as the air was forced from his lungs. A structural warning alarm sounded near Spartan, but he ignored it and instead watched the enemy fighters on the rear display.

Here they come.

With the bomber already slowing, the pursuing craft flew past him and into a position half a kilometer ahead. They were quick to realize what was happening and slowed down before spinning about to face him while continuing on the same vector. Spartan activated the main weapon coils and depressed the primary trigger. As the button clicked, he held his breath, waiting for the inevitable failure.

"This had better work!"

The hull of the spacecraft shuddered as the massive weapon accelerated a dense projectile the size of a man's fist toward the fighters. The railgun was a simple weapon that had been shrunk down to a manageable size in the craft. Even so, it used up vast reserves of power and would not be able to fire for another ten seconds. Spartan watched with glee as the ultra-high velocity round slammed into the nearest Biomech fighter, smashing a hole through its center. Sections ripped off, and it drifted on its original path, now lifeless and useless.

"One down, three more to go!" he laughed.

Khan would love to have joined in, but he was back to the main computer system and checking their route. He looked at the scanners once more before crosschecking with the data on the bomber's navigation computer.

"Spartan, none of this makes sense. The computer has no idea where we are."

The gun was ready again, and Spartan released another shot; but this time the Biomechs were ready and altered their velocities just enough for the dense charge to flash by them.

"Who cares? The scanner still shows the open Anomaly, right?"

Khan checked it for what felt like the fiftieth time.

"Yes, it's open. There's one cruiser blocking access."

"Good. Then we're going for it. How much further?"

Khan looked at the shape of the three Biomech fighters before answering.

"About ten more hours, assuming we can get past those three."

Again the main gun fired, but there was little chance of them striking the smaller Biomech fighters. They were half the size of an Alliance Thunderbolt Heavy Fighter and reacted with great speed. The shapes were anything but streamlined and looked something more akin to a small, crewless resupply shuttle but bristling with weapons. Large retro thrusters were fitted to each corner, and a single powerful engine was planted firmly in the center of the rear. Khan watched one fire a blast at them, and a single round penetrated the starboard armor and opened multiple breaches. Alarms activated, and small clouds of sealant rushed to the small tears, sealing the craft to stop it ripping itself to pieces. He turned back to the computer system and tried once more to redirect power from one of the communication arrays to the turret controls.

"Work…you useless piece of…" he shouted before spotting an override lever.

He turned away from his system and pulled at the fallen storage box near the side of the computer. He hadn't seen it before because a crate of spare parts had covered it. The chase must have shaken them free, revealing an entire engineer's panel. As well as a computer display, it was fitted out with mechanical overrides to a number of systems. Without thinking, he pulled on the lever. A low hum spread through the inside, followed by the whine of motorized turrets.

"Khan? What have you done?" asked Spartan in an accusing tone.

He didn't need to ask any further. Lines of status lights lit up all around the cockpit.

"Uh, Khan, we have power," he said, barely believing what he was saying.

Khan laughed back at him, and Spartan tapped the icons for each of the enemy fighters. The turrets were fully automated and tracked the craft, each turret taking careful aim with their twin automatic cannons. They were simple affairs, nothing like the railgun, yet perfectly suited for use in the coldness of space. There was no trigger for these weapons. Instead, each turret adjusted its fire pattern based on their current trajectory and velocity as they fired. Two turrets eliminated their targets with minimal ammunition, but the final turret fired once and then exploded. It caused no major damage to the bomber but did tear the weapon from its mount, whereupon it vanished into the darkness. The other two turrets spun around as though in a race and tore the last fighter to pieces with a final burst.

"Uh, is that it?" Khan asked.

Spartan checked his scanners and then the damage indicators for the bomber. A sickening feeling ran through his body as he checked the gauges and status bars, each time expecting to come across the one result that would leave them stranded in uncharted space for the rest of their lives. The four-engine heavy bomber was a resilient war machine, but it had already been considered obsolete when captured two decades earlier; and previous battle damage showed along its long fuselage. They had escaped from the Biomech fleet almost a month earlier and had followed the telltale trail of debris and fuel emission through four separate Rifts before coming to this one.

"Looks clear to me, just that cruiser guarding the entrance."

Khan nodded and finally unclipped himself so that he

could pull himself through the interior of the craft to the gunnery position just behind Spartan. The space was far too small for him, so he pulled the straps from two seats around him in an improvised but useable fashion.

"How many does that make it now?"

Spartan checked the scanner before answering.

"Eleven fighters so far. I think that one might be more of a problem."

Khan shrugged.

"I don't care. Anything is better than being a prisoner on that dammed ship."

Spartan nodded ruefully. It was true; both of them had experiences aboard the Biomech command ship they didn't want to remember, and neither knew how long they were there. It might have been weeks, but it could as easily have been months or even years. The interrogation, punishment, and torture had taken its toll on the two of them. Their escape had been violent, and it had taken no small degree of skill and ingenuity to slip the fleet and make it this far.

"Yeah, I'm not arguing with that."

He nursed his stump where one of the Biomech machines had torn away his arm. The pain had long gone, although he was convinced he could still feel where his hand had once been. The machines had done that to him, but he was certain it was for nothing more that perverted pleasure. The thought of the blades cutting into his flesh made him queasy, so he shook his head and concentrated on the pulsing shape waiting for them at the end of the debris field. It was one of the largest Spacebridge tunnels he'd seen so far.

"What do you think is on the other side of that Rift?"

Khan lifted up the side of his lip, an expression he often gave when confused.

"It might be a friendly region of space; it might be another region they have passed through. Either way it won't be here."

"What happened here though?"

He pointed to the debris circling the planet.

"This was no skirmish. It looks like hundreds of thousands of ships, and a lot of them are as big as very small moons."

Khan looked at them. Spartan watched him, wondering if his friend was merely examining their shapes, or if he genuinely had an explanation for what was going on. Neither said anything for almost a minute before Khan turned back to him.

"I'd say this was an extermination battle. Just look at the numbers. We have capital ships, remains of transports, and smashed space stations...and what about the planet?"

Spartan looked at them and tried to visualize the scene of what must have been the greatest ever space battle. He had seen enough battles in his time, but even the massive battles in the Uprising had rarely involved more than a score of major ships on each side. Even the accounts of the Great War fifty years before had shown battles with no more than fifty ships as the norm.

He's right. This is a graveyard.

The planet showed no signs of life, its atmosphere was toxic, and there were clear signs of destructive activity showing up on the scanners. Spartan used the long-range targeting cameras to examine the area in more detail before the glowing entrance moved into view. It instantly brought his attention back to their current predicament.

"Remember the Biomech fleet, Khan, how many ships were there?"

Khan lifted his shoulders slightly.

"Who knows…a lot I would think."

"Hang on," said Spartan; shifting slightly in his seat, "that's not a cruiser, look."

He turned the scanning unit toward the ship guarding the entrance to the Rift and activated the passive scanning equipment. They had made that assumption based on the size of the vessel. The shape was different though, and as they watched, it became clear that it was something else.

"You're right, look at the configuration. A control station," said Khan.

Spartan altered the settings to show an even closer view of the station. It looked in poor shape, but even from that distance, they could make out the outlines of a substantial powerplant that was attached via a series of reinforced gantries.

"Exactly. This must be one of the entrances to more enemy space. Why else have a station to monitor and control it?"

Khan placed his chin in his hand and considered their problem.

"In that case, how the hell will we get through without them stopping us?"

Spartan had already returned to the small tactical map shown on a computer display to his left. It showed the dead worlds and the debris field, as well as this destination.

"We can't stay here. Look, the carrier that followed us here is moving up out of orbit. I'd say three, maybe four hours, and they'll catch up with us."

"Unless we make for the Rift?" he asked rhetorically, "But if we do, that station will just shoot us down as we enter the place."

Neither seemed to have much of an idea. Instead, Spartan made the final adjustments to leave the higher layers of debris prior to breaking out to the Rift. Khan watched the station and scratched his forehead.

"It's not right, Spartan. We can't make it this far, kill so many, only to be stopped by that thing." He pointed at the image of the station on the screen. Spartan twisted his head around and smiled at him.

"I have a plan."

He said it with a firm tone and familiar look that

brought a grin to Khan's tired and scarred face.

"Does it involve doing some serious killing?"

Spartan nodded, his smile wide.

"Have my plans ever been anything else?"

Khan wasn't particular bothered by what the plan might be, just as long as there was one, and if it involved violence, then that was even better. He watched Spartan and noticed him checking the escape sequences for the bomber. It could mean only one thing.

He means to jump ship. Sounds just like one of Spartan's plans.

* * *

Jack lifted the glass of port and threw back yet another mouthful of the reddish liquid. No sooner had he swallowed it, he grabbed the bottle and poured out the last drops into his glass. He dropped the bottle back down on the unit at the side of his desk and drank back the last of the fortified wine. Unthinkingly, he had not bothered to filter the wine, or even to decant it prior to drinking. A small amount of sediment dripped into his mouth and snapped him out of his daze. He almost choked as the dry pieces clung to his throat, and he was forced to grab the bottle of tepid water nearby and gulp down mouthfuls. The water ran down his cheeks and mouth, covering his stained marine tunic and even his pants. The door swung open, and a bright yellow light filled the room like a blazing sun.

"What the hell!" he muttered, knocking the water over.

His eyes could barely adjust to the light conditions, and the levels of alcohol in his body blurred and slowed everything into a dreamlike state. He tried to stand but staggered and fell to the ground, directly in front of whoever had just entered his bunk space.

"Private Morato, on your feet!"

Jack tried to lift his head, but he couldn't find the strength. Instead, the face of his dour NCO, Sergeant Stone moved in front of him. As usual, the Sergeant sported a grim, angry looking face devoid of any emotion. The man was a scarred veteran, many years older than Jack, and yet a marine with experience in dozens of theaters. Unusually, he was wearing his dress uniform, although Jack was in such an inebriated state, he barely noticed. He turned and slammed the door behind with such force that a gust of air blasted into Jack. He bent down, grabbed him by the collar, and dragged the sorry looking Private to his feet.

"I know your mother is in a coma, and your buddies ain't coming back. We've all been there. I've been there, and it will happen again. I promise you."

He released Jack but stayed in the position.

"You have responsibilities, and it's been far too long. Every veteran in the Corps has had to face this."

Jack's head tilted slightly as though the weight of his own head was proving too much to hold up. The Sergeant grabbed him and held him upright.

"Listen to me, marine. If you want a court-martial, you're going about it the right way. Pull yourself together!"

He moved away from the inebriated marine and watched him drop down to his knees. He shook his head while looking at the pitiful Jack and bit his tongue before he continued his rant. He was well aware the young marine had suffered more than most. Even so, Sergeant Stone could recall the stories from the marines that fought in the Uprising, and although he'd been too young to join-up at the time, he had witnessed some of the fighting first-hand; especially the attacks on urban areas that had killed many of his friends.

"Private, now...get to your feet!"

Jack summoned as much willpower as he could muster to stand up straight. He swayed, and for the briefest of moments almost vomited onto the Sergeant. He held his breath and regained his balance, and then finally looked at the man carefully.

"I...uh..."

"I what?" barked the Sergeant. "I'll tell you what you'll do. You will get showered, dressed, and down to the dry dock. The scuttlebutt is that Conqueror will be relaunched in less than an hour, and you will be there, Private!"

He stepped to the doorway and looked back at the pitiful excuse of a marine.

"Son, you and the rest of your squad excelled yourself

on Helios. Don't let them down by falling apart."

With that, he was out of the door, and Jack was left standing in his barely conscious state. He staggered to the small bathroom and missed the washbasin, crashing into the wall. He tried to avoid hitting his head but only managed to move quickly enough to strike his cheek on the cold metal. It opened a small cut, and a trickle of blood ran down to his neck.

It took Jack fifteen minutes to shower and change his clothes, as well as time to swallow painkillers and wash his face for the tenth time. He eventually staggered out of the small room and into the corridor. The door swung behind with a clunk, and he found himself in the bright open space of the secondary passageway in the marine quarters of Saratoga Naval Station; the brand new Alliance base situated in the heart of what used to be T'Kari. A group of five Jötnar marched past, each wearing their black marine uniforms with pride.

It didn't take them long, did it?

It wasn't that long ago that Jötnar had been unable to join the military, even after their sterling work fighting for the Confederacy during the Great Uprising. Now it seemed they were joining the marines in larger numbers. One nodded as they moved past, but he didn't recognize him.

Come on, you idiot. Concentrate, the dry dock.

He looked first to his left and then in the direction the

Jötnar had emerged from. There were lit signs throughout the station but most referred to sections by numbers and letters only. Finally, he spotted the sign to dry docks, at least the Alpha Three docks. He just hoped they were the right ones. It took Jack almost ten more minutes until he reached the great observation deck that looked down onto the dry docks. The term was an anachronism, as the docks themselves were actually external to the station, and in reality, positioned in the void of space where they could be worked on in a weightless environment by scores of robotic workers. The docks were arrayed like a line of coffins, and in each was a ship in different stages of completion.

It's her!

Jack stopped in his tracks and stared at the massive shape of the Alliance's infamous Battlecruiser. He couldn't believe that the two hundred and sixty-two meter long capital ship was finally repaired and ready for battle once more. The last time he'd seen the ship was when he had escaped from its burned hull, following their high-speed crash onto the surface of Helios. He looked at the ship and tried to count how many months ago it had been since the violent incident on the planet of Helios. No matter how hard he tried, he couldn't remember.

"I told you we'd rebuild her, and quickly too," came a familiar voice.

Jack spun about and almost lost his footing. His body

moved, yet his head felt as if it were still in the same position. He almost fell to the ground again before righting himself and taking a lungful of air.

You idiot!

The shape of a man in a naval uniform moved about in front of him before he regained his balance. He focused carefully until he could make out the grizzled features of the commander of the station. He lifted his hand in an awkward salute that luckily the Admiral ignored. Anderson pointed to the gray warship.

"The damage wasn't as great as you might think. The internal systems were fully functional, even after the crash. The major problem was the layer plating."

Jack blinked and rubbed his eyes.

"Plating?"

Admiral Anderson could see the face of the Jack and recognized the hollow eyes and long face, an expression he'd seen hundreds of times before through three decades of war and loss. He extended an arm out to the ship and the flanks near the bow.

"The layered plating extends all around to protect from kinetic projectiles. That is what took most of the thermal damage before the crash finished off the rest."

He turned back and smiled.

"Engines, navigation, and weapons are all still working, apart from the keel turrets. We lost every one of them."

Jack was still stunned. He recalled the stories in the

media about the loss of the ship and the ensuing public investigation. In the end, the blame had been laid squarely at the feet of the Helions.

"I...uh...I never expected to see her again, not like this."

Admiral Anderson nodded in complete agreement.

"You had better fall in with your unit."

He tilted his head slightly, pointing in the direction of Sergeant Stone and the rest of 3rd Platoon. He saluted as best as he could, and then marched to join the rest of his unit. As he moved, he noted the scores of military personnel, each selected from the Marine Corps and Navy units stationed on board the largest and most significant Alliance base in the Orion territory, the newly constructed Admiral Jarvis Naval Station. Built in the heart of former T'Kari space, it was perfectly positioned as a strong foothold inside the Orion Nebula. One of the marines stuck out more than the rest.

Wictred.

His loyal friend was the only member of his team that survived the bloody battle on Helios. It was a memory he wanted to avoid, and as he moved in with the rest of his platoon, he lowered his eyes and tried to concentrate on the ship rather than the people around him. Admiral Anderson had moved back to a large group of high-ranking officers while the hundreds of assembled people waited in silence. Finally, he moved away and faced them.

"Marines and sailors, you have been invited by your commander to witness the relaunch of our most advanced warship. Even after the controversial attack and crash landing on Helios, she is ready for action. Her hull is the toughest ever built, and she's spent the last months being fully restored and upgraded to serve as heart of the Orion Fleet that is to be based here."

He lifted his hand and beckoned towards the massive warship.

"I give you the Alliance Navy Ship, Conqueror. The heart of the Alliance Navy!"

In perfect timing with his gesture, the navigation and internal lights activated to bathe the ship's superstructure in a myriad of tiny dots. Massive lamps lit up the ensign of the Alliance Navy, as well as the thick black letters marking out the name of the warship. He moved his head slightly as he surveyed the many units waiting, stopping at the grim face of Gun, the commander of the 17th Battalion.

"As of today, there will always be at least one complete Navy Heavy Assault group based at this station plus one or more disembarked Marine Regiments. For the next nine months, it is you, the 2nd Marine Corps Regiment. I welcome you to your new commanding officer, General Daniels, former commander of the 17th Battalion."

The middle-aged man stepped from the crowd of officers.

"Thank you, Admiral."

He gazed out at the men and women of the two battalions.

"When the 4th Heavy Battalion gets here from Carthago, it will be the first time all three of our battalions have been present since the Uprising. The Orion Nebula is a fractious place, and with five thousand marines, including the newly equipped Vanguard platoons and armored units, we will make our mark."

CHAPTER TWO

The collapse of law and order in the Helios system was the trigger point for a series of calamities that would befoul the Orion Nebula. The similarities with the past troubles on Prime and other Alliance worlds served as stark reminders as to what might come to pass, if action was not taken to avoid the rot spreading outside of Helios and to its neighboring star systems. As the quarrels and troubles spread, so did the strength of the enemy grow.

Orion – The future?

Admiral Lanthua looked out at his assembled fleet and smiled with satisfaction. It was one of the largest peacetime fleets ever assembled, and his core of Khreenk Federation battleships formed the strongest part. Most of the ships were actually moving backward with their engines on full burn to slow their approach. The Khreenk ships were different though, and their engines were able to swivel one hundred and eighty degrees to alter the direction of thrust, without changing their actual heading.

"Report?" he called to the captain of the fleet over the communication array. One by one they submitted their information, including readiness, speed, and status. Every ship was functioning as expected, apart from the small Alliance contingent. He glanced briefly at the Alliance officer, snorted, and then looked back at the disposition of his fleet.

What do these primitives know of war?

The assembled Narau fleet was now in its final twelve hours of deceleration as they approached the third planet of the Anicinàbe. Until then they were a race the Alliance knew little of, though rumor had it their people controlled the largest and most diverse empire of the eight known powers. The Helions implied they had control over more territory than the Alliance, the T'Kari, and the even the great enemy, the Biomechs, all combined. There were more than sixty ships in the fleet, with the majority supplied by the Khreenk Federation. A scattering of Helion ships drifted toward the rear, but most of their effort had been forced to remain at home to deal with the growing insurrection or because their own crews had sided with the rebels.

"What happens next?" asked Alliance Liaison Officer, Captain Tory Campbell.

He waited amongst the group of aliens and stood out like a Jötnar in a room full of humans. On his ear was a translator unit that seemed overly large for what it actually did. Much like the more advanced T'Kari models, it was able to convert his conversation directly in a number of native languages, including the common tongue of the Khreenk. Their language sounded nothing like the dialects used by the Helions, and he was forced to try and ignore the sounds coming from the device as he spoke. The small group of Khreenk officers continued speaking with each other, and he could do nothing but wait. He was a middle-aged man and had moved from politics to military service just seven years earlier. Though he was only of average height, next to the officers of the Narau Fleet he was taller than almost every one of them. His light blonde hair and large blue eyes seemed to draw attention no matter where he traveled on the Helion ship. Finally, one of them moved toward him.

"Alliance officer, what is it?" he asked through his own translator.

Captain Campbell could easily identify the look of scorn on the man's face. They were very similar in build and coloring to those human oriental people, yet of smaller build. Each had been augmented in some form or other, and this one was no exception. Part of his face was missing and had been replaced with a skin color metallic plate.

"I asked, what happens next?"

This time his voice was raised slightly so that he was almost shouting. Several of the other Khreenk looked at him, but none actually responded. Captain Campbell looked at the man's face and recalled where he had seen the officer before. It had been three days earlier when the fleet had broken free of the Khreenk Rift and met up with a scattered formation of Anicinàbe ships. He had come aboard from one of the other ships.

"We move to the target and scout for the enemy."

He then turned and walked back to his comrades. Campbell watched him go and shook his head as he was once more left alone.

This assignment is a waste of time.

He looked down at his secpad for what must have been the hundredth time and relooked at the article assembled by the Alliance intelligence agencies on the Anicinàbe. He had so far managed to avoid meeting a single one of this illusive race, even though they occupied a vast region of space. According to the article they controlled large numbers of planets, yet refused to be governed by a single central authority. There were factions made up of people from all the races through the Anicinàbe system, each of them in a state of permanent competition with the other. It reminded him of the stories of the ancient indigenous tribes back on Earth in its glory days. People like the North American Indians who had never been one nation.

Is that a good thing, or not? he thought, now even more confused.

They were positioned near the front of the ship and in a room able to take twenty or thirty people. Tiny computer screens ran around a circular central area where the commander of the ship stood. On the outside of the room on three sides were massive windows, each almost the exact size of the outer wall itself. Campbell found himself wondering quite how strong they might be, especially as they were in such an obvious and vulnerable position. He could see the shapes of the nearest vessels, as well as the tiny squadron of three Alliance frigates that had been sent to assist. They were nowhere near powerful enough to do anything of note, but they did fly the flag of the Alliance and guaranteed them a place amongst this diverse group of people.

The commander now spoke, but his crew seemed to spare him no attention. He walked about the center of the bridge, taking special note of the work conducted by each and every one of them, especially one of the taller Khreenk who was trying to show him something on a display screen. The translator seemed to take an age before it altered his voice.

"All ships, destination approaches. Check weapons, Raiders forward."

It was a strange message, especially once the translator had torn it apart into English. They were a long distance

33

from their final destination, yet the Khreenk commanding officer appeared apprehensive, perhaps even nervous at their mission.

What the hell are Raiders? he wondered.

He grabbed his secpad and put in the details, but the closest match was a vague reference to Khreenk Special Forces and something about piracy. It meant nothing to him other than that it implied asymmetric warfare.

Scouts perhaps? Or skirmishers.

He wanted to ask the Khreenk officer about the destination, but his eyes were drawn to a line of light yellow dots off in the distance. He lifted his hand to point, but two of the navigators had already spotted it and drawn it to the attention of the commander. His expression changed, and he looked about at each of them. Campbell couldn't tell if he was excited, angry, or both.

"It's a trick! All ships separate!"

There were no internal alarms or emergency lighting inside this alien vessel. Instead, the commander and then the senior officers below him walked about and shouted at the crew. It seemed a slow method, but the results were surprisingly fast. Campbell watched from his position a short distance from the commander, as the formation of ships used their maneuvering thrusters to slightly alter their trajectories.

So, we have twelve more hours to go with our engines on full reverse before we reach the target. If we change our angle of attack, the fleet will be separated when we get there.

It was a serious problem, and the more he considered it, he realized they could end up hours apart and right in the middle of a potential deadly enemy. Even more worrying was he still had no idea who the enemy was, or what they would do when they reached their destination. His secpad vibrated, and he pulled it out to look at the screen, the face was a young man in a naval officer's uniform.

"Captain Campbell, we're detecting a shift in the Anicinàbe Rift. The Narau commander is ignoring our hails."

It was the commander of ANS Spearfish, the lead ship in the frigate squadron. Though small compared to most of the Alliance fleet, there were still hundreds of men and women on board, and they were capable of taking on anything up to a cruiser when working together.

"What kind of shift?"

The commander of the ship looked surprisingly concerned.

"A serious one. My chief engineer says it could be a prelude to closing down the Rift. You know what that will mean."

That caught his attention immediately. If the Rift shut, they would be trapped in Anicinàbe space for who knew how long. There was always the fear the Rift might never be opened again, and that would leave them stuck in another part of the galaxy, perhaps forever. He nodded to the commander.

"Understood, I will speak with him."

Captain Campbell marched over to the Khreenk leader of the fleet, but two of his officers spotted his approach and blocked his path. He tried to move past them, but they sidestepped and then physically halted his progress.

"I need to speak with the Admiral."

The two muttered and growled in such a way that his translator device was completely incapable of doing its job.

"Captain," said a quiet voice from his secpad, "we don't have much time!"

Captain Campbell could sense the concern in the ship commander's voice, and he knew too well the risks they faced if they were trapped out there. He reached out to step forward, and as the Khreenk officer grabbed his arm, he took his chance. With a quick movement, he grabbed the alien's forearm and yanked him forward. Taken by surprise he stumbled, and Campbell chopped him in the middle of the back with his right fist. The Khreenk fell down, and he was past him and in front of the Admiral. More Khreenk rushed to assist, but not before he was able to speak.

"Admiral, my Alliance frigates are reporting trouble with the Rift."

The Admiral looked at him impassively, even as a trio of Khreenk moved around the Alliance officer and held on tightly, preventing him from drawing any closer to the Admiral. It seemed he was ignoring him, but then his eyes drifted to the right so that he could check the computer displays. Finally, he looked back.

"I will speak with your commanders."

He then turned his attention to his officers and barked an order. They released him before Campbell's translator even uttered a sound. The Admiral engaged in a short discussion with the Alliance officers then turned and shouted at his own crew. It must have been in code of some type because the translator once again did nothing. Eventually, the Admiral looked back at him. He lowered his head slightly in a passive gesture.

"On behalf of the Khreenk, I apologize."

Campbell nodded politely and answered.

"What now?"

The Admiral shrugged, using both his chest and his shoulders. It was almost comical, and he might have laughed if it hadn't been for their particular predicament.

"Perhaps if I had listened to your officer's counsel, I might have left scouts at the Rift. Instead...I fear we are soon to be trapped here..."

He looked at the massive glass display at the front of the ship and took a step closer, as if this would somehow allow him a better view of whatever it was that waited out there for the fleet. A clicking sound came from somewhere in his body, perhaps his throat but sounded more like it was coming from the center of his chest.

"We are not experienced in war. The Narau fleet is for show, for politics. We cannot turn back, not until we have finished our deceleration..."

The Admiral turned and looked at Campbell.

"...and we are on our way to destruction in this place, look."

He indicated to a dot in the distance. With a simple gesture, the window image transformed and enlarged as if a massive telescope. Captain Campbell was fascinated by the technology but forced himself from asking the obvious and looked at the shape. It was a ship, but of a form he was unfamiliar with. It was impossible to gauge the size, but the design was like two long cylinders fitted around a wide central box structure. Thick ribs ran down its length between which were scores of openings.

"What is it?" he asked.

The Admiral let out a long sigh; it was almost like the hiss of a snake. He reached up and scratched at the metal plates fitted to his cheek and forehead.

"Yes, I've seen this type of ship before. It is a ship of the Enemy. One we have not seen for hundreds of years. Have you been to Helios before?"

Captain Campbell nodded.

"Yes, only for a few days. I didn't get to see much. Why?"

The alien Admiral considered his reply before finally

speaking.

"There is a famous painting in the capital. It shows one of the great space battles between the Helions and the machines."

He pointed at the ship ahead of them.

"Those ships were the heart of the enemy fleet. There must have been dozens of them in the painting. I think the Helions named them Ravagers. Yes, that's it. They are large warships that carry troops and fighters and attack moons and small colonies."

He sighed, a sound and gesture that was surpassingly human.

"I never believed it until now, perhaps the prophecy that the Enemy would return is true. When the comet rises, Helios will burn. Soon my friend, soon…we shall face them."

Captain Campbell was shocked at the news of the ship. Yes, there had been rumors that there were small numbers of Biomechs still remaining throughout the galaxy, but not like this. From the assessments already coming in from the Alliance escorts, this ship was big. He checked back to the vessel that had tried to break through to Helios when the Alliance had first made contact with the Helions, and it showed up as bigger in every way.

"How powerful are these things?" he asked, dreading the answer.

The Admiral looked at him with slightly glazed eyes.

"If this is a Ravager, then many of my ships' captains will want to flee. The Helions lost an entire task force to one of these ships in the war. It is a famous story. The Helions were sending a small force to reinforce one of their colony moons. There were two famous battleships, the pride of the Helion fleet and four escorts. The Ravager caught them and destroyed them all with fighter attacks."

Now Captain Campbell was starting to understand. The description and design matched his assessment of the powerful warship.

"So, the Ravager is a hybrid aircraft carrier. Do you have any idea how many craft it can carry?"

The Admiral shook his head.

"No, we have never captured one. I would estimate over a hundred though, a mixture of fighters and bombers."

Captain Campbell could see the difficulty they were in, both as a fleet and as individual ships. The Narau fleet was substantial in number but lacked carriers and fighter cover. For fighting fleets of warships they should be just fine, against a major carrier they would be vulnerable. But what really concerned the Captain was the suggestion that discipline was poor in the fleet. He suspected this might be because it was only a polyglot force that held a fragile allegiance to its elected Admiral. The mission had been a simple one of a reconnaissance in force in the Anicinàbe sector, due to distress signals emanating from a number of their colonies, not a call to war.

"What about the Rift?"

The Admiral nodded at the glass once more. Campbell looked at it and spotted the silhouette of a ship he didn't recognize. It was the long, sleek shape of a large class of warship. The design was long, smooth, and it bristled with antenna.

"Anicinàbe cruisers?"

"Yes, they must have been forced to help the Enemy."

Campbell shook his head.

"Or they have sided with them. I wonder what they were promised."

The Khreenk Admiral pressed several buttons on his console and then shouted orders to his officers. Every one of them pulled at strapped and harnesses.

"What's going on?"

The Admiral looked at him and smiled.

"We are preparing for an emergency direction shift; we need to get to the secondary Rift before they can trap us."

"What Rift?"

"It will take us back to the border of the Klithi. We can regroup with their fleet."

The ship began to shake as the engines put in massive amounts of additional thrust. Captain Campbell could feel the change in gravity, and he immediately felt heavier.

"Strap yourself in, Captain, before it is too late."

He was already heading for one of the emergency seating areas, and an officer helped strap him in just as another series of bursts from the engines almost caused him to vomit. His secpad flew from his left hand, but he stopped it with the right hand before it could crash into the bulkhead. The face of the Alliance officer still showed.

"We're too late!" said the man on the screen.

Captain Campbell had no idea what he meant and looked up at the glass windows. They had changed again, and this time showed a view of the fleet as it scattered, each trying to slow down and change course. It was a mess because they were all still traveling at great speed to their destination. Each of the factions had set a different course while a small number continued onward. Two vessels must have hit something because they were engulfed in a blue flash that spread through their hulls like burning hot plasma. That was when Campbell spotted it.

Mother of God!

It was a ship; identical to the ship they had been looking at near their destination. This one was right in the heart of the fleet and had somehow matched their overall course and heading.

This can't be, he thought, even as he tried to calculate the complex trajectories to be able to do that. He gave up after realizing it was irrelevant right then. All he had to worry about was surviving. Ripples of light ran down the hull of the ship, and each one was matched to a series of explosions and flashes on the ships of the fleet. One Khreenk heavy cruiser took a volley of gunfire that tore the top off its superstructure from the rest of the ship. He counted a dozen ships that were already burning before a single vessel returned fire. Unsurprisingly, it looked like the Alliance frigates were the first to respond. His secpad lit up, and he grabbed it and brought it close to his face.

"Captain, we have to get out of here. I'm sending you and the fleet coordinates. Persuade the Admiral to follow us."

The secpad faded to black, but the face of the commander of the ship and the sparks and flashes behind him stayed firmly in Campbell's thoughts. The secpad flashed for a second, and then a number of schematics and navmaps appeared. He gave it a cursory look and called out to the Admiral. The commander of the fleet twisted his head to look at the young Alliance officer.

"The coordinates, they are an acceleration vector. You need to move the fleet."

It was obvious to Captain Campbell that the Narau commanding officers had no idea how to act in a battle situation. The Alliance had been involved in battle since its early inception back in the Great War, roughly seventy years earlier. Even when not at war, they faced insurrections and pirate raids throughout the scattered colonies. Thankfully, the Admiral seemed to appreciate this and quickly deferred to the man as he checked the incoming signals.

"Yes, this is good," he said without even looking at him.

He gave a series of coarse commands to his crew. Most were surprised at what he said, but not one of them dared to question his orders. In seconds, the ship shuddered once more, and vibrations spread through every part of the mighty vessel's hull.

The engines, he's changing direction!

The Admiral threw him a quick glance.

"If we survive this, I will owe your commander a life debt. Now, hold on, we have a small chance of getting through this."

The ship shook violently as dozens of kinetic rounds slammed into its hull. The Khreenk warships were well built and very strong though. After a minute of nearly continuous bombardment, they were away from the ruins of the fleet and accelerating on a vector that would move them slightly from their original destination. More importantly, by accelerating, they were making use of their already substantial momentum, and each second took them further from harm.

* * *

It was a large room, easily capable of holding fifty officers, perhaps more. Models of dozens of ships from the Alliance and the Confederacy's past adorned the walls, and in the center stood an oval table; on it a model of the station that was still under construction. Everything seemed smart and clean, perhaps too clean. It was a measure of the brand new station that every part of it looked as though it had just arrived from an Alliance factory. At one end of the table was a floating video projection showing multiple feeds of violent events on the world of Helios. There were a large number of explosions before all but one of the feeds turned black.

"This is the most important section," said the officer on the right-hand side. His face impossible to make out while the unit ran and the lights were dimmed.

A crowd of people ran down a shattered street, and small ducted fan bikes and vehicles flashed by overhead. A large tower structure crashed to the ground as the camera team ran for cover before being washed with dust and debris. The aircraft slowed down and opened fire at those running, finally striking an area near the camera crew. The last shot was of the camera on its side, facing down the street toward four dead Zathee, the largest ethnic group of Helions that were now in open revolt.

Captain Hart, a rough looking officer nodded as though the footage had just answered any question they might have. A dozen people sat around the table, including Rear Admiral Lewis, the commander of the 4th Heavy Strike Group. General Daniels, the commander of the 2nd Marine Corps Regiment plus the captains of the largest ships in the fleet.

"Our tactical reconnaissance drones have avoided

detection so far, but without boots on the ground, our information is sketchy at best," explained Captain Hart.

"Captain, thank you," stated Admiral Anderson, the commander of the station.

He looked toward the virtual presence to his right of General Rivers, the Chairman of the Joint Chiefs. He was the highest-ranking military officer by law in the Alliance. His word carried the weight of the President and of the Alliance's civilian authority.

"So, with this limited intelligence, we have been called on to assist in organizing a task force. To do what, exactly? Can you apprise us of the situation on Terra Nova?"

The time delay from the Admiral Jarvis Naval Station through T'Kari space and then to Terra Nova took considerable time. The signal was collected and repeated at Rift Spacebridges in T'Kari space, Prometheus space in Proxima Centauri, and finally Alpha Centauri, the home star system of the capital of the Alliance. A counter ran next to the video display, and it ran down as they waited for the General. While waiting, Admiral Anderson looked at the others.

"Since the start of the rebellion on Helios it has spread. The Khreenk Federation has offered assistance and to mediate a peace settlement. At the same time, T'Kari scouts report similar uprisings on many of the Helion's other worlds."

"Other worlds?" asked Captain Alyani Tinychai,

commander of ANS Serenity.

Anderson pointed to Captain Hart who brought up an image of the Helios System on the projector unit.

"Helios is just one star and one planet. They use the term interchangeably. Just as we do though, they have many moons and dozens of other stars and worlds. They have been cagey at telling us everything, but so far we have already charted three more stars, each with inhabited worlds. All of them within six light years of Helios."

Captain Tinychai seemed intrigued at this information.

"So the rumors of the Helions commanding a large empire were true, after all?"

Anderson shrugged. Captain Jose Pezal pointed at the Rift on the edge of Helion space. It was marked as the exchange point between Helion space and the Khreenk Federation.

"Admiral, where do we stand with the other empires, then?"

Before he could answer, the counter ran to zero, and a fuzzy image of the General appeared, correcting itself as more data arrived.

"Admiral Anderson, thank you for arranging this important meeting. There is urgent news from our new ambassador on Helios, as well as from our other contacts throughout the Orion Nebula."

He paused while a clerk handed him something.

"As you are all aware, we have been collating data on

these new regions of space. There are planets, races, and factions we had no idea even existed. Our big concern is this prophecy that the Helions keep referring to. We have analyzed all records we have access to, and it is clear they are convinced the Enemy will return to Helios for vengeance."

Admiral Anderson nodded as if he were in a discussion with the General.

"Now, this prophecy is a common theme with each of the races, and there are even hints on Hyperion in our own territory. Normally, we would ignore this, but there is one thing they all have in common. It is this."

His face moved to the side and was replaced by what looked like a common comet.

"This is C34A, a well known comet apparently amongst the races close to the Helions. It was last present during the defeat of the Biomechs and their incarceration on their own worlds. As you know, the Black Rift is the only fast route to cover the thousands of light years to their domain."

The image returned to General Rivers.

"This comet is on its way back, and according to the Khreenk, the Helions, and all the rest, will signal the start of the next war."

One of the younger officers muttered something and was quickly silenced by a nearby captain.

"Now, because of this potential threat, our entry into

the Narau military as a temporary member has been accelerated. Our strength has already been recognized, and this places us at the heart of the political sphere of the Great Powers."

The officers in the room looked at each other and then back to the virtual presence.

"The troubles on Helios have stark similarities with the problems we faced back on Proxima Prime at the very start of the Uprising. For those of us who were there at the time, you'll recall how the situation changed from insurgency and terrorism to outright war."

His image vanished and was replaced by a vast model that seemed to include all the territories of the Powers, including the Alliance. Helios was in the center and surrounded by four flashing stars.

"We know there are small groups of Biomech forces and their supporters, perhaps even around our own worlds. Alliance Intelligence has examined everything from the evidence left by them on Hades and Hyperion through to the prisoner that Admiral Anderson has on your station. Everything points to one thing; a long-term Biomech strategy to return to Helios."

He paused to let that piece of information sink in. The video was not in real-time, so he had no way to gauge exactly how they would react. Even so, the short pause was about right as they started to chatter with surprise and confusion at his news. His voice finally returned.

"We have every belief that the remaining Biomechs will seek to exploit this situation anyway they can, perhaps to try and reopen the Rift to their worlds. The President has therefore authorized me to take major action in this sector as part of a Narau Force under the authority of the Helion government. These forces will operate from an orbital deployment area based upon four capital ships. Admiral, if you would continue."

He stopped for just a few seconds as a number of further documents and video files continued to arrive. Admiral Anderson then continued the briefing.

"The T'Kari will conduct patrols of the Helios System, especially the access points to the other Powers while flying the Alliance flag. Their ships are ideally suited to this kind of operation, and it will leave us to concentrate on Helios. We will also be sending a smaller fleet to meet with contingents from all the other Powers to guard the Black Rift."

"This is madness," snapped General Daniels, without even thinking.

"The Helions have treated their people like dogs. The uprising has spread, and the Zathee have already offered us support if and when war comes to us. And now we plan to send ground forces into the middle of all of this? This will simply allow the Helions to maintain control."

Admiral Anderson exhaled slowly, the sound getting all of their attention.

"You're missing the big picture, General. It is our job to ensure peace and stability for the Helions. This will guarantee resources and warriors for the fight, if it ever comes to it. If we send in troops right now, we will start a war with the Helions, a war we cannot afford to become embroiled in."

General Daniels opened his mouth but Anderson stopped him.

"I know, we could handle them, but what about the others? What if the Klithi or the Khreenk side with them? In minutes, we could be at war with every single one of them, all so that we can offer military assistance to the Zathee, a culture we only knew of months ago."

He pointed at the display.

"As you can see, General Rivers has already sent us the dispositions for Helios. Additional forces are en route so the entire 4th Heavy Strike Group can be committed to action. That is twelve ships under the commander of Rear Admiral Lewis plus the 2nd Marine Corp Regiment that will operate from orbit over Helios. I will ensure this station is made available for support craft, resupply, and anything else you might need."

He paused for a second, getting his breath before continuing. In that brief moment, he looked at each of them and could see the tension in their faces. This was evidently far more serious than any of them had expected.

Captain Harris, the commander of ANS Crusader, one

of the most famous ships now in the fleet, lifted the palm of his hand slightly to get attention.

"Admiral, this all seems hasty. Have we learned something new from the Biomech soldier? Why the rush? Comets have been the harbingers for a long time, even on our worlds."

That one question turned the room to total silence. It was common knowledge that the soldier captured during the initial foray into Helios had been brought to this place for study. What wasn't known though was what had happened since. Admiral Anderson looked at the man and smiled in a gesture that was hard to fully understand.

"Captain, it is a good question but perhaps not one for today."

The video stream from General Rivers returned. Admiral Anderson signaled for his audience to turn their attention to his image.

"I am sending over all intelligence required for this operation. I must take my leave of you. You have everything you need, and I expect nothing but the utmost professionalism in your approach to this problem. Any requests may be made through Admiral Anderson, who is in command of all Alliance forces inside the Orion Nebula. Good luck to you all."

With the General now gone, Admiral Anderson switched off the video feed and looked out to the men and women.

"The Admiral Jarvis Naval Station is fully operational, and it will now be your permanent base of operations, as well as the most remote border fortress we have out here. It is our job to stabilize this part of space, to prevent the enemy from taking ground, and most importantly, to ensure that no Biomech ever gets within a single AU of the Black Rift."

His image vanished, and at the same time the Admiral stood up. He looked about the table at each of them. They looked eager for information, but there was no way he would be telling them any of what he had learned.

"That is all for now. Admiral Lewis, General Daniels, if you would stay behind please. We have further details to discuss."

The rest of the officers left the room as quietly as they had arrived, and only the three senior commanders remained in the room. Anderson said nothing until the door shut behind them, and he was left with the other two.

"Well, what did they decide?" asked General Daniels.

Anderson scratched his chin for a second. The years had not been kind to him, and like General Rivers, starting to show his age. His skin looked tired and his hair a brilliant sheen of white. His eyes, however, glowed brightly, and he showed all the intellect and intelligence that he always had. He considered the General's question. The other officers knew roughly what the plan was, but they were not privy to the overall strategy being adopted by High

Command back in Terra Nova. He, on the other hand, had spoken with General Rivers six hours earlier and had argued vehemently against the decision that had been made. He looked at the two men and raised an eyebrow before speaking.

"Our strategy is...unexpected."

General Daniels shook his head in an irritated fashion.

"Isn't it always? We do have a plan then?"

Anderson opened his mouth in a narrow smile and reopened the star map that showed the known borders of the Great Powers. Each of their regions of space was colored differently, clearly showing the territory of the Anicinàbe was the largest in terms of star systems.

"We have the Helion League, the Khreenk Federation, Klithi, Byotai and Anicinàbe territories out here."

He then pointed at the small region of space off to the left.

"This is us and our six star systems. We, of course, have territories in Alpha Centauri, Proxima Centauri, and Sol, plus our newest mining outposts and colonies at Epsilon Eridani, Gliese 876, and Procyon. And in the last few years, we have included T'Karan to this to make a total of seven stars."

He looked back at them, clearly waiting to make a major announcement.

"Do you have any idea how many star systems the other Powers control?"

There was silence as the other two men looked at him impassively. Anderson knew all too well they would not know, even he wasn't completely sure about the information passed on via the diplomats on Helios.

"I'll tell you, gentlemen, forty-five stars and hundreds of worlds. Half of those are in Anicinàbe space. There could easily be as many again that we do not know about. Why do you think we have allowed our frigates to join the Narau fleet on one of its patrols?"

"Intelligence," replied Rear Admiral Lewis in a slow, deliberate tone.

Anderson stood up and walked toward the nearest wall where he stopped and examined the model ships. Most he recognized, and some even brought back painful memories. The wrecked hulk of the Battlecruiser Crusader was the one that made him the think the hardest. It had been the pride of the fleet and the flagship of Admiral Jarvis, the heroine of the Uprising.

"Precisely," he said, his back still to them.

He took the model from the wall and examined it with interest, finally turning to face his two guests.

"Stability for the Alliance is our priority, and the worry is that the Rift network is larger than anticipated and poorly mapped. The enemy is still out there, and all of our worlds are vulnerable."

He walked back and placed the model on the table.

"It is simple, gentlemen. Our job is to keep these forty-five worlds stable and friendly. We must do all we can to explore the Rift network, and ultimately prepare for the day when the attack will come."

Rear Admiral Lewis didn't appear convinced.

"Attack? Who's to say the Biomechs aren't smashed or weakened beyond chance of recovery? If they're so strong, then why aren't they already here, taking us apart like before?"

Anderson smiled and returned to his seat. With a single tap, he brought up an image of a vast hangar type structure. Inside was an object bathed in white and yellow lamps. Both men leaned in closer to examine the shape. It was a large creature, like something from hell itself but a sickening mixture of machine and flesh. It moved a little before a fluorescent green fluid was automatically pumped into its body via a machine to its side.

"The Biomech soldier?" asked General Daniels.

"Yes," answered Anderson.

Daniels shook his head in horror.

"What are you doing to it?"

Anderson was surprised at his discomfort. The Biomechs had been responsible for so much death; he would have thought the man would relish seeing the thing suffer.

"This is nothing, just drugs to stop it from turning on us. It has already killed eleven technicians since we brought it here."

That piece of information seemed to placate him, at least for now.

"From our detailed studies, we have learned a great deal. Firstly, the living creature inside the machine is old."

Daniels didn't seem impressed.

"What do you mean, old?"

"Well, this particular creature is almost six hundred years old, yet its armored exterior is much older again."

Admiral Lewis and General Daniels looked shocked at this revelation. Neither seemed to know what to say, so Anderson continued.

"There is more though. In our interrogations, we have established three key points. None are confirmed, but each of them makes sense in its own way. First, the Biomechs are an ancient but dying race. Our biological analysis confirms the genetic decay, but they have managed to avoid the worst effects in a way we do not understand. It is not completely clear, but we suspect they have a finite number of soldiers, and they cannot be replaced."

Admiral Lewis lifted up his hand in surprise. He was one of the younger senior commanders in the Alliance military and known for his somewhat abrasive attitude on occasion.

"Wait a minute, how the hell was this decision made? Unable to reproduce, I just don't believe that."

General Daniels seemed to accept this point quite quickly, however.

"It makes sense though. Think about it. These armored machines must be to protect their ancient bodies, so they build the armored cocoons that turn them into something like demigods. If you lived pretty much forever, would you want more people to share what you have? Soldiers are usually the youngest. What if this guy is the same?"

He pointed at the image on the display.

"Hmm, that is a rather tenuous link. What is it based on?" asked a dubious sounding Admiral Lewis.

Anderson tapped the button, and the video feed zoomed in much closer to show the large head of the thing. All three stared at it with a mixture of fascination and horror. One similar creature had led the forces of Echidna back on Hyperion, but at the time, it was assumed the thing was some type of massive war machine.

"It is through a mixture of interrogation and biological study. According to the captured soldier, it considers its own race some sort of master race. They learned to control life before they met the other races."

Admiral Lewis lowered his head to his hand.

"If they can control life, why not simply create more? They can always use cloning. It's not like they can't do that. We are somewhat familiar with Biomechs and their creations. Do you remember the AI Hubs that took control of our ships?"

Anderson seemed to like what he was hearing. The last thing he wanted was senior officers that simply carried out orders. He also knew that both of them would do whatever was necessary to protect the Alliance.

"Yes, that is all very true. But if you remember, the genetic material of the Biomechs that we fought and the AI hubs was proven to be new, some of it a mere few years old. It was either harvested or created from scratch. Neither the soldier that tried to arrive at Hyperion, or this one were like that."

He pulled out his secpad and ran his fingers along the front. It was a simple gesture and sent a secure digital packet to both of them.

"Look at that."

General Daniels had his device out first and was past the first page before his Navy opposite number had done the same. It was a modest report that had been assembled based on information gathered on Helios over the last three months. It included pictures of their paintings, sculptures, and artworks along with audio testimonials. Admiral Anderson only gave them a minute to read it before interrupting them.

"I'll let you read that in your own time. You'll note the title is the Desperation War. It is the name the Helions and their allies used in the great battles against the Biomechs. You'll note the reports describe all manner of Biomech creatures and machines, yet the soldiers like this one appear infrequently. In fact, there is a song that the Helions sing, one about the great battle of Pylos."

General Daniels face lit up.

"Yes, I heard this when I visited the capital. It is about the surrender of a Biomech garrison, if I'm not mistaken."

"Indeed," said Anderson.

He reached forward and tapped a button. A recording of young Helions filled the room, and the three of them listened in silence, trying to imagine what was being said. It was short and over in less than a minute. Anderson leaned toward them as though revealing a great secret.

"The song is about the fall of the T'Kari colony called Pylos by the Biomechs. A combined Helion and T'Kari fleet broke through and prepared an atomic bombardment for the world. According to legend, there were over a million Biomechs and six of the Biomech soldiers, this leadership caste. They surrendered the world and withdrew rather than lose six soldiers."

"I think I'd be more worried about losing a million Biomechs to be honest," said Admiral Lewis with barely concealed sarcasm.

Anderson nodded as though he were correct.

"True, except the million were executed autonomously by the soldiers as they left, all so that six might avoid death by the atomics."

This silenced the Admiral, at least for now.

"With this information, we can determine the Biomechs were broken in this war. We know that small numbers of their soldiers, like the one we have here and the one destroyed during the collapse of the Hyperion Rift remain, each of them hiding and waiting."

He straightened his back and again took a deep breath, as if preparing for some great speech.

"They have soldiers and ships throughout the old worlds, including our own. Their homeworld lies beyond the Black Rift, almost two thousand light years from Helios, and if the Helions are right, they have been working on their revenge since they were forced into exile."

He then pointed at the image on the wall of the first photograph ever taken of Helios. It was becoming one of the most widely copied images in the history of humanity.

"Helios is the Nexus, the point at which every one of our races reaches the rest. High Command has determined that the Biomechs remain as a clear and present danger. We must therefore prepare ourselves and the other races if we want to avoid extinction."

He looked at each of them, gauging their expressions.

"The days of wondering are over. From today, we are on a war footing, and we must do everything necessary to ensure we are ready. Because when they come, we will see a war that will make the Uprising look like a picnic."

CHAPTER THREE

Many people have questioned naval tactics and strategies ever since the first armed spacecraft clashed. The first battles were between modified conventional craft with ultra long-range missile systems. Neither ship would usually see the other, as they would be attacked and destroyed at a distance of hundreds of thousands of kilometers. With advances in electronic warfare in the middle of the twenty-first century, the ability to strike at long-range became more and more difficult. The battles soon changed to the great battleship duels of the Great War and the carrier battles and ship skirmishes of the Great Uprising. Looking to the future, all hopes rested on the idea of the universal ship design, with a mixture of weapons, armor, defensive systems, and embarked fighters. Events in the Orion Nebula would put this idea to the test.

Naval Cadet's Handbook

The training scenario on board the Alliance warship

was not the most well prepared that Jack had ever seen. Since the news that the entire regiment was to be shipped out, they had been practicing a great variety of different missions, and this was the fourth in the last fortnight. The entire training hall and barrack area had been converted to represent an urban warzone, but it was hard to visualize the place as anything more than a glorified Marine Corps kill house. The buildings were wood and plaster, most of which were unpainted, and the destroyed vehicles no more than stacks of crates and boxes with camouflage nets and sheets laid over them to give form. He inhaled, but the fully enclosed PDS armored suit removed anything that could be a contaminant so he took in the clean, yet slightly oily air the built-in storage tanks provided.

"I'm in position," he said quietly.

The others in his team were spread out, and according to the computer generated overlay, were also ready and waiting. He looked at his target and then checked on both sides for signs of anymore of the guards.

"Sentries eighty meters ahead. No sign of the hostage."

He dropped to one knee and moved into position behind one of the broken walls. In a single fluid motion, he took aim through the optical sight of the L52 Mark II carbine and placed the target drone directly in the center. It moved slowly, its imitation arms moving about as it did its best to act like a realistic target. To the right of the sight were a number of details that constantly updated, including wind speed and distance. That was when he identified two more guards that were standing around the prisoner. He took careful aim at the sentry to the left and flagged the others for the rest of his team. Lines flashed around the others as each marine selected and tagged a target.

"I have a shot," he said in a calm and clear voice.

As he looked at the robotic target, the memory of his last fight on Helios flooded back. It wasn't the Animosh, or even the flyers that rushed about near them; it was the unstoppable artificial creation that had been landed to fight them. In all his life, he'd never experienced such helplessness than when fighting the unfeeling machines. The drone reminded him of how they looked and moved, and it unnerved him. He'd lost a lot of friends that day, and try as he might, he couldn't get their faces from his mind.

Concentrate, this will get you killed!

To the flanks of the drone appeared another two mockups of Helion civilians. They looked like static dummies and were fitted out in a very rough approximation of the types of clothing seen on the planet. Jack remained hidden behind a fake wall, with the carbine resting on the top. He could see the positions of the rest of his fireteam to the right where each waited for the order.

"Take the shot," Wictred said slowly.

It was the sound of his Jötnar friend, and the only

member of his team to make it back alive from Helios. He winced at the calm sound and wondered if the losses affected his synthetic companion the way it did him. He moved the weapon just a fraction and then squeezed. The recoil was modest, and it used nothing more powerful than what was in reality a glorified heavyweight beanbag round. It hit the target in the center mass, knocking it back. Half a dozen more rounds struck about it as the other marines added their own fire.

I don't think so, he thought.

He recalled his ineffective shooting at the drone on Helios. It was nothing like the drones in this scenario, of course. This one was designed to mimic a human, nothing more; whereas the beast of a machine he'd faced on that hot planet was a combat drone, a heavily armed and armored fighting machine, more like a twentieth century tank than a man. In the end, it had taken concentrated fire from Hammerhead gunships to destroy it.

"Now!" called out Corporal Wictred.

A dozen rounds landed around the targets before another team of bayonet equipped marines lurched from cover and rushed in to grab the hostage. He didn't recognize the markings on their armor, other than to see they were not from his squad. The plan had been for a fast firefight that would remove each of the targets.

"Wait!" he called out.

Jack moved his carbine to the right as he checked for

signs of the enemy. The briefing had suggested there might be up to eight, and so far only three were down. It wasn't his call though, and the second team of four was in the target area in seconds. He spotted two drones lifting rifles; after taking careful aim, put one on the ground. The second was blocked by one of the marines, and he was unable to take the shot without striking his own comrade.

Idiots!

The team reached within three meters of the drone that held a hostage to its front. They spread out, each pointing their weapons at the machine. It moved its block shaped head as if looking at them and then vanished in a green haze. The paint bomb on its chest exploded, effectively killing the hostage and the entire rescue team. Even from this far away, a glob of green paint managed to strike his visor.

Dammit!

A klaxon sounded, and a bright lamp switched on, bathing the combat area in a warm yellow light. Sergeant Stone emerged from a raised balcony area to look down at the tired and painted covered marines. Jack stood up and wiped at the visor, leaving a narrow smear on the front of the reinforced transparent housing.

"Great job, gentlemen. You managed to neutralize the hostage and two teams of marines in the process."

He grinned, but it wasn't one of pleasure, just simple annoyance mixed with expected disappointment.

"You failed two of the three objectives. You did at least kill the hostage takers."

Two more marines stood up. One of the younger marines, a tall man of well over two meters, opened his visor and then threw his weapon on the ground in disgust.

"You've got something to say, Private?" snapped Sergeant Stone.

The Private looked up at him, and Jack could easily identify the arrogance and self-importance in the man's posture. It was odd. That kind of attitude rarely made it past the initial training. It was something that had little to offer the Corps.

"There's no way to win this, Sergeant."

The battle-hardened drill instructor laughed a low, hearty sound that should worry any marine who heard it. He walked to the edge of the balcony and surveyed the sight below him. There were nearly thirty marines, and every one of them looked fed up.

"The mission was to rescue the hostage from a terrorist cell that had promised to kill them if you attacked. You attacked. You died. What other outcome did you expect?"

He shook his head in disappointment while a number of heads lowered. Jack watched but found himself almost smiling. He looked out at the training hall, to the marines, and finally at the grizzled Sergeant. He then lifted his arm slightly to the air.

"Sergeant."

The man moved his eyes, but not one other muscle appeared to move.

"Yes, Private?"

"We could have shot them down at a safe distance."

Sergeant Stone's right lip lifted slightly, appearing to be amused.

"Yes, that's true. But what about the hostage?"

Jack laughed to himself before speaking.

"The hostage wouldn't make it, but our marines would have."

Stone nodded at the last words.

"Very true."

He lifted his right arm and pointed to the spread out groups of marines.

"There will be times when you will be forced to make difficult decisions. Helios is a nest of backstabbing vipers, and your friends could become your enemies in seconds. When your backs are to the wall, you must always remember to look out for the marine next to you. A marine is the only person you can rely on when you get there."

He looked back to Jack and gave him a short nod. It wasn't much, but it was probably the only positive comment or expression Jack had ever seen him give.

"Now, get some food inside you, and report back here in three hours."

Jack was one of the first to leave and went straight to his quarters at the rear of the habitation section of the ship. Unlike on the space station, his was no longer a dedicated room. Now he had no more than a small bunk plus personal stowage area and a display terminal. He jumped up to the bed and tapped the screen. It flickered on and accepted his credentials, showing him the same basic information as the much smaller secpad. In seconds, the unit accessed his communications log and identified a series of new messages. One in particular caught his eye.

What's this from Terra Nova?

He swiped his hand, and a progress bar appeared as the data was decrypted for him. Terra Nova was an unimaginable distance away, and without the communication repeaters now installed at every Rift, it would be impossible to ever receive a signal. Finally, the front image of the military hospital appeared to be replaced by the face of a doctor.

"This is Doctor Barcheta, of the Terra Nova Medical Institute. I have a progress report on your mother, Ms Teresa Morato."

Jack took a deep breath, almost sighing as he waited for the inevitable. He had few really family left and with Spartan missing, his estranged siblings hating him, and his mother in hospital, he found the Marine Corps to be more his family right now.

"The gunshot wounds to the right thoracoabdominal region are showing rapid signs of healing, and there is no sign of peritonitis. Ms Morato's head injuries, however, are more serious. The lacerations are healing, but it still too early to tell if there will be any permanent neurological damage."

Jack was gladdened that the news hadn't been more serious. The last he'd heard she had been admitted after falling into a coma and that her wounds were of a serious nature, potentially life threatening. The real worry to him now was the coma. It had been months since the battle, and he'd already read multiple accounts where casualties had remained in a comatose state for years, sometimes even decades.

Will she ever come out of it?

There was no more video from the doctor, but there were a number of private reports, as well as x-rays and still imagery of his mother. He stared at them for almost ten minutes before shutting off the system and rolling over onto his back. He hadn't wanted to remain with the Corps and would have been much happier staying with Teresa until she recovered; he was loath to lose what little he had left. But with her injuries being so severe, he couldn't even speak to her. He knew his time was better spent with his remaining friends in the Corps, and Gun, the commander of his battalion had requested he return as soon as possible. The door opened, and the remaining marines in the barracks walked out, leaving him on his own. One entered and held the door open.

"Jack, get out here!"

It was Wictred, his oversized Jötnar friend that he'd

fought so many battles along side. Both Wictred and his Jötnar companion Hunn had joined the Corps at the same time as Jack, but Hunn had fallen in battle. Jack hesitated, not wanting to spend more time socializing with the others, but the expression on Wictred's face gave him no leeway.

"I'm not asking, Jack. I'm telling. Now move it!"

It was a pleasant order, not the kind barked by Sergeant Stone, but the tone was clear.

"Yeah…yeah," he answered and threw himself down.

Wictred shook his head and stepped out into the passageway. The blast door started to close behind him as he called back inside.

"Maybe change your clothes before you join us?"

Jack looked at him while the door slammed shut with a clunk. He looked down and only then realized he was wearing his marine issue clothing from the previous training session. But there was no paint. They were dripping in sweat.

You idiot.

He ripped of his tunic and pants and walked to the shower entrance at the end of the barrack room. He was inside and the water pouring down over his body before he even noticed the dozen other marines busy washing. Over half were women, and on any other day, it would have been a reason to stay a little longer. Today he wasn't in the mood.

It took Jack and the others nearly an hour before they

were changed, showered, and in the ship's canteen for their lunch. The ship operated like vessels through the ages, on a twenty-four hour system. Marines came in for lunch at multiple times of the day, depending on their shift patterns and operations. It wasn't an issue, as all foodstuff consumed were dehydrated and shipped in packets from forward naval bases throughout the Alliance. He walked in and moved to the counter where the staff handed out the meals in bowls.

"What are the options today?" he asked glumly.

The tall black marine behind the counter grinned with a gleeful expression.

"Private, we've got the best for you today. Lamb casserole, chicken in herbs, and today's special, chili con carne."

Jack looked at each in turn and gave up. He just grabbed at the first piping hot bowl and moved to one of the long tables where Wictred and three other marines were sitting. He moved around the table and sat on the opposite side to face him. He looked down at the portion of lamb casserole and breathed in the taste. It was served in a white bowl and gave off a faint green hue from the broccoli and vegetable bouillon. Pieces of meat and carrot floated about to give it a less than appealing look. Jack took a spoonful, chewed, and then swallowed it down.

"Nice?" asked Wictred with a wide grin.

Jack took another mouthful and watched as the rest of

his new squad sat down. At first it was just a handful, and then as quickly as the first sat down, the rest were there and making themselves comfortable. There were thirteen of them in total, and each acknowledged Corporal Wictred as they sat down. He looked about the canteen, recalling his time many months ago when the ship had been fresh and brand new. Although the exterior and systems of ANS Conqueror had been fully repaired and improved, the interior sections had seen far less time spent on them. The canteen showed signs of electrical scarring, and the patched bullet holes on one of the walls had been filled and painted in such a hurry, the marks were still visible.

"It could do with more salt," he answered finally.

Wictred had been promoted following the Helios incident and was now the senior corporal in the squad. That meant he was responsible for the other twelve that made up the three fireteams, as well as liaising with their platoon commander.

"So," started Wictred, "we screwed that one up, and Sergeant Stone wants improvement."

Private Jana Jenkell, the squad's medic spoke first. Her jet-black hair had been cut short, and her dark blue eyes almost matched the color. Her faced was grim, and as Jack glanced at her, he wondered if he'd ever seen her smile. As she spoke, he remembered she was the new one with the stutter.

"Well, they set off the bomb because they were able to

activate a trigger. Why not eliminate that ability?"

Frewyn, the oldest of the group shook his head. He was stoutly built and spoke with a common accent that gave the impression he was far less intelligent than he actually was.

"How exactly would we do that?"

Jack swallowed another piece of lamb and then spoke.

"Gas or a stunner of some kind."

Private Riku laughed at this idea. Of all those, seated she was the most unusual looking. Tall and attractive, she could easily have been a model if it hadn't been for a hideous scar that ran down her face. There was something else that in Jack's opinion made her probably the ugliest woman he'd met; it was her miserable fixed expression.

"You have one of those lying about, Private?"

"You're such an asshat," said Private Jenkell.

The young woman took another mouthful of her lunch and laughed at the taller and more attractive woman. Several of the others sniggered at her insult, and it was clear that Riku had few real friends in the unit.

Jack looked at Private Riku with the same kind of irritation Private Jenkell had and shook his head with a look of disinterest. Once more Private Riku displayed a look that bordered on contempt of him. Wictred had told him it was how he imagined a woman chewing a wasp would look like. Jack smiled as he thought of that, and then spotted her watching him. He lifted an eyebrow, and she scowled in return.

Would it kill her to smile? Maybe.

Jack recalled the last three conversations he'd had with her, and they'd always ended up the same. No matter the subject, it reverted to her, as if she always had an experience that trumped the rest. She loved complements and seemed to ask questions and make comments designed to make people feel obliged to add something nice about her. Amusingly, this never appeared to work. It seemed to encourage bitterness amongst the rest of the marines with almost every word that came out of her mouth, and that encouraged her to try even harder.

"Good attitude, Private Riku. What would you do then? Oh, I remember, you waited at the back."

She scowled at him, and he nodded as if thanking her for some kind of concealed complement.

"You're most welcome," he added, much to her annoyance.

A tall, wide man, looking more like a wrestler than a marine, scratched at his nose before speaking. His face had been burned badly in the past, and he had a number of marks and scarring running from his left ear down to his chin. His lip was slightly squashed and of them all, he looked as though he'd been in a number of fights.

"You have an idea, Corporal?" Wictred asked.

The big man nodded.

"Yeah, we have a few options if we don't want to lose

people. What if we take in a hostage of our own and send them in, right in front of them and in plain view."

"Nice," announced Jack at the idea.

"Good idea, Callahan," said Wictred, "So either we use a form of nerve agent to incapacitate the target, or we use a decoy of our own. Those are both options that could save marines."

"There is one more," said Jack.

Private Riku shook her head as he spoke.

"We could make sure we kill them all this time."

* * *

Spartan and Khan clung to the interior of the bomb bay fitted to the bulbous flank of the aged bomber, as it continued on its course toward the increasingly large shape of the space station. By all accounts, it was larger than any ship either of them had ever seen. Spartan guessed it must be around fifty percent larger than a Confederate battleship from the previous war. The station moved off to the right and then vanished from view for a moment.

Hold on, whatever you do.

Both of them were attached via improvised harnesses they had taken from the small crew area in the middle of the bomber. Without it, they would have been thrown about as the craft moved. They had set the spacecraft on a spinning course that while slow in its rotation, still gave the impression the craft was out of control; either because of internal damage or more likely the crew had been incapacitated. Although the bomb bay was sealed, it lacked heating or an independent air supply. Spartan was okay, as he had been able to fit inside one of the crew's emergency space suits. Khan, on the other hand, was forced to use one of the spare oxygen units and helmet; the rest of his body would have to manage as it was. Spartan just hoped the doors would stay closed and sealed because exposure outside of the spacecraft would kill Khan in less than a minute.

"Spartan, you think this will work?" asked Khan. His voice rasped from inside the mask, and Spartan could tell he was already feeling the cold. It was probably the tenth time his old friend had asked the same question, and once more he was forced to encourage him.

"Of course, when do my plans not work?"

Khan sniggered to himself, both of them were well aware that Spartan's plans were far from perfect. In Khan's experience, they always required a little extra muscle to make them work. He looked up and at the side of the space station as once more they spun about to face it.

"What's stopping them from seeing us?"

It was a good question, but Spartan had thought of that already.

"Look, we're next to the damaged bomb mount. There are fuel leaks and electrical damage all around here. Unless they examine this section with advanced scanners, they'll miss us. Anyway, why bother looking?"

It was true. With the spacecraft drifting through space, it presented no great problem and could easily be left alone to continue its path out into the black void of space. On its current trajectory, it would pass right between the Rift and the station. The bomb bay was completely sealed from the exterior of the ship until opened to give access to its internal bays. There were four small windows, each no bigger than a man's hand, at the far end to give engineers visual access for loading and maintenance. It wasn't much but enough to allow them a good view out of the spacecraft and toward the station. It was when Khan was looking through the nearest window that he spotted it.

"Spartan, look."

He nodded to his left and kept his movement to a minimum. It wasn't that he was clinging to the outside of the bomber, but he was familiar enough with the various scanners onboard Alliance vessels to know they could detect heat changes, and that could easily be taken for movement.

"What is it?" Spartan asked, moving to the window and looking out.

He could see the shape of the Biomech transport ship as it moved toward them. It immediately filled him with dread. It was larger than the bomber, but nothing the size of the cruiser that had been pursuing them. There were two small drones attached to its dorsal armor, neither had been detached. Instead, it moved into position underneath them and then even closer.

"See, I said it would work," Spartan said.

Khan smiled inwardly but could sense the relief in this friend's voice. The vessel took nearly five minutes to finish moving into position and matched their rotation before it connected using some form of grav clamp. Once joined, they could feel a slight jolt as the ship's engines activated, and their course was corrected. Another minute later, and they were heading directly for the station, the cruiser waiting not far from where it must have released its spacecraft. It took them to the right of the station where three docking mounts were located. As they approached, the two were able to get a good look at the exterior of the metallic construction.

"Seen anything like this before?"

Spartan moved his head slowly.

"Nope, this isn't ours, and it doesn't look like the gear the T'Kari use either."

"Biomech?"

Spartan tried to shrug but found it hard to move the muscles while also trying to be as quiet and still as possible. There were no windows on the outer parts of the structure, but as with most stations, there were a large number of antenna and communication masts that extended in almost every single direction. Spartan looked at the individual details but finally concentrated his attention on one small part near the airlock. It looked like a spider but on closer examination was a dry dock. Underneath it were three large buildings, each almost big enough to house one of the new Alliance frigates. There were also a dozen gantries and sat atop them were Biomech drone fighters, much like the ones that had attacked them during their escape.

"Yeah, that sells it."

Khan looked in the same direction and recognized the shape of a Biomech ship, like they'd seen while on board the T'Kari Raider many months earlier. Every second brought them closer, and the size of the ship increased until they could appreciate the scale.

"It's got to be one of those carriers," Khan said.

The shape was certainly familiar, but this wasn't as big as the mighty cruiser class ships they had seen before. These were something closer to the smaller escorts and scouting ships used by the military. Along the side of the hull were markings and a black shape of some kind of snake beast. Spartan sighed at the sight of the shape.

"Echidna."

He looked irritated but not surprised.

"Man, why can we never shake these guys? We keep finding them."

Khan looked at it for a second and started to speak

while watching the ship.

"At least that tells us who they are. This must mean we're at a Biomech outpost."

Spartan took several short gulps of air and felt an immediate rush of cold oxygen in his chest. It felt like heartburn, but he ignored it, knowing very well his friend was in far more discomfort than him.

"Even so, this is hardly well protected. What do we have? One Rift, a control station, and a shipyard with a couple of ships and a dozen drones. Hell, I'd say this is a way station for long-range ships."

"Maybe," replied Khan. His voiced lacked conviction.

It was another thirty minutes before they reached the docking mount. They drifted into position, and the bomber shuddered as they were locked into place. At this range, they could make out every single detail, and the more they looked, the more alien the place appeared. The base was static, and on the way the spacecraft interacted there was no form of artificial gravity. As they waited, Khan spotted movement.

"There," he said, pointing with his forehead.

The shape of a large Biomech machine appeared, its body completely exposed to the elements. It moved slowly with one foot connecting securely before it moved the other. It seemed nervous, or perhaps it was just taking its time.

"One of our metal friends?" asked Spartan.

They both watched the thing with barely concealed bitterness. Khan clenched his fists, and Spartan could see his friend's muscles contracting as he squeezed the straps. Khan was angry, very angry. Spartan extended his one good arm and placed his gloved hand on Khan's shoulder.

"Easy friend, I know. We'll have our revenge. I promise you."

The machine looked like one of the incredibly rare Biomechs. Not one of the artificial monsters they had fought on a dozen worlds, or even the completely synthetic warriors like Khan that had been built as frontline soldiers for the War. No, these were the machines with biological minds, the leadership caste of the entire race they knew simply as the Biomechs. This one looked just like those that were responsible for their interrogation and torture for so many months. It appeared to be smaller, and its metal outer housing was in a poor state. The black paint had been rubbed or worn down so much there was more bare metal than paint remaining. It was bipedal and appeared to be a rough match for Khan in terms of height and girth. Its head was sunk down low and looked more like a beetle than a machine. It moved toward the spacecraft and waited like a statue just five meters from its side.

"What do we do now?" asked Khan.

He looked to Spartan and could just make out the wide smile on his friend's face through the armored visor. The chill was now spreading through his body, and he was starting to wonder if he could still move his legs. The bomber shook and then moved toward the large metal structure ahead of them. When they were halfway there, the doors opened and revealed a dark interior.

"When we get inside, we'll get out of here."

Khan winced. "And then?"

Spartan pointed at the Biomech craft lined up inside the structure.

"We'll find a way out of this place, I promise you. Maybe we'll take a few of those bastards with us."

He beckoned with his hand, and his thumb extended out to the machine.

"And I think he should go for starters."

Khan nodded but was forced to hide a rough cough before answering.

"He will do...for now."

Spartan looked away from Khan and smiled.

Don't you worry; we're getting out of here and back home. We're going to get our friends, the fleet, and the Corps, and we'll grind these animals until there's nothing left but ash and waste.

CHAPTER FOUR

By electing to involve itself in affairs outside of Alpha Centauri, humanity exposed itself to great risk. New species, empires, and technologies would come to the forefront, as well as the rumors of the Enemy long thought defeated. There were positives for the Alliance, however, not least the benefits that come from the meeting of different peoples, including trade and science. Ultimately, without the contact with other people, the Alliance would have been completely unprepared for the realization of the Helions' ancient prophecy, one that would affect the worlds of the Alliance, no matter what decisions were made.

The Unforeseen Consequences

The Narau fleet had lost a quarter of its number in the ambush laid by the Biomech warship and its allied Anicinàbe cruisers. The timing had been perfect, as had their positioning. By waiting at that point in space, the ships hadn't been detected until the Narau fleet was already moving too fast. Only a few ships had been destroyed, the others had either scattered and vanished or surrendered rather than face destruction. Of those that remained, the Alliance frigates were the most prominent. Moving in a wide formation at the rear, they used their large numbers of automated turrets to shred any Biomech fighters in pursuit. Unlike the ships from the other Powers, the Alliance ships were heavily equipped with defensive firepower, a valuable lesson learned in the violent battles of the Great Uprising where human fought human in bloody civil war.

The scene inside the Khreenk flagship was very different to how it would have been without human intervention. Instead of panic and confusion, the crew had been given implicit instructions and was making substantial progress in avoiding a direct and bloody confrontation with the Enemy; a confrontation that they would be unlikely to win.

"Admiral, a group of their ships has changed their course. They must know our plan," said Captain Campbell.

Unlike before, the Khreenk Admiral immediately listened to the advice of the young Alliance Captain. In the last few hours, the low-ranking Alliance officer had saved a dozen of the Narau ships, and he seemed happy to accept any more advice from him, even to the annoyance of his own officers. Now the Captain stood alongside the Admiral at the heart of the ship. He looked at the data carefully.

"They are accelerating at speeds we cannot match; no living crew is capable of withstanding those levels of acceleration for more than a few minutes."

Captain Campbell smiled grimly; it was clear to him what was happening. He knew enough about ship design, physics, and directional vectors to see it.

It's Biomechs all right.

With massive computerization and minimal crew, there was a good chance this warship was actually completely devoid of life. That meant the Enemy would be ruthless, fast, and very quick to make decisions. Those were all advantages, but ones that humans had beaten in the past. What really interested him though were the other ships. The Biomechs were a flexible race and usually made use of others to fight their battles. Either through or coercion, the Biomechs had encouraged these Anicinàbe to help them. Based on the speed of the larger vessel, it was no surprise to him that the Allied ships were unable to match the pace of the larger vessel.

"Yes, they will reach the dead zone at the Rift before us. What do you suggest?" asked the Admiral.

"She's automated, just look at the acceleration. None of our ships can come even close to that. We're pushing just over our safe limit, and this ship is moving at triple our maximum speed. Either that or it just has Biomech warriors for crew."

The Admiral nodded in agreement but still didn't quite understand how this would help them in their battle. He said nothing for a moment, and Captain Campbell was forced to repeat himself before even receiving an acknowledgement. It was clear the Admiral had never faced a situation like this, and Campbell was starting to wonder if he'd ever actually even been in a battle before. That then reminded him that, of course, neither had he, apart from skirmishes with black marketers and pirates out on the Rim.

"How does this help?" asked the Admiral after what must have been nearly thirty seconds thinking.

Campbell lifted his datapad and held it in front of the Khreenk commander. It showed a detailed schematic of the large Biomech warship. Unlike the Anicinàbe, this vessel was ugly and covered in multiple layers of armor, making it look more like a giant slug than the beautiful aesthetics used by the others. Red and green circles pointed out potential weapon locations as well as exit tubes for spacecraft.

"It means they will be faster and more powerful than anything we have here. The single advantage we have is manpower, and that is useless in a space battle, especially one where they may not have living crew."

"So we use our numbers, firepower, and maneuver to

beat them."

Captain Campbell half nodded in agreement. It was far from the ideal solution for such a major threat. He was acutely aware he could only push so far before his suggestion would be construed as an affront to the alien's ability to lead the fleet. That could be very dangerous for the operation.

"Partially, don't forget there is no realistic maneuver that can be conducted at these speeds. We have to use all available power to get to the Rift. Captain Hampel of ANS Spearfish suggests a bombardment corridor, and that we do not decelerate for the Rift."

One of the Khreenk officers moved from a computer system as he listened to what was being said. Unlike the Admiral, he was not wearing any kind of translator equipment and was forced to rely upon the Admiral to explain. They argued for a short while before the Admiral lifted his arm to silence him.

"A bombardment corridor? Explain."

Captain Campbell tapped on his secpad as he sketched out the details and showed it to the two officers. It showed a large force of ships with a rectangular path in front of them. Neither seemed to understand the image. He turned it around, suspecting for a moment he may have switched it off by mistake, but no, he hadn't.

"Okay, we position the fleet so that every ship is able to fire on the same course we are traveling along. Well before we reach the target, we open fire with all projectile weapons at the Rift, as well as up to fifty kilometers around it."

The Admiral seemed to grasp this last part.

"I see, but what of us? We will still hit the Rift entrance. No, we cannot do this."

For some reason, he looked horrified at the suggestion and explained it to his junior officer who seemed equally incredulous. To make matters worse, he then walked away and back to his computer, completely ignoring the Alliance Captain. The Khreenk Admiral beckoned to him instead.

"You want to break through a Rift at speed? Are you mad?"

The same officer as before called out to the two of them in his native language. Luckily for the Captain, his translator was able to catch most of it.

"We cannot do this. The Klithi have scouts near their side of the border, and they can come through to assist if we ask for aid," he said firmly, but the translator was unable to add the intonation.

The Admiral didn't seem keen at this suggestion, and Campbell could only assume it was down to some past or ongoing rivalry between the two peoples. He didn't know a great deal of the Klithi other than that they were the pacifists, evolutionarily advanced, and equipped with sophisticated ships. Though their craft were potentially the most impressive he'd heard of, it was rumored the

Klithi only used civilian ships. He was dubious that a few of their scouts could be of much use.

"What are their ships like?" he asked.

The officer said something untranslatable and then turned away, leaving the Alliance officer with the Admiral.

"The Klithi ships are unlike anything you have ever come across, Captain. They have access to surface shielding, a technology that surpasses even the T'Kari, yet they refuse to build ships of war."

"So they cannot fight?"

The Admiral shook his head at the question.

"Oh, no, their ships are a match to ours; even their civilian transports. If they were to ever build something for war, we would all pay the price."

He smiled in a way that reminded him of somebody about to do something very bad. The ship shuddered slightly, and some of the officers' voices increased in volume as they did their best to manage the gun crews and defensive systems. The battle was a long-ranged affair, but every now and then a small group of fighters would make it inside the protective cordon of the escorts and inflict damage on one or more vessels.

We need decisive action here. This is too damned slow.

Campbell was in direct communication with the captains of the three other ships, and tactical data was being sent directly to his datapad regarding attackers, vectors, and damage assessments right from the tactical officers of each of the three frigates. He pointed at the large formation of ships that was clearly visible through the glass.

"Our ships are keeping the fighters away, but we have to make it through the Rift. If we decelerate, our ships will be scattered by the Biomechs."

The Admiral looked confused.

"I don't understand your plan," he said, and this time the translator seemed to convert the words almost in real-time. Campbell noticed the Admiral was speaking more slowly to give the technology time to do its work.

"Can you close the Rift behind us if we get through?"

The Admiral smiled in that strange way again in response to his question.

"I see. No, few races have that technology. Trust me, we fought a war over this long ago. The T'Kari would never share it and neither would the Helions. It is the reason the Black Rift is still sealed."

Captain Campbell pointed at the shape of the vast Biomech warship that was moving toward the Rift in space.

"What about them?"

The Khreenk Admiral took in a lungful of air before answering, and it gave Captain Campbell more time to examine the alien. He had tried to work out where the metal and flesh were fused, but the work was impressive. It was as though the metal plates and augmentations had been melded together. Even though the metal sections were colored the same as flesh, the end result was something more akin to Frankenstein's monster than the synthetic warriors he knew as the Jötnar. The Admiral must have noticed the attention and he raised an eyebrow, an oddly human characteristic.

"You wonder about our…improvements?"

Campbell nodded, not sure it was wise to try and hide his curiosity.

"The Khreenk are a proud people, but we are not as advanced as the others. The Klithi are millennia ahead of us genetically. They live longer, and their mental capacity exceeds even our greatest scientists. The Byoti are stronger and capable of living in places that would kill us. The T'Kari and Helions both possess technology they refuse to share with us. All of this left us vulnerable many centuries ago."

"So you augment yourselves to rectify that?"

The alien looked uncomfortable with that question.

"We fix and repair problems with our bodies and try to improve what we can. Synthetic limbs and body parts help us to live longer. Warriors are fitted with stronger implants to improve strength and agility. It has allowed us to keep what is ours…for now."

He pointed to his temple.

"But so far we have failed to improve the mind, and in time this will be our downfall."

One of his officers shouted out something, and he looked at a computer screen before returning to face Captain Campbell."

"The Klithi are ready and waiting behind the Rift for us. They have mobilized five traveler ships. What do you suggest?"

The young Captain was listening to every word as he made notes. No sooner had the Admiral finished, and he was already on his secpad and speaking with Captain Hampel. It didn't take long before he looked back at the Khreenk commander.

"My commander wishes to speak with you," he said and then handed the device to the alien, saying no more.

"This is Captain Hampel, ANS Spearfish. Can you give me the capabilities of these Klithi ships? What are their armaments?"

The Admiral was now forced to wait, and for a moment, Captain Campbell thought there might be a problem. Then he realized he would need to wait while his own translator system did its work. Even so, he couldn't see anything on the alien's ear that might do the job.

The implants, of course.

"Captain, the Klithi ships are passive. They are heavily shielded; they are not designed for open warfare. They are not a people accustomed to war; with their technology they have never been threatened."

Captain Campbell lifted his hand to get the alien's

attention.

"They must have some weapons on board, something to protect against pirates or Raiders?"

The Admiral's eyes lit up at the mention of pirates.

"Yes, all Klithi ships have territorial blockers. They use them to disable ships that stray past their patrols."

There was silence inside the ship, and the Khreenk Admiral waited for the next question. Instead, Campbell simply tilted his head in a questioning manner. It still took the Admiral a few more seconds before he really understood what the Captain wanted.

"Yes, of course, their weapons. The Klithi use self-targeting charges that approach ships and discharge electromagnetic attacks through their armor. They can leave swarms of thousands of them; each is no bigger than my hand."

He extended his hand to demonstrate.

"Mines?"

"Perfect," came a dulled voice from the secpad.

The Admiral leaned in closer as he listened to the suggestions from the Captain. They spoke for nearly half a minute, and he passed the device back.

"Your commander wishes to speak with you," he said.

Captain Hampel's face waited patiently. As before there were people moving about in the background, and he could easily tell that the frigate's crew had their hands full, trying to keep the almost inexhaustible supply of fighters from the rear of the column.

"The plan is simple. The Admiral is going to contact the Klithi and get them to mine the Rift on the other side. They will then come through and wait on this side of the Rift as bait."

Captain Campbell was confused at his suggestion.

"I don't understand, Sir."

"It's simple," came back the curt reply. "Just make sure the rest of the fleet uses this set of coordinates and maintains their acceleration. When we reach the target, we have to be traveling as fast as possible."

Captain Campbell looked at the figures, and a narrow smile began to form across his face. The plan was simple, incredibly simple. He just hoped the rest of the fleet would do as ordered. There was just one part he wasn't sure of.

"Sir, what about the enemy ship and its fighters?"

"Yes, that is what the bombardment corridor is for. Every single ship, apart from our three frigates and the Helions escorts, will open fire on my target vector. We will create a ten kilometer wide path to break through."

Will they be able to navigate a vector that small?

It was as though the commander of the frigate could sense his apprehension.

"I know it's a tall order, but if we do it, we'll come out of this in one piece. Double-check on the details with the Admiral, and make sure he understands the plan. The bombardment is on a fixed vector. Any deviation will destroy the mines and risk damaging the waiting Klithi ships."

"What about the Klithi?" he asked.

"Don't worry about them. I've already spoken with them. When the time is right, they will travel back through and scatter on the emergency route I have mapped out. Understood?"

He saluted smartly.

"Sir."

"Good luck, Campbell. It's going to be close."

* * *

Admiral Anderson tapped the display to show the video streams from the Alliance frigates once more. As was now standard, the ship's logs and video feeds were combined to give a detailed picture of what was happening inside the ship as well as outside during such an encounter. He sat alone in his office, his long wooden table looking out of place with the modern materials elsewhere. He'd appropriated the model of the old Crusader to place on the right-hand side, and a number of plaques and images hung on the walls.

This is insanity, he thought. The smile on his face implied otherwise.

The large group of ships was the Narau fleet, commanded by Admiral Lanthua of the Khreenk. He counted the ships and noted a good number were missing from the force that had been sent on a scouting operation. The current sequence showed the escorts, led by the Alliance Captain Hampel, fighting off Biomech fighter waves. The automated turrets were especially effective, and he found it hard to hide his smile.

Good work, Captain. At least somebody out there knows what they're doing.

He rotated the three-dimensional model of the battle about on his monitoring system while the ships continued to move. In one direction was the Rift into Klithi space, as was a small formation of their civilian ships. His intercom beeped, and the face of his secretary popped up.

"Admiral Lewis for you, Sir."

He nodded in response. "Send him in."

The door opened, and in walked the smartly dressed Admiral. There was barely a decade between their ages, yet Anderson seemed to have aged far more quickly than the slightly younger man. While Admiral Anderson was the perfect example of discretion and caution, Rear Admiral Lewis was something of a loose cannon. In the days prior to the Uprising, men like him would have been demoted or kicked out. Things had changed though, and commanders that were quick on their feet were extremely important to the military. Once their greetings were over, he sat down and found it impossible to not look at the battle.

"The Klithi – Anicinàbe incident?"

Anderson nodded.

"I still cannot believe the Narau Fleet was so unprepared and unable to defend itself against such a pitifully small force. Have you read the ship assessments?"

Admiral Lewis nodded.

"Yes, it looks similar in capabilities to the ship that tried to break past Helios and on to the Black Rift. You remember how many ships it took to stop that thing?"

Anderson could remember only too well. The small task force of the latest Crusader class ships had managed to keep it busy, but it took Helion reinforcements and an assault by ground troops to finally win the day.

"Oh, yes, but this one is different. According to the reports from the Khreenk, it was entirely automated, as opposed to the other ships we've met. I have run the data through my labs here and at the Prometheus research station. They all came back with the same. It's a fast battleship type vessel, something designed for long-range interdiction."

The two officers looked at the model of Admiral Jarvis' old ship, one that Anderson had been the executive officer of back at the start of the Uprising. Crusader was the first and only ship of her type to have been constructed, and with her now gone, there was nothing quite like her in the Navy's inventory.

"So, the Biomechs have constructed their own Crusader. Why?"

Anderson shrugged.

"We built her to respond to situations quickly. CCS Crusader was a pioneer, a battleship with the speed and armor of a new generation cruiser. These ships would allow them to intercept our fleets and convoys before we can bring in warships to assist."

He turned and nodded at the display and the space battle.

"Have you seen Captain Hampel's plan? It was a stroke of genius."

Admiral Lewis shook his head.

"No, I read the report, but the video feeds hadn't arrived. I've already put him and his officers up for a commendation. They are responsible for saving the entire Narau fleet."

"Quite," replied Anderson before restarting the stream.

The Narau forces moved at massive speeds toward the Rift while the Biomech warships chased after them with all their guns blazing. Many of the projectiles were able to strike the ships, but the return fire managed to keep most of them away. The scores of turrets quickly dispatched any fighters that managed to reach the capital ships. By the time the fleet was within a thousand kilometers of the Rift, the larger Biomech vessels were amongst the fleet and firing their weapons into the heart of the force with powerful broadsides. A single Khreenk warship ripped apart from the gunfire before they struck the Rift. With a flicker, the Biomechs and the crippled Khreenk ship vanished while the rest of the Narau fleet continued past it, missing the entrance to the Spacebridge by just a few hundred kilometers and rushing on into space.

Anderson banged his fist down hard on his desk and paused the footage.

"Do you know what was waiting on the other aside for them?"

Admiral Lewis smiled grimly. He would have probably turned the fleet on the Biomechs, but the solution advocated by Captain Hampel had surprised even him. He did his best to not look a little jealous at the solution selected by the young escort Captain.

"Klithi anti-ship mines, if I'm not mistaken."

"Exactly. Apparently, the Biomech warships crashed into the mines with such force the debris alone tore them to pieces. The remnants were finished off by the waiting Klithi re-entering the Rift to deal with them, and even better, the wrecked ship is being brought here for us to study."

He pressed the button and the display turned black.

"Interesting, I'm surprised they would give up the wreck quite so easily."

Admiral Anderson took a sip from the glass on his desk before answering.

"The Khreenk are grateful. Actually, that is one of the biggest understatements I think you'll ever find. The

Narau fleet would have been annihilated. Because of our forces most of them lived, and we have received the credit for that, as well as the Khreenk Admiral. How would it have looked if we had been refused?"

There wasn't time to a response as he continued almost immediately.

"There was more than one ship anyway, and we're just getting part of the wreck. It's a win-win situation. Anyway, that isn't why I called you in here. Have you seen the latest from the Alliance News Network?"

Admiral Lewis leaned forward slightly.

"About the rebels on Helios?"

Anderson's expression turned grim, and he nodded slowly.

"Yes, the attacks throughout the colonies of the Helions are becoming a major concern. Government forces have lost control and are resorting to gas attacks and wide area munitions. High Command has requested a full strategic summary of the situation, especially with regards to these new sightings of the Biomech warships. We are in a position where the entire Helios System could fall apart, just as the Biomechs return. If Helios falls, then so does the Nexus of all the other Powers. Some of them have linking Rifts, but most need the ones to Helios to reach the others. I do not find this a coincidence."

Admiral Lewis appeared confused at the last part concerning the ships.

"Warships? I understood there was just the one incident, on the Klithi–Anicinàbe border. Have there been more?"

Anderson tapped his secpad and transferred a new report to him.

"When you have a chance, read through this. It's going to be useful for your operation."

Admiral Lewis raised one eyebrow.

"Operation? We aren't set to leave for another three weeks."

Clearly from the expression on Anderson's face, something had changed. He knew the fact that a number of Anicinàbe tribes had sided with a Biomech force was a concern, but the last report he'd read said there were over a thousand separate factions among the Anicinàbe.

How serious could it really be?

"The situation is very fluid on the ground. The Helion government has been weakened. A large number of government hardliners were killed with the failed attack on the capital two weeks ago. Those left have been trying to negotiate peace terms with the Zathee and as might be expected, the minority Irkerk, Yuulen, and the Sh'Dori ethnic groups are not happy with this. They want to retain control."

Admiral Lewis took all the information in but still wasn't exactly sure why any of this mattered to him.

"How exactly does this affect my orders?"

Anderson grinned ever so slightly. The man's disinterest

in politics reminded him of a time when he'd been nothing more than the executive officer on a Confederate Battlecruiser. It had seemed much simpler back then he seemed to remember.

"It is like this. The Helion government has requested Narau assistance to provide humanitarian relief and support while they try to stop the fighting."

"Okay?"

Anderson lifted his hand to show he hadn't quite finished.

"That is rubbish though."

He paused; letting those words sink in.

"There are rumors they are doing this as a precaution against the Animosh. It is my guess the Animosh themselves might start a coup, with support from the other three ethnic groups if they find the right moment."

Now Admiral Lewis understood what was happening.

"So, if we sit back and wait, we could be left with the same as before, a planet where the majority are kept in thrall to the other three cultures, but with a hardline government that has a mandate to crush the Zathee that dared to rise against them. That will turn into a full ethnic war."

"Exactly, and that is why I have given approval for 4th to be sent in to assist with this."

"And they said yes?"

Admiral Anderson's lip lifted slightly, almost betraying

a smile at his answer.

"I need your troops in position within seventy-two hours. We have to retain control of the situation, no matter the eventual outcome."

Admiral Lewis looked confused.

"I don't understand. Which side are we helping? The Helion government or the Zathee rebels?"

Now Anderson nodded without actually answering his question. Admiral Lewis understood immediately that there was much more going on than he had been led to believe. He knew enough to not push it any further and so stood up to leave. Already the complications of arranging the rapid advance of such a major force filled his mind with a multitude of potential problems, and the individual details were something he would have to work on over the duration of their trip.

"We need Helios and its colonies secure and ready to react aggressively if, and when the Biomechs rear their heads. Stability is more important than either of the two sides. Understood?"

Admiral Lewis nodded. "Admiral. We will be ready to leave within the hour."

There was a short pause before he made for the door.

"I will be in touch when we reach the orbit of Helios. I'll await your orders."

The door shut and Anderson was left alone. He looked back at the screen and brought up the reports from the

Intelligence Division. One in particular had arrived direct from the office of Intelligence Director Johnson. On the front it was marked with nothing but the code 57D. To anybody else it would mean nothing, but to Anderson it could mean just one thing, the internal codeword given for a decapitation strike. He opened the file, and the very first set of images showed the schematics for the government buildings, barracks, and mass transit system on Helios. The next set of pages showed an organizational tree and those in key positions throughout the government.

As I thought.

He flicked through the many pages before finally reaching the transportation hub, a massive city-sized segment of the capital that was fitted out with dozens of landing pads, platforms, and docks. The Alliance agents had taken many still images and video sequences from this part of the city, especially around the three largest pads. They were marked in red.

That is the place.

He looked at them for a few more minutes, especially the details from a number of key contacts Johnson had made among the different Zathee groups that were being known in the intelligence community as the Helion Alliance. The name implied something organized, but in reality it looked as though the Zathee groups had almost as many disagreements with themselves as they had toward the government and its Animosh state security forces.

The details in the report were nonetheless impressive, not that he would expect anything less from a man such as Johnson.

That's good enough for us. All we need now is official recognition.

He brought up another page with a list of key officials in the government and the Zathee community that promoted peaceful revolution. Most had been flagged as agitators and were being hunted by Animosh security units. He stopped when he came to the dark skinned face of an old Helion.

Naglou, so, you are the one chance of ending this without total war on Helios.

The details around the Helion man showed he was actually one of the Sh'Dori, the largest of the ethnic groups on Helios after the Zathee. In theory, the Sh'Dori should have little interest in helping the Zathee gain any degree of power in the Helion administration. According to information sent from Alliance agents on Helios, he carried a great deal of weight among many of the factions on Helios, even those normally anti-Zathee. The information on Naglou suggested he was something different. Although Sh'Dori, he was married to a Zathee woman and promoted a program of equality and rights for all Helions. He double-checked the numbers once more before tapping the camera unit on his desk and activated the secure video log.

"This is Admiral Anderson with a priority one message

for General Rivers, Chairman of the Joint Chiefs, concerning Operation 57D."

* * *

"Jack, look at this!"

He opened his eyes and glanced to his left in the direction of the sound. He was sure he'd only just fallen asleep after yet another extraction training exercise with units from the other two battalions. He was finally starting to enjoy himself, yet the fatigue and depression always returned after coming back. A group of at least a dozen marines were crowded around the communal computer unit they used for news reports, public briefings, or for catching up on entertainment in the few hours of downtime they received each week. He recognized at least a few of them, but there was no sign of any officers, not even Wictred, who seemed to be wherever the unit was.

"What is it?" he asked, without climbing from his bunk.

Private Frewyn separated from the others and walked the short distance to Jack. He grabbed his foot and tugged at him.

"It's started."

Jack rubbed his eyes and then grabbed at the side of the bunk to avoid being pulled from it. He kicked out and caught the marine in the shoulder, much to his chagrin. For a second he felt bad, but the shouts of excitement from the others distracted him.

"We've recognized the Zathee government in exile. This is it."

Jack was a little stunned at the news. The last he'd heard the rebels had attacked the government, but they'd been repulsed, and the feared political paramilitaries were engaged in reprisal attacks.

"It's Helios. The Animosh have assault the government buildings and taken over in a coup. Have you heard of this guy? He's called Lyssk, a senior commander in their forces. He's been granted a full term as something called a Justitium."

Jack sat up and looked at them with a bemused expression on his face.

"Justitium, it's just a fancy term for a temporary dictator."

They had been on their way for the last two days, yet this was still a surprise. Everything he'd heard so far suggested the uprising would drag on for months, perhaps years. He rubbed his chin while thinking.

"I thought the government was negotiating peace terms with the Zathee rebels? Now this Lyssk is in charge. What the hell happened?"

He jumped down and landed hard on one foot. The pain ripped through his body, but he simply chose to ignore it and limped over to see what was going on. The computer unit was a combined virtual presence for the command staff and a multi-layered visual display unit. In the center was a briefing from the Alliance News Network; around it were a dozen smaller feeds showing sub stories. He looked for his secpad but couldn't find it to hand.

"Hey, Jana, your secpad?" he asked the black haired Private.

Without answering, she reached down and tossed the device over to him. His hex access code gave him the same front page as on his own device. He then lifted it up to the news feeds and dragged the current stories to the device. It was a seamless transition, and now he could examine the extra pages of detail on his own. The first thing that caught his eye was that the military government forces appeared to be in control of all the important locations. All government and military installations were under their control with only a few exceptions. Even so, it seemed that the Zathee had come out in force to the streets, and there were pitched battles right across Helios.

"This could go really badly," he said quietly, but Jana still heard him.

"What do you mean? The Zathee have taken over ninety percent of the urban areas."

Jack handed her back the secpad. He'd seen enough already.

"The Zathee already occupied three-quarters of the urban areas down to their numbers. The Animosh will regroup and then starve them out, or turn the big guns on them. Don't forget, there are three other ethnic groups on that planet. I tell you; unless somebody helps stop this, the revolution will turn into a massacre. What if the other Powers send in troops to help them? The Zathee are not ready or equipped for war."

He looked away so that they couldn't see his face.

They aren't soldiers. If this Lyssk is smart, he could crush them in days.

Jana sighed as she walked back to the rest of the group and stopped. For a second she contemplated asking another question, but the latest report took her attention from Jack and back to the display unit.

"I don't believe this," said one of the marines.

Jack moved closer and nodded at the scrolling piece of information. It was as if the new report was directly answering his points. Another of the marines called out, this time a stunted looking man with an arrow-shaped tattoo on his cheek.

"The network says the Alliance has voted to assist the civilians. What the hell does that mean? Assist? Which civilians?"

The door opened and in walked Wictred, as well as Sergeant Stone. They were as menacing as any two people could ever be. Both wore their black Marine Corps uniforms and were equally grim. Sergeant Stone looked serious, much more so than normal, whereas Wictred looked almost excited. As a juvenile Jötnar, he wasn't as big as his cousins such as Khan and Gun, though he looked just as dangerous. Even so, he still looked like a troll compared to the others in the room. He nodded briefly at Jack before speaking to them all. He glanced at the Sergeant who simply nodded.

"You've heard the news?" he asked.

Most of the marines nodded, but Jack spoke first.

"The fighting is getting worse on Helios, and we have recognized the government in exile."

"Almost. It's much worse than the press are saying," replied Sergeant Stone, with no obvious emotion.

Wictred nodded in agreement before continuing.

"The coup by the Animosh and their commanders was just the beginning. Harlan, the Minister for the capital was killed along with most of the civilian command structure. With the earlier losses in the uprising, there are very few left with any idea about what's going on. A small number of survivors are in hiding with the Zathee, but they won't last long."

Every one of the marines seemed excited at the news, even though none of them had a single idea what their role would be in whatever might unfold over the coming days or weeks. Sergeant Stone could see the video feed behind the group and spotted one of the clips he had watched just twenty minutes earlier. It showed a civilian transport that had been shot down while trying to make a break for the atmosphere. The burning wreck was scattered over twenty city blocks, and the casualties were substantial. He looked back at the marines with his hard, cold eyes.

"They have sent in their troops to put down the uprising. Casualties are over sixty thousand so far, and it's going to get worse and fast."

"Sixty thousand?" spat out Jack, "When news of this spreads, the Zathee will turn this into a full-scale war. This will go on for decades, and now we are involved?"

Sergeant Stone opened his mouth as if about to speak but instead took another breath. All the marines watched and waited for him.

"That's why in eleven hours we will be joining units from our sister battalions on the surface of Helios."

He looked at each of the marines, and all but Jack seemed ecstatic at the news.

"That's right, marines, we will be part of the operation to stop this before it becomes a full-blooded war. The military coup was against what was left of the civilian government. Those that survived have contacted us directly and requested military aid. We will end this in the way only we can."

"End what exactly, Sergeant?" asked Jana.

Wictred beamed at her, his large uneven teeth glaring.

"The fighting. The other Powers have voted to use the Narau to intervene to halt the bloodshed. But we will be landing with the first wave, and we will do things our way."

Wictred and Sergeant Stone walked closer to the

marines, not that it was necessary anymore, as each was listening intently to everything they had to say. Sergeant Stone finally stopped and stared at Jack.

"The rest of the Corps will assist in humanitarian operations; we have a different job though. You up for this, Private?"

Jack looked up at him, seeing nothing but the cold, emotionless eyes of the Sergeant. It was strange, but the idea of battle seemed to fill Jack's body with adrenalin, and in an instant the depression and the bitterness had vanished.

So, this is it then? Fighting is the cure, for now?

"Yes, Sergeant, I'm ready!" he shouted out, and for the first time in days, he felt human.

CHAPTER FIVE

The realization of the ancient Helion prophecy would focus attention on a hundred worlds. One of the most peculiar would be the old worlds of Sol. Long abandoned by those with the money or means to do so; the worlds of Sol were a shadow of their former selves. Their natural resources had been squandered over millennia of abuse, and of those areas still populated, many had long ago turned to crime. Earth itself, the cradle of humanity was a desolate planet with poisoned oceans, polluted skies, and a populate that had been forced to shelter in massive shielded cities dug just below the surface. Long ignored by the prosperous worlds of Alpha Centauri, Earth would return to significance in ways that the citizens of Helios or Terra Nova could never imagine.

The Lost World

General Daniels surveyed the strategic map inside the heart of ANS Conqueror with great interest. This part of the ship had been extended and improved as part of the massive repair work undertaken following the ship's last unfortunate incident in orbit around the planet. A dozen other officers manned the computer units at the mapping unit that filled the center of the room. The walls were made of smoked, semi-transparent aluminum, and one of the sides was open and led directly into the CIC of the ship. He could make out the form of Admiral Lewis as he managed the fleet. A middle-aged Captain Hardy approached and saluted. He was the liaison officer between the Navy and Marine Corps, and the critical link between the vast forces now in position around the planet.

"Sir, all ships' captains confirm the fleet is in position. We have forward elements from the 8th and 17th ready to drop."

He nodded at the Captain and then looked back at the three commanders of the battalions. Of the three, the only one he knew particularly well was Gun, the Colonel of the 17th Marine Battalion. In the middle of the group of officers was the young Lieutenant Colonel Diego Koerner, another veteran of the last year of the Uprising and the commanding officer of the 8th Marine Battalion, the force that had already seen action in this part of space. The wildcard was Colonel Horst Brünner. He was by far the oldest and looked like he was in his early seventies. He wore a white mustache and looked every part the upper-class officer of Terra Novan ancestry.

"Well, there we have it. Zathee forces are reeling from chemical weapons, and the Animosh are leveling airstrikes on the urban areas. I have the authority from Admiral Anderson, commander of the Orion Sector, to contain this situation. You have seen the plan and made your preparations for operations in the capital."

He tapped a button and up came a schematic of the areas under dispute. There were four large red spots on the map; each centered on government buildings, precincts, military bases, and landing platforms. A fifth in the center was larger and darker than the rest.

"You will note the entire planet is one massive urban area and technically a giant city. Our numbers are limited though; we will perform surgical strikes at key areas in and around the capital."

He pointed at an area almost a hundred kilometers in diameter.

"This is heart of the planet, the place that will decide the future of both the planet and the rest of the Helion colonies."

"General, what about the other colonies?" asked Lieutenant Colonel Diego Koerner.

General Daniels lifted his finger slightly as if remembering an important fact.

"Narau forces are operating a blockade of any military vessels moving between the colonies and Helios. This conflict is being contained, and if we are smart, we'll be successful here. According to Alliance Intelligence, the other colonies are agitating, but it hasn't moved to full-scale insurrection…yet!"

He held his chin in his hand for a moment before launching into the details of the operation. The assembled officers waited patiently and double-checked the details with those on their secpad.

"Now, let me summarize the overall plan. We have a multi-pronged operation that will stabilize this situation and return Helios to its people. First, we need to find and evacuate key Helion personnel that are on the run. Without them, the uprising will be without solid leadership. Second, we need to protect the civilians, and third, we will assist the government in exile at defeating this coup."

All three of them had gone over the details of the operation a dozen times, but General Daniels was leaving nothing to chance. He wanted to ensure they knew both their own objectives as well as the overall strategy. In his experience, it was critical that everybody involved knew the plan from a high level. It was all too easy to get caught up in individual details and then ignore the big picture.

"Phase One is the rescue operation, and it will be conducted by Captain Carter of the 8th Battalion."

He looked at the young man with a thin black mustache. He was by far the youngest and most junior of those present, yet he stood up smartly and with an air of supreme confidence about him. Lieutenant Colonel Diego

Koerner had selected him, as being his most experienced and dynamic officer. He'd had little time to check the man's dossier, but from what he'd seen, there were few better at such a risky operation. He nodded at the man and then returned to his briefing.

"The Captain's forces will land at the besieged Animosh precinct that has been taken over by Zathee rebels. Some of the survivors of the Helion government are trapped inside and completely surrounded by Animosh forces."

The General placed his hand over the red shape on the map. An aerial image of the site showed the precinct was the size of a shopping center and flanked at each corner by large towers. It was the largest structure in the area, apart from a large domed building on the opposite side of the street.

"We're in sporadic contact with them via an Alliance operative that is inside there. At last count there were over two hundred Zathee and a dozen Helion officials, including the Helion Vice President. There is more than just the precinct though."

He moved the image to show the domed structure.

"Underneath this building is the crossover point for six major road and rail systems. Whoever controls this key location can slow the flow of weapons and troops. Right now, the Animosh are using it to move their forces underground and away from the street levels. If we block it, they will be forced to move overland and in plain view of our aircraft. We must secure this underground location for as long as it takes."

He nodded in the direction of Lieutenant Colonel Diego Koerner.

"This is an aerial assault operation and will be conducted by your recon elements under Carter. It will be a high-speed smash and grab operation, right under their noses. They will secure the precinct structure, evacuate the officials, and then hold the precinct and transport hub until elements from Phase Two to link up with them. "

He turned his attention to the vast bulk of Gun. Colonel Brünner seemed to pretend that Gun wasn't there, and General Daniels made a mental note to examine this further.

"Colonel Gun, you will have the honor of leading the ground operation itself."

He let that sink in for a moment and watched for the reactions of the other two Battalion commanders. As he suspected, only Colonel Brünner seemed to have any issues with having a former Biomech in charge of such an operation. Even so, the man said nothing, but he suspected he would be hearing about his decision to use Gun via other channels. Colonel Brünner was certainly well connected with High Command.

"Phase Two will, in my opinion, be the riskiest of the three phases. I've therefore decided to hand it to our renowned expert in direct action."

Gun smiled at this, especially when he mentioned the phrase 'direct action'. He couldn't think of a better description for his preferred method of battle.

"This will be a major show of force, and the Colonel will land the entirety of the 17th on a broad front in the capital city. The Zathee have been alerted of this, but there is still a chance some will not have heard the news. You will act as a buffer and engage any forces attempting to strike the civilians. Nearly two thousand marines will secure a dozen strong points and box in the Animosh and any Helion troops still fighting for the generals that instigated the coup."

He looked at Gun and noted the change in Gun's face. He was now serious, and it reminded him of the grim determination he'd seen on his old friend's face many times before.

"Spartan relied on you in the past, and now I will. You will need an iron will to maintain this line against any aggressors. Without you, our foothold will be temporary, and we could be forced to abandon our operation. I need temporary landing zones cleared for the next phase."

Gun grinned.

"I've never let Spartan down, and nothing will change with you, General."

The battle-scarred Jötnar was greatly out of place alongside the other officers. They may have been wearing the same uniforms, but there was no hiding the great monster of a warrior standing in their midst. General Daniels nodded in response to his words and then turned to Lieutenant Colonel Koerner.

"Colonel, you will command the relief troops for Phase One. Using the ground secured by your own recon units, the rest of the 17th will land armored vehicles and bring in the heavier equipment. Once assembled, you will send in an armored column in support for Captain Carter and the rest of your forces at the precinct. Your remaining units will support Colonel Gun on the ground, wherever he deems it necessary."

He looked back at the map and tapped it. The image changed to show the ground taken by the marines, as well as the precinct sitting directly in the middle of the Animosh defenses. It was clear Carter would have his work cut out holding this position, but there was nothing else he could do. It was the center point for the entire operation.

"Yes, General," Koerner answered smartly.

Then he turned to Colonel Horst Brünner.

"Colonel, the 4th are only recently reformed. As you know, I have decided to keep them on standby as a mobile reserve. You have the largest number of Vanguards and Jötnar assault units in the regiment and will need to be ready if the call comes. The Helions are a paradox, and we barely understand their people, let alone the many factions and cultures. I want options if things head south."

Gun didn't seem particularly happy about this and

turned to look at the man. He wanted to say something, but Daniels spotted him trying hard to keep quiet. Though he had his own battalion to command, there were no more than a score of the Jötnar spread over more than fourteen hundred marines in his battalion. Brünner, on the other hand, was in command of the newly designated Heavy Battalion, and that included over a hundred of his kin under his command, marines that Gun felt personal responsibility for, even though they were now technically equal to any other citizen in the Alliance.

Don't say it, Daniels thought, as he watched the scarred warrior. *Perhaps in the past he might have spoken, but over the years Gun has learnt something of diplomacy. Good.*

The man simply nodded in acknowledgement, refusing to utter a single word of complaint in the presence of the Biomech. Daniels could see what was happening but decided that was a battle for another day.

"I thought you were some kind of spiritual leader for your Biomech friends?"

It was a low blow, but Gun seemed to take it in his stride.

"I still am, ask any Jötnar."

"But your council, isn't it now disbanded?"

Gun gave him a wicked smile.

"The council, but our tribal system remains, as does my place. We are now Alliance citizens, no different to you, as promised by the Senate. Most of my kin still live on Prometheus, Hyperion, and Luthien, and they are all colonies of the Alliance, as those of Carthago and Kerberos."

"But you are not the..."

"Colonel," cut in Gun, "you know nothing of our people, or what we have done for you. My people still consider me the first...because I am."

Those last words made the other men laugh, and it bizarrely managed to calm things down a little. Admiral Lewis had been wondering at what point the deconstruction of the Jötnar political system would be brought up. It had been gradual but necessary if they were to become a full and active part of the Alliance. The benefits to the Alliance were already being felt as hundreds of Jötnar signed up to join the Marine Corps. As he looked at Gun, he did wonder if the Jötnar would ultimately replace normal humans, due to their natural size, strength, and toughness. That was for another day though; it would be generations before they would need to consider this. At least that was what he hoped.

"As you can see, gentlemen, we have a busy day ahead of us. Remember, we have specific objectives to achieve. Triple-check your briefings; the enemy is a violent regime that has turned on its own people. They are a ruthless people with the full force of the state security forces, known as the Animosh under their command. We estimate their numbers at a little over thirty thousand operatives in the capital alone. We are also aware that they utilize over a hundred combat drones."

General Daniels took a short breath before giving them the final piece of information.

"There are also rumors that citizens from the pure blooded ethnic groups are volunteering to form citizen militias to help the Animosh. This is unconfirmed. Remember, this battle will be fought and won by the Zathee themselves. They have millions on their side, along with local knowledge. If we do our job, the Zathee will be able to finish theirs."

* * *

Spartan drifted from the bomber and pulled himself to the ground of the station. He kept as low as possible and was pleasantly surprised to find the pressure and breathable oxygen indicators in his suit were both showing as green. He looked up at the cold figure of Khan and shook his head at him.

"Khan!" he whispered, as quietly as he could manage. A pair of emotionless eyes looked down at him.

"Follow me."

There was a series of deep incisions in the floor of the hangar, much like pits in a garage, and he was able to move inside and out of the line of sight of anybody in the station. Khan pushed back and drifted down from the bomb bay toward Spartan. As soon as he was free of the craft, he found himself spinning uncontrollably. Spartan reached up, grabbed his foot, and dragged him into the blackness. With a hiss, his visor slid open to reveal a beaming smile.

"Can you believe it? We're on a Biomech station!"

Khan showed no signs of amusement.

The bomber itself now sat in the center of one of the smaller hangars and attached to four long spindles extending from the sides, top, and bottom of the spacecraft. It would have been impossible in a building with normal gravity, but this section was like any other part of space, and the outer hangar there so that it could be safely pressurized.

"They must have people here, otherwise why bother with the air?"

Khan shrugged, but he was thinking about something.

"Why have people here? Maybe it's being used to store prisoners, like the ship we were on."

The mere thought of the ship they'd escaped from sent a sickening feeling through Spartan's body. He looked down at his stump of an arm; doing his best to hide the bile he felt building in his throat.

"Bastards," he muttered.

"There's something else it could be," suggested Khan.

Spartan was breathing quickly and tried to calm down for a few seconds before speaking.

"What do you mean?"

"You remember the inside of the T'Kari Raider, all those pods and the clones. What if this station is being used to store more like that?"

Spartan nodded but didn't look convinced.

"Who knows?"

A sound from their right caught their attention and both fell silent. It was a clanking sound, and instantly took Spartan back to the ship. It was the sound the Biomech machines made when they walked, an odd mixture of servos, gears, and motors. Unlike the machinery used by the Alliance, the Biomech machines had a smoother, quiet sound, and it was unmistakable to him. The sound became louder, along with the clunk of large metal feet. Just as each foot moved, there was an odd suction type noise as the mag seals on its feet activated and deactivated in sequence so that it could move about ion a zero gravity environment. Then it appeared above him.

Another one of those things!

It took a great deal of self control not to hurl himself out of their dark hiding place and up into the hangar, so he could strike a blow against one of the hated machines that had caused him and Khan so much pain and suffering, and over so many months.

"Spartan, isn't that the one?"

Spartan watched with interest as the shape went past. He could make out the coloring of the thing, and it seemed to be a dull yellow where any kind of paint was still intact. Most of its metalwork was worn down to the original material and was simply a matted gray that reflected little.

"No, this one is different and smaller. Watch how it moves."

They both stayed as low as possible while high enough to get a narrow view of the machine. It was bipedal and about two and a half meters high. Unlike the machines on the ship, this one was equipped with four arms, and two were equipped with a selection of large tools. It moved up to the side of the bomber and turned to face the right-hand door nearly halfway along the length of the spacecraft.

"What's it doing?" asked Khan.

Spartan watched and for a moment had no idea what was happening. Then the angular piece on one of the right arms started to spin and gave off a high-pitched screaming sound. It leaned toward the bomber and placed the tool directly onto the metalwork. A great blast of sparks flew from the outer skin, and in seconds the machine had ripped through the outer layer and was pushing its two tool arms inside the aircraft. Khan had lifted his head up enough to watch, but Spartan grabbed him and pushed him back down.

"There's more of them!" he said, almost in a panic.

Two machines came from the other side of the hangar, but these were smaller eight-legged ones. Spartan kept low and watched them move by following their shadows on the wall. It didn't take him long to recognize the form. He moved back down and faced Khan.

"Remember those eight-legged things on Hyperion?"

"The robotic fighting machines?"

Spartan nodded.

"Yeah, those things. Well guess what's just arrived?"

Khan clenched his fists, gnashing his teeth as he listened to their approach. They were a powerful foe, and one he had a great deal of experience of. On Hyperion, one of the Alliance's newest colonies, the Biomechs had attempted to build a portal. A large force of marines and Jötnar had defeated them at great cost. Khan himself had fought the machines in hand-to-hand combat and remembered the adrenalin and excitement, as well as the carnage when fighting them. Khan pulled Spartan close to his face.

"If they have those machines here, then they are expecting trouble."

Spartan considered this for a moment.

"Us?"

Khan raised his eyebrows in disbelief.

"Are you serious? They would fill a station with machines, just in case we stopped here?"

As Khan explained it, Spartan did his best to hide his embarrassment.

Of course it's nonsense to think they would take such measures for two people. It's far more likely they're here for something a little more substantial.

"You think they are part of an assault force. Yeah, makes sense."

The two were quiet and listened to the sound of the machines moving about above them. Neither enjoyed skulking about in the dark. It was the exact opposite of their preferred method of combat. Spartan was the classic marine, always wanting to close with the enemy and engage them with every weapon to hand. Khan was the epitome of the Jötnar, a powerful monster of a man with the intelligence of a marine and the body of a Vanguard. It wouldn't have taken much to get them out of their hiding place and into action. But neither was armed and both were feeling the effects of their deprivations on board the Biomechs' ship. Spartan flared his nostrils slightly and then moved up very slowly to take a look.

"I'll tell you something, old friend. We aren't leaving this place until we have some answers."

He started to pull himself away further, but Khan grabbed him.

"And some weapons, decent weapons."

The Jötnar's expression had changed already and into something more resembling the old Khan Spartan remembered. It had taken them a long time to make it out of that hole, but finally they were free, and neither was going back. He reached out and placed his hand on his friend's shoulder.

"Don't worry, we'll find something, and I promise you,

we'll have our revenge."

He almost spat at the ground but quickly remembered they were in a zero gravity situation. It was best avoided, so he kept his thoughts and anger deep down and inside.

It's time these machines were taught a few things.

Spartan was already watching those above them and must have spotted something because he was out of the dark gap in the floor and moving through the air. He turned his head and looked back at Khan.

"Come on, we have an opening."

There wasn't a second's hesitation on Khan's face, and just like a hundred times before, he was following Spartan and expecting to run into trouble at any moment. They were past the bomber and heading toward an open area to the rear where four oval doors were fitted. Each was large enough for a Biomech machine to move through, and one had been left open. They drifted toward the door, reaching the railings that ran around the frame. Spartan pulled himself to the right, but Khan landed by accident directly in the middle. He should have moved but just stood there, gazing at the object on the other side of the open door.

"Khan, get back!" muttered Spartan, but his friend was captivated.

Spartan glanced over his left shoulder at the bomber. There was no sign of the Biomech or its machine siblings, only the aged spacecraft and the cavernous hangar. He noticed the markings from the days of the Confederacy, and for the briefest moment felt a pang of nostalgia for those days. There had been no Alliance, no Biomech war machines, and no alien races back then. The walls of the hangar were fitted out with scores of racks and mounts from which hung a variety of tools from simple hand tools to complex and unrecognizable heavy devices. A sound from near the bomber drew his attention. As he watched, a pair of humanoid shapes moved around the craft.

Dammit!

"Khan, with me!"

There was no time for contemplation or thinking. He pulled at the rails and swung inside the doorway and into the next section. Khan needed no encouragement, and both slipped inside just as the two figures emerged from the side of the bomber. Spartan observed them carefully and was surprised when the two forms stopped near the front of the craft and began speaking to each other. Both wore spacesuits but of a totally alien form of manufacture. They were about the same height as Spartan but more slender in build.

"Who are they? More Biomechs?" asked Khan bitterly.

Spartan detected an odd tone in his friend's voice, and when he looked at him could see the interest he had in these creatures.

Why is he so upset? Is it because he feels an attachment to them if they're synthetic as well?

132

Spartan shook his head.

"No, I don't think so. Look at them; don't they remind you of somebody?"

Khan's lip curled slightly as the realization dawned on him.

"T'Kari?"

Spartan nodded.

"Yeah, the suits are different, but they move the same, and listen to them speak."

The one to the left was busy chatting away, and although it was impossible to understand what they were saying, it was quickly obvious they were speaking the language of the T'Kari, or at the very least a dialect of theirs.

"Do you remember any of their language?"

Khan almost laughed at the question, and Spartan nodded apologetically.

"Yeah, well, it was worth a shot. These must be captured T'Kari. You remember what the others said?"

Khan barely moved his head in silent acknowledgement. Spartan looked back at the two, almost feeling sympathy for them.

"They were taken from their homes in Biomech attacks and forced to serve the machines. They must be holding hostages."

The large Biomech emerged from the shattered side of the bomber and pulled at the metal framing to extract itself from inside. It caught on part of the metal as it moved, and several chunks tore and split before it was out and attaching itself to the floor. The body language of the two potential T'Kari transformed in an instant. They stood up straight and watched the machine. It moved close to them and swung one of its arms at the nearest. It struck with a low-pitched thud, and the alien was sent spinning about in the weightless environment before striking the wall. Spartan shook his head and reached out to hold Khan back.

"No, we can't...not yet," he said as quietly as he could.

The Biomech machine stopped and looked straight at him. Spartan felt his heart drop but kept completely still. Khan did the same, and it looked like it might have worked. It was nonsense, of course; the Biomechs would certainly have access to finely tuned sensors. After all, even the Alliance Vanguard Marines had access to that level of equipment, and the Biomechs were centuries ahead in most regards when it came to science and engineering.

"What about that?" asked Khan.

Until now Spartan hadn't even looked inside. He looked behind him for a brief moment, gazing at the hundreds of cylindrical shapes fitted like shelves in a warehouse. At first it took him back to the T'Kari Raider they had been on where the enemy had been transporting clones to his own worlds. But this was different, and he was shocked to see the layout was almost identical to the ones he had seen back at the start of the Uprising. He had been on board a ship where the foul Biomech creatures had been created. These cylinders looked exactly the same as those used in the harvesting sites; a place where living prisoners were mulched down and used to create new and terrible monsters. He looked back to Khan, and he could see a change, one that he hadn't seen for months.

"I can't, not anymore," Khan said.

He leaned out of the doorway, pried a bar from the wall mount, and then kicked at the wall and toward the Biomech. He bared his teeth at the thing as he moved silently to it. Spartan watched him go and was instantly reminded of the bond between them. Khan, after all, was related to the Biomechs and all their plans. By all accounts the final stage of manufacture. It seemed they had first started by cloning key individuals, such as the human leader Typhon, to help spread dissent through the Confederacy while doing the same with dozens of other races. Then came the foul creatures, those that left cities as burning pyres, and the very last stage was the completely artificial, synthetically manufactured monsters that included him. At the same time, these machines had managed to encourage every race to side with them from the Zealots of the Confederacy to the T'Kari Raiders in New Charon. It was a long and complicated link, and one that Khan was less than happy about. The warrior spun about. He hurtled toward the machine with shouts of anger bellowing from his lungs. Spartan didn't hesitate and pulled around to the left to find a tool.

Come on! Find something, anything!

The sound of hand-to-hand combat had already started as Khan smashed his own improvised weapon against the armored housing of the machine. It had turned its four arms against his friend, and Spartan couldn't imagine he would last long against such speed and savagery. The machines would always have the edge in this kind of encounter.

"Khan!" he cried out in a mixture of fear and anger.

There were small items that he didn't recognize, but on one unit was a series of metal splinters for fabrication work. They were studded, and he could only assume they were for bracing heavy equipment. It didn't matter; he needed something substantial to swing. He grabbed the largest and rested the weightless bulk on his shoulder like a club. For a second, he looked like a battered and wounded version of the ancient Herakles, the famous human hero. He looked at the fight and then tensed his muscle against the doorframe like a spring.

"I'm coming!"

He pushed back to compress his legs, flinging himself off and back toward the bomber and the direction they had come in from. As he flew at the machine, a series of sparks flashed off the Biomech. Spartan cried out in surprise as Khan tore off one of its arms. He cast it aside like a piece of garbage and swung behind it to carry on striking. Then Spartan was in range and drifting to the right of the Biomech. It seemed to have completely forgotten about him, but as he tried to stab at it with his metal club, one of the arms twisted about and blocked it.

"It's like that, is it?" he snapped and grabbed at the arm.

Rather than trying to avoid the powerful limb, he used it to drag himself closer to the thing. It flailed with one of the engineering arms, and a serrated edge slashed Spartan's leg. It was a quick attack, but the cut was deep and nearly ten centimeters along his flesh. He winced and then jammed the metal splinter into the machine's neck joint.

"You might be a machine, but I know what's inside you!" he shouted.

The metal splinter was shaped like a large wedge and pushed down the side of the head and into the torso. There were flashes around its body, and the lights in its armored helm went black. Both grabbed at the floor and the bomber, as the machine halted like some dormant statue. The magseals on its feet still stayed active, so it remained upright but to all intents and purposes, dead.

"Good timing," Khan spluttered.

Spartan tried to smile, but the blobs of blood from his wound were drifting away. He felt a little sick and would have tipped over if it hadn't been for the lack of gravity. Khan pulled himself to his friend and looked down at the wound.

"I did all the work, and you still got cut," he laughed.

Neither of them had noticed the two T'Kari that had been watching the fight unfold. In their bloodlust, they had concentrated on tearing the machine apart. The T'Kari had vanished from their thoughts, but now both waited in silence and with firearms raised and pointing directly at their surprise guests. One chattered excitedly to the other before tapping something on its suit. The helmet opened up to show a face they both recognized. It was that of a female T'Kari. She bowed slightly and lowered her rifle.

"Uh, what's going on?" asked Spartan.

"How the hell would I know?" muttered Khan, doing his best to nod.

More noise came from the right, and all four turned to see one of the eight-legged machines coming into the hangar. It moved with a horrific gait unlike any other machine or creature. Spartan lunged at the T'Kari and lost his footing. As he drifted in the air, he pulled the weapon from the T'Kari and took aim. The weapon was unfamiliar to him but was equipped with a rudimentary iron sight and trigger. He squeezed the trigger, and a blue discharge blasted out at the machine. It tore a hole through the metal but did nothing to stop it.

"Not once you fool, kill it!" growled Khan.

Spartan was spinning now, and he rotated completely around before he could fire again. This time he held down the trigger until the weapon stopped firing. It must have loosed nearly thirty rounds. It was more than enough to leave the eight-legged machine a lump of molten ruin that floated past them in the hangar.

"Okay, Spartan, I've had enough of this place. What now?" Khan asked, pulling his friend back to the floor.

Spartan looked to the T'Kari and tried to hand the weapon back, but the one refused and instead pulled out a small pistol from a leg holster. The other alien with its visor still closed, pointed to the doorway next to the massive room full of cylinders. It said something quickly, yet with a stern tone that was obvious even in an alien language. Spartan listened intently, as he had spent a considerable amount of time with their people. He recognized just one of the words. It was their word for exit, and he had seen it written in their own peculiar script at T'Kari research sites and on ships.

"So, they know a way out," he said both to himself and to Khan.

His friend seemed to positively shake with excitement at this news.

"All right, let's do this!"

CHAPTER SIX

Spartan was punished again and again after the Great Uprising, even though he was one of many heroes to have lived through it. Unable to climb through the stifling structure of the Marine Corps, he forged his own path with the infamous APS Corporation. This high-tech private security company was torn apart by controversy, however, and once more he was cast aside. Many had forgotten his name when he vanished aboard a T'Kari Raider, one of the many ships forced to serve the Biomechs. Few expected to see him return, and even fewer could imagine the change they would find when he did.

The Rise of Spartan

Jack looked out of the tiny armored window on the side of the Hammerhead. None of the other marines could see it, but his forehead was covered in a fine sheen of cold sweat. He took in a series of harsh breaths and tried to slow

141

his pulse, but it wasn't working. He could see the flashing indicator icons on the overlay inside his armored helmet, but it did even less to help him calm down. An image of the battle with the Animosh returned, one where most of his friends lay dead around him. It was the thought of Hunn, the Champion of Hyperion lying in a growing pool of black blood that returned time and time again.

"Hold on!" shouted a marine.

The craft shook and buffeted as they hit the warm air above the urban sprawl of Helios. It was enough to snap him out of his thoughts and put his mind back on the mission. He tapped the release button, and the visor opened to let in the cool conditioned air of the spacecraft. He reached inside; his armored hand tried to wipe away the sweat, but with the glove it was difficult. He cursed and closed the visor before anybody could see his face.

Get it together, idiot!

He looked back at the tiny window, remembering the last time he was in this position. It had been inside the damaged hull of ANS Conqueror as she had made her way through the atmosphere. It ended in a violent emergency landing, followed by hours of hiding and fighting. This time was different though; at least he tried to tell himself that. Now they were heading down by choice, and it made him feel strangely distant to his comrades. He could see the swirling light brown clouds in the skies, as well as layer after layer of roads, rail systems, and tall buildings. It was how he had imagined Terra Nova would be until he actually went there many years earlier.

"Jack, you ready?" Wictred asked.

Jack said nothing but lifted his thumb in the universal gesture. Wictred seemed satisfied with that, looking about the craft at the other marines as they sat and waited. All of them wore their latest issue dark gray PDS Alpha armor and black tiger strike camouflage pattern. The gear had been introduced prior to the Helios Expedition and was a minor upgrade to the old version of the armor that had been used in the Corps for decades. It was designed to provide protection against the environment, as well as moderate enemy fire. It fitted close to the skin. Contrary to most people's thoughts, the suit wasn't designed to turn each marine into a tank, more it had been created to allow them to operate in any environments within a fully sealed suit. The visors on their helmets were a smoked black color, and the reinforced gorget section at the top of the chest covered the neck and chin; this was the most obvious visual change to the equipment.

"Remember the briefing. Our job is to secure the officials and to get them back to the birds. We go in fast and get the job done."

The marines replied back on the affirmative, and Wictred nodded slowly. Unlike the other marines, he could never have fitted inside standard marine issue gear. Instead, Wictred wore the heavily modified armor produced back on Prometheus and based on specifications laid out by the Alliance military, with the assistance of engineers on Hyperion. The color scheme was identical to the PDS Alpha armor that Jack wore, but it more closely resembled a non-powered version of the exo-skeletal armor used by the massive Vanguards. For a second, Jack actually thought he was looking at one of those pieces of equipment, but the finish was completely different. The slab plating and rougher finish marked it out as a functional object, like everything Wictred's people used. It was the first time Jack had seen Wictred wear it, and it looked much more aggressive than he'd expected.

"What do you think of the JAS gear?" called out one of the marines.

Jack heard the man's voice and glanced at Wictred to hear his response. The armor's name was a simple one, and he was pretty sure he'd heard it described as a Jötnar Assault Suit, as opposed to the Personal Defense Suits used by everybody else. At least that was what he'd heard in the barracks.

"It's tight, not how I would have designed it," he said smartly.

Two more of the marines looked at Wictred as he flexed his muscles. There was no fancy powerplant or hydraulics. Everything that moved was done purely through the strength of its wearer. He looked directly at Jack and lifted up both fists as if boxing. It gave Jack a perfect view of the serrated blades on the arms.

"I like the weapons and armor though. It's a start, and it is a good match for the Vanguard gear."

Jack looked at the arms of the armor and noticed the obvious changes that had been made for the Jötnar. Their propensity for violent close ranged combat had meant the removal of anything designed for ranged combat. The limb joints were stronger, with multiple serrated edges on the arms all the way to the elbows. He imagined this type of new armor would make them even deadlier killing machines. It wasn't surprising they were being mated up with the Vanguards to create heavy units. Jack looked at the rest of the marines in the Hammerhead and was still surprised at how small they were compared to the enlarged bulk of Wictred. He shook his head, doing his best to hide a laugh.

This is not going to do anything for Wictred's ego!

"Don't forget the rules of engagement, Corporal," he called out to his friend.

Wictred frowned at this, and to others it might have looked as if it was more of a rebuke. Jack knew differently. This was Wictred being annoyed that he wouldn't be easily able to use his new toys, at least not until they were in serious danger. Wictred protected his face with the left paw and struck a mock punch with the right.

"If any of them get too close, I'll have to introduce them to my friend here."

It was a modest distraction, but as he looked at Wictred, the thoughts of the Helion synthetics that had been far from his mind were now back and in full form. They had been much like Wictred, though more slight and closer to Jack's height than his friend. He wondered how many were still on the planet and then banged his helmet hard against the bulkhead.

What the hell are you doing? Sort it out, now!

It was the continuous buffeting of the spacecraft that had brought him back to reality, and he was actually thankful for it. The memories of what had been were impacting him, and he needed to focus. Jack looked back to the window and spotted another of the Hammerheads moving in formation. The craft was smaller than the spacecraft normally used for this kind of mission, and it was part of the great change that had swept through the Alliance military. The days of all operations commencing with a massed landing craft assault were long gone. With better vehicles, weapons, and armor, the marines of the Alliance could make use of a host of new vehicles, from the small but fast Hammerheads to the eight-wheel Bulldog armored personnel carriers to launch lightning attacks ahead of the larger landing vehicles.

Do more with less, Jack thought, remembering one of the many briefings as units had been cut and new vehicles introduced. The only good thing was that as they had discovered more worlds and people, so had public demand for protection. It seemed the citizens of the Alliance were feeling nervous, and perhaps a little vulnerable after seeing the first footage of the alien worlds.

I remember one of my instructors telling me that nothing draws people together like the threat of a more powerful competitor. I'm not entirely convinced with that argument, but at the very least there have been substantial increases in defense spending throughout the Alliance, and that means more marine battalions, more bases, and most of all, more ships.

"We're going in hot!" said one of the marines to the laughter of the others.

"This ain't hot," laughed another while he played about with the slide on his carbine. Wictred shot him a withering look from across the Hammerhead.

"Marine, this is combat, not some lame ass game. Keep your weapon stowed and your game face on unless you want to be first one with their head in the mud when we make landfall!"

It was harsh and unexpected from his friend. Wictred was young compared to his kin, yet this promotion in the Corps and his recent experience seemed to have changed him. Jack looked at the other marines and wondered why they had changed in such different ways since the last operation.

"What's up his ass?" muttered Private Riku, only loud enough for the three marines including Jack around her to hear.

Jack almost snapped at her, but something deep down forced him to keep his mouth shut. Only a handful of those in the Hammerhead had seen combat, and those hadn't seen anything like the combat he and Wictred had witnessed. Jack forced himself to stay calm and looked at each of them, making sure he could remember their faces. It wasn't easy as the visors made it almost impossible to make out detailed features. Luckily, the insignia on their chests and the occasional individual markings on the armor helped a little.

"Hey, Morato. We're gonna kick some serious ass down there!" said Private Callahan.

Jack looked at him and said nothing; his mind had turned blank. He knew the excitement and bravado was just as much a coping mechanism as was the alcohol still lingering inside his body. It had dulled his senses, yet everything around him seemed to be moving slowly, apart from the view out of the window. He looked back and watched a pair of Lightning Fighters drop down to avoid a burst of thermal cannon fire. One was hit on the left engine, and it quickly caught fire. Jack watched in fascination as the fighter's internal fire suppression system stopped the fire. The engine was out of action and streamed a long trail of black smoke. That was when the internal speaker activated, and Jack knew immediately it was Captain Carter, their commander for this operation.

"Marines, this is it. Reports from embedded drones

show columns of armor on the way to the precinct. Time is of the essence. Remember, the priority is the rescue of the Helion officials. Once secured, we moved onto Phase Two and hold the entire side until relieved. Good luck, people. Keep your heads down and your eyes open."

Jack had only met the man briefly before boarding the Hammerhead, along with the rest of his team. He was a wiry man with a thin black mustache and a peculiar accent to his voice that Jack found difficult to place. He'd looked calm and confident as filed past and stepped to their positions inside. Jack looked at the rest of their formation from the window and found the Hammerhead with the black arrows near the nose.

That's him, he thought.

"Marines, we've been spotted, and now they know we're here," said a familiar voice over the platoon's private audio channel. The sound was crystal clear for a change.

They'd better have the comms working right this time.

"Animosh ground forces have blocked off the remaining route back to rebel lines. The precinct is now on its own and won't hold against a combined assault. Our schedule has been stepped up, so we're going in fast. You know your targets and extraction points, so do not dawdle."

Jack looked to the other marines and could almost smell the raw nerves.

"We have three minutes on the ground before Helion aircraft will be on us. Good hunting," said Sergeant Stone.

It was strange to not hear him ranting and raving at them. This was the first time they'd been into action with the Sergeant, and Jack was actually quite impressed with the reassuring tone of the Sergeant.

Perhaps I misjudged him.

"Twenty seconds!" said the pilot over the same channel.

It was the final signal for Jack, and it sent a massive surge of adrenalin though his body. He scanned the rows of indicator icons on the visor overlay to check everything was ready. Then he noticed the red icon that monitored his weapon.

You idiot.

He looked down and saw his L52 Mark II carbine sat there dormant, its power unit switched off, and its powerful energy coils completely impotent. With a quick twist, he activated the capacitor charging system and readied if for action. It didn't take long for the weapon to charge, but it still sent a chill of mild panic through him.

"Five seconds!"

The Hammerhead was now shaking considerably as the engines redirected their power. Until then, Jack had barely even noticed the slowing descent. Even in simulated landings, they didn't come down this hard and fast. His body seemed to increase in weight, and he thought he would be unable to breathe. The side door hissed open, and a dull yellow haze filled the horizon. The smoked visor quickly adjusted to the lighting conditions.

"Go, go, go!" shouted Wictred.

The dispersal from the Hammerhead was automatic, and it didn't even feel like a real combat operation to Jack. Half of the marines were out before it was his turn, and then he was outside. Even as he moved out, he could see the shape of the two armored mules, now known colloquially as the Ram due to its reinforced frontal section. The machines were as big as farm animals and stood on two pairs of inward facing legs. Slabs of lightweight armor hung around their bodies, and as they were fully unrevealed and dropped to the ground, the differences between the two became clear. The first had open cages fitted to its top and flanks for the transport of supplies, ammunition, and equipment. The second Ram carried a dual L48 rifle fitted inside a motorized housing where its shoulders should have been. The frontal armor of this model was much more substantial than the other, and along its haunches were two reinforced cases for recon drones.

"This way!" called out a faceless marine, as he leapt over a piece of rubble and rushed away from the Hammerhead.

Okay, let's go, Jack thought.

Jenkell, Frewyn, and Callahan spread out in front and moved toward the tower, with the Ram clanking after them. Jack followed right behind but kept his head down. His boots made a loud crunching sound as he crushed small stones to powder. From memory, he knew this structure was the captured Animosh precinct and was guarded at each corner by a massive tower. Green lines on his helmet's overlay showed where he needed to go, and small green diamonds marked out known friendlies.

"Keep moving!" said Wictred.

He lurched past Jack. His friend's large bulk and longer legs meant he could move faster over a distance, and he was in position and waiting for them by the time they reached the base of the tower. At this distance, Jack could see the improvised barricades that formed an almost continuous wall around the precinct, roughly ten meters from the structure itself. He jumped up and over the rough wall, almost landing on top of Private Frewyn's foot.

"Hey, watch it!" he snapped back gruffly.

Jack automatically dropped to one knee as the rest of the marines swarmed ahead. The scream of engines pulled his eyes toward another Hammerhead that had moved into position over the central structure. The engines rotated around, and as they did so, let out a roar that echoed for kilometers. The downdraft kicked up a storm of dust and dirt, striking the armor of the marines.

More Hammerheads flew down low, and in less than sixty seconds; an entire company of marines was deployed around the base of the precinct, both at the barricades and just inside the building. He looked at those still hovering over the lower part of the building between the towers. Three squads, a full platoon of marines, had now landed on the central roof, and Jack could monitor their progress inside the building. They moved quickly and in seconds were on their way to their rendezvous.

"Watch your sectors, people," said Wictred in a calm, yet stern voice.

Jack turned his attention back to the barricades. At least thirty Helion civilians were hiding behind the obstruction with a variety of weapons. Jack gave them a quick glance, noting that less than half were equipped with firearms. The others carried hand tools and some nothing at all. One spotted him looking and lifted his hand to signal in the human fashion.

Where did he learn that? Jack wondered.

A black circle appeared in the man's forehead, and he staggered back and to the ground. Another was struck in the shoulder before all of them ducked down.

"Incoming!" Callahan cried out.

Sensors on Jack's armor detected the source, direction, and type of fire being put down on them. He glanced at the information and noted one important point; they were thermal rounds.

"Animosh!" he spat out.

Private Riku kept down low behind the barricade but twisted her head to look at him.

"How do you know that?" she asked angrily.

Jack moved down next to her, lifting his head just high enough to look out across the open ground at the blocks of buildings about forty meters away and on the other side of the wide open road system. There were no vehicles anywhere near the precinct, apart from those dragged into position to form part of the barricade. Jack pointed at a partially demolished three-story structure.

"In there, I promise you are Animosh fighters."

She took aim with her L52 Mark II and looked at the distant rubble. As per their rules of engagement, she kept her finger off the trigger. They were not allowed to open fire indiscriminately.

"I see movement, are you sure?"

Jack nodded.

"Oh, yes, only the state political forces are allowed to carry thermal weapons."

"You've seen them before?" she asked incredulously.

Jack had forgotten how little the others in the squad knew about him. Since his platoon had been reinforced, over half of the marines had been shipped in from other units. He'd only really talked with Wictred and never about what had happened on Helios. There had been rumors amongst the other marines but few facts about Jack. He nodded.

"Yes, they are fast and well equipped. Keep your eyes open."

Wictred's voice came over the platoon channel.

"Hold your fire."

Jack looked to his left, then his right. His comrades were spread out along the barricade at intervals of about five meters. Each kept down low but took careful aim with their carbines. The two Rams reached their position, and the one fitted with cages moved closer to the base of the tower and then lowered itself to the ground. From there, Jack could see the spare ammunition, medical kits, and backup radio gear.

And the other?

He glanced about and spotted it moving to a damaged part of the barricade. Without any human intervention, it pushed its way into the rubble, dropping down so that only the upper part of its structure was visible. The motorized turret activated, and the weapon pointed up at a light angle, waiting for a target and permission to fire. Jack was fascinated as the side case flicked open, and out flew a small hex-rotor multicoptor. The device was about the size of a marine's helmet, but around it were six small ducted fan engines, each almost silent in operation. It powered up with a gentle buzzing sound and then vanished into the sky. He checked the overlay in his helmet and nodded to himself, as the other marines tagged the Helions and were already on their way to the evacuation Hammerheads overhead.

"Extraction in fifty seconds, stay frosty," said Captain Carter over the audio channel.

Red threat indicators suddenly appeared on the overlay. The drone had detected them from its high position and was sending back detailed information on direction, vector, and velocity. Captain Carter's voice returned, this time sounding less than impressed.

"Hostiles are in the area. If you are fired upon, you are cleared to engage."

It was a minor change, but now Jack had permission to return fire, if and when the Animosh attacked. He could see the enemy's aerial units moving ever closer, and the number underneath each object showed they would be in range of the precinct in just over a minute.

Damn, this is gonna be close!

"There!" cried Wictred from his position fifteen meters away to the right.

Jack tracked to the right and spotted the movement. At first it was just a handful of dark shapes, but then there were scores of armored figures, the dreaded Helion paramilitary forces. They wore a heavily faded and discolored orange uniform that looked almost blood red in the daylight. From their shoulder hung cloaks that partially obscured their forms. What really surprised the other marines were the weapons the Animosh carried. Unlike the uniform equipment of the Alliance, the Animosh utilized a variety of ranged and close combat weapons, including thermal rifles, maces, and lightweight shields. It gave them the look of a ceremonial riot police unit.

"Wait for it!" called out Wictred.

The Animosh moved out from cover and ran across the open ground toward the barricaded position around the tower while at the same time another Hammerhead swept down to land on the roof. A dozen Alliance fighters circled above them, each looking for any sign of trouble. The thirty or so Helions at the front stopped, dropped to one knee, and planted their shields on the ground; the rest formed up so that they were three deep and rested their weapons on special mounts cut into the meter tall plates of armor.

"I don't like this," Private Riku said, her normal nonchalance fading and being replaced with raw fear. Jack looked at her and nodded back at the Helions in the street.

"Keep your finger ready on the trigger," he said, reassuringly.

There must have been hundreds of the Animosh, and the modest number of Helions on the barricades opened fire to little effect. Only the odd captured thermal rifle was able to smash the shields while the rest did little more than scratch the metalwork. It was then that Jack realized the only noise around him, apart from the odd round of gunfire, was the chattering and shouting of the Helion defenders. The Animosh were almost totally silent as they waited in their odd formation. Jack was reminded of some of the old films he'd watched depicting warriors in the nineteenth century on Earth. A time when large blocks of soldier would march into battle and line up to blast away with gunpowder weapons.

This is just wrong.

Then it came; a great flash of energy and then a volley of heat as a hundred weapons unleashed their firepower.

Jack almost missed the thermal blast as he dropped down to the ground. Chunks of the barricade tore off, and pieces of metal flew about like razor sharp pieces of glass. One thermal round struck a marine on the far right. It hit the man hard in the chest, burning a hole nearly a centimeter into the armor. Incredibly, he staggered, dropped to one knee, and then righted himself before moving back to cover. A loud sound, low in tone reverberated about the precinct, shortly followed by dozens of Helion rebels surging out of the precinct and to the barricades. Jack looked at them and recalled how similar they were to the T'Kari. They were generally slightly shorter than the average human, yet far slighter in build. They were quick, but that didn't count for much in this kind of battle. Three were cut down in the gunfire before they could reach cover.

"Fire at will!" came the order.

Jack didn't even bother checking who had said it. All he needed to know was that it was a flagged command order on his helmet overlay, and that they were under fire from the Helion paramilitaries on the street. He took aim at the center of the armored line and pulled the trigger. The L52 thumped into his shoulder as it accelerated the three magnetized slugs at the target. Wictred had already sent the silent command over the squad network to use the high-power setting. The rate of fire was heavily reduced, but the weapon did discharge its capacitor in one go, turning the carbine into something more like a railgun, but with the kinetic impact of light artillery. Three holes, each the size of his fist ripped through the shield, slightly to the left, and about the height of the Helion standing behind it.

Yeah, he thought with grim satisfaction.

The Animosh warrior moved, and he could only assume it was a kill. Even so, the damaged shield remained, and another gun barrel appeared and took aim. The staccato sound of the Alliance marines firing was the exact opposite of the steady and controlled volley fire of the Animosh. A Helion to his right dropped his rifle and ran to return inside the safety of the tower, but he was hit in the back of the head. The impact sent a shower of blood and brain matter over the wall.

Idiot.

Jack returned his gaze to the line of Helions. Some were standing their ground, but few had the training, skill, equipment, or even the inclination to join them. The marines went to work as if they were in yet another training scenario. He flicked the firing mode to normal rapid fire and aimed at the same point as before.

Let's try something different.

He held down the trigger and could easily make out the buzzing sound as he emptied the entire magazine in a short burst. Through the small magnification in the optical sight, he could see the pattern the magnetized rounds made as they moved from left to right, hitting six separate shields. While he fired two high-power shots from another, marines slammed into the shields, joining him to create a hole three-men deep in the line. Wictred must have spotted it because the gap was immediately flagged as a priority on the visor overlay.

"Jack, to the left!" Private Frewyn shouted.

He lifted the carbine and twisted thirty degrees. One of the mechanical combat machines was moving from cover and into the open ground between the buildings and the Animosh precinct. It was slightly smaller than Wictred, more like a large man and bipedal. Its armor was closefitting and smooth, and resting in its hands was a thermal weapon that looked like a support version of the weapons the Animosh used. It moved quickly and was halfway across the open ground before it was hit by fire from three marines. Dents appeared in its armor, yet it kept going before ducking down behind a burning Animosh troop carrier.

"Wictred, combat drone, Sector Four. It's heading right for us!" Jack shouted on the communication channel. He tried his best, but there was a surprising note of panic to his voice at the size of the machine. Then he spotted the other two moving behind it and also taking cover. He opened his mouth to speak, but Wictred had beaten him to it.

"I have them, three combat drones, flagged for support fire. Bring them down!"

The icons for the support units lit up and surrounded the three shapes instantly. It was all part of the new firmware for the PDS, and Jack had to admit, it seemed to be working well. The only problem was that the support units were lightly spread out with just a single sharpshooter for each squad of twelve.

I need to help them.

He looked behind him and located the support Ram. It had dropped down to avoid being hit. With a simple request through the comms system, it activated and moved over to him while keeping as low as possible. It was alongside him in less than ten seconds. Jack clipped his L52 onto the special mount on the front of his armor across his chest and reached into one of the mesh cages on the side of the Ram. It detected his IFF signature and unlocked to give him access to the weapons cache inside.

Where are you?

On the right were three of the old L48 rifles, weapons that dated back to the Uprising and well before. He grabbed the nearest, checked it was loaded, and then twisted back to his position. The Ram made a quiet clicking sound and scampered off almost like a dog to a group of three marines, presumably to take them more ammunition. He lifted the weapon to his shoulder and zeroed in on the three machines. They were hard to hit as each had taken up a solid position in cover. Every few seconds, one would push a weapon out and fire, and with each blast came a casualty. He counted two marines and as many Helions killed or wounded before he was ready.

Just to the side.

Jack squeezed the trigger halfway, and the laser rangefinder instantly calculated the distance to the target. A single button tap then added on an extra meter. He finished the pull and fired a single large-caliber projectile from the rifle toward the machines. With any other weapon, this round would have been wasted, but the L48 was a different kind of beast. Where the L52 was the latest state of the art coil weapon, the L48 was a traditional firearm that utilized advanced variable ammunition. The heavy explosive round rushed past the machine and exploded a meter behind them, showering the two nearest with ultra-hot metal fragments. Jack fired three more times before the return fire forced him back into cover. As he waited there, he could see on his overlay that one was damaged, but all three were still in the fight.

"Hammerheads are leaving, good work, marines," said the Captain on the Company wide channel.

Jack looked up and saw the shape of the three Hammerheads flying away from the precinct. A group of Lightning Fighters took up flanking positions around it as a flight of Animosh ducted fan scouts arrived. These vehicles were just big enough for a single rider and were powered by a ducted fan fitted front and back. They opened fire on the Hammerheads, but it was too late. The state-of-the-art craft tore them apart with their automated turrets while they lifted up and accelerated up into the sky.

Well, that's done. Now all we have to do is hold this place.

He lifted his head from cover, noting the Animosh formation had broken up into smaller groups and had moved even closer to the barricades. More fire from the machines raked across the line, and he was forced to give his attention to them rather than the advancing Animosh.

"Corporal!" he called to Wictred.

"Here," came back the quick reply.

Jack wondered where he was, looking quickly at the visor overlay to find his friend just inside the tower of the precinct. He was heading for the door, now that the Hammerheads were on their way.

"The machines are drawing our fire from the Animosh. It's a diversion."

"Yeah, I thought so."

The door burst open, and Wictred appeared like an iron-plated titan.

"Concentrate your fire on the Animosh!" he called out, both on the audio channel and through the external speaker on his armored suit. He then turned his head and looked at the three machines out in the center of the street and in cover.

"I'll deal with them!"

CHAPTER SEVEN

Commander Gun was the first of the Jötnar to break free of the shackles of the Echidna cultists in the Great Uprising. Named for the great gun that was strapped to his arm, he turned to become one of the great heroic warriors of that war. By the end of the struggle, he had emerged as the leader of the Jötnar and a great friend of the Confederacy. His return to the military would see him promoted to the command of an entire battalion. As more Jötnar signed up for military service, they would become a common sight in the ranks of the Marine Corps where their strength and military prowess was greatly valued. Gun would forever be remembered as the first of his people though, a creature born to destroy humanity, and one that instead became one of its greatest heroes.

Heroes of the Great Uprising

The three Alliance Thunderbolts screamed across the dull skies of Helios, each leaving a vapor trial in their wake as they chased a group of heavy Helion fighter drones that were making for the scores of marine transports, landing craft, and landers. Unlike the squat ducted fan fighters, the Thunderbolts were small craft with a recognizable silhouette, due to the pair of sloping wings from which two mighty hybrid engines sucked in air to compress, ignite, and then blast out behind them. They were the fastest and most agile fighter in the Alliance inventory, but even they were slow, compared to the pair of Animosh low altitude drone interceptors. They moved around them with agility only possible with unmanned aircraft to try and protect their heavy fighter brethren. The Alliance pilots did their best to avoid their pursuers and focused their efforts on the heavy fighters, the craft most able to harm the marines' land operation.

"Now!" cried the pilot of the lead fighter.

All three craft opened fire with the nose-mounted cannons. Round after round blasted about the Animosh craft, and two were quickly destroyed, leaving just a single one in the air. It pulled up, trying to escape, but a heat-seeking missile launched from one of the Thunderbolts chasing it exploded just a meter behind its engine unit. With a red flash, the fighter tore apart.

"Gotcha!" shouted the pilot of the second.

"Cut the chatter Yellow Two. We've got bogies, three marks right behind us."

These interceptors were much smaller than the larger

fighter drones, and although lighter armed, they were prefect for high-speed chases like this one. Every time the Thunderbolts tried to evade, the interceptors closed the distance.

"Break formation, keep them off the landers!" the Squadron Captain ordered.

The Helion interceptors were an advanced form of ornithopter, shaped like winged insects, and had been nicknamed Bugs by the Alliance fighter pilots. The wings vibrated so that they left a barely discernible blur along the flanks of the craft and darted about almost as if able to ignore the rules of physics.

"Yellow Two to Yellow Leader, they have me!" the pilot on the left called out in a desperate voice.

"Break low and run hot!" called out the leader.

Without hesitation, the fighter turned upside down and dropped down nose first toward the ground, its engine burning almost white hot. One of the interceptors chased it, but the young Captain in charge of the squadron rushed down after it. They lost almost a thousand meters of altitude before they reached the highest peaks of the city. Yellow Two ducked between the massive structures while the interceptor fired burst after burst. All the while, Yellow Leader moved to get the perfect shot. Then he had it, and with a short burst, the interceptor spun out of control and struck a tower beacon.

"Thanks, Yellow Leader, I owe you!"

Behind the swarm of dog fighting Thunderbolts and Helion drones, followed the Marine Corps landing craft. These massive landers could place an entire company of marines into the heart of battle. They were armored and equipped with the best defensive systems available. This was the latest iteration of the model, now known simply as the Mauler, due to the battery of twenty-four spigot mortars that were arranged in armored housings on each side of the craft's front section. It was a heavy assault lander and perfect for attacking contested positions. One of the Helion Bug interceptors moved around it to attack, but two automated turrets tore it apart before it could fire its weapon.

"Yellow Squadron, return to formation!" called out the Squadron Leader.

Their formation had scattered, and it took almost a minute for the three fighters to pull back to join the rest of the fighter cover for the Maulers. No sooner had they formed up, more interceptors returned. The Maulers stayed close together and used mutually supporting gunfire, much like the massive blocks of heavy bombers used back on Earth in the wars of the twentieth century. More interceptors rushed in from the east, and Yellow Leader tagged them on his helmet display.

"Hostiles, intercept!"

They peeled off and were quickly surrounded by a formation of the Bugs. One Thunderbolt exploded as it collided with the group, and gunfire flashed around the two survivors.

"We're under fire!" called out the pilot of the lead Thunderbolt as it banked to the right. The pursuing interceptor drones raked it with gunfire, shattering one engine and putting a dozen holes in its fuselage.

"Mayday, mayday, I'm going down!"

The remaining fighter dropped its countermeasures as it did its best to shake off the interceptors. At this altitude the drones had a massive advantage, and it was unable to strike back before they could shoot. Another Thunderbolt from a different squadron was hit before the turrets of the following Mauler were in range. Two more fighters plummeted downward, along with the wrecks of a dozen interceptor Bugs. Meanwhile the wave of landing craft rushed down to the waiting landing sites, each preselected by Alliance agents and their rebels allies. Though the fighters were taking heavy casualties, they'd done their job and kept the drones away from the landing craft.

"Bastards!" Yellow Leader swore, as he punched the eject button.

The entire crew section of the fighter blasted away from the burning wreckage, and retro thrusters cut the speed before three parachutes deployed to slow the descent. The Captain watched as the pilot from the first fighter dropped down with his parachute fluttering above him, and the first of the landing craft swooped down to an open street.

A handful of Helions, presumably Animosh fighters, moved to intercept but were quickly engulfed in a massive barrage, as all twenty-four assault mortars devastated an area a hundred meters wide in front of the craft. The pilot smiled as he saw the cloud of smoke, knowing full well that from within that craft a hundred marines would surge out and overwhelm the scattered Animosh in seconds.

Now it's our turn! he thought happily, then realizing the predicament he was in. His chute had caught a strong current, and he was moving away from the landing zones and into Helion controlled territory.

Oh...great, this is just what I need! he thought bitterly.

* * *

The gun line was thin, with just a small number of the Alliance's marines intermixed with rebel fighters. Yet the combined fire of L52 carbines, and the occasional L48 rifle, was impressive and gave the impression of far more defenders. It was continuous and also extremely accurate. More of the Helion rebels had joined them, now that they could see the Alliance ground forces would stand and protect them. The coilguns blasted holes in the armor while the L48 rifles exploded charges inside the formation. It didn't take long for the three blocks of Animosh to start to crumble. Jack fired again and then dropped the now empty L48 to return to his carbine. Movement to his left caught his eye, and he turned slightly to see Wictred leap over the barricade on his own.

"Wictred!" he shouted, fearful for his friend.

The Corporal ignored his shout, and sporadic fire from the buildings on the other side of the street forced Jack back to the safety of the improvised precinct defenses. He fired a short burst at one of the muzzle flashes and then saw Wictred out in the open. A dozens thermal projectiles struck his armor, yet one only managed to do much damage. He ignored them as if it was nothing but rain and jumped onto the debris sheltering the three machines. One of the combat drones opened fire directly into his chest. He stumbled and fell down into the cover. A shattered arm flew out and landed on the ground.

"No!"

Then Jack spotted the Wictred stumbling to the side. It wasn't him. He found himself unable to fire as he watched his friend smash his great armored fists into the combat drones. They tried to return fire, each of them refusing to give ground. The fight reminded him of what his father, Spartan, had told him of the fighting on Hyperion against the Biomechs. The machines had no interest in protecting themselves. They were simply given their orders, and Wictred was taking full advantage of that fact. It was only then that Jack noticed the guns had fallen silent. The Animosh waited patiently with many of them watching the machines battle away. Even the marines and the rebels had halted their shooting.

"What's going on down there?" demanded Sergeant Stone.

Jack was sure he could hear the Sergeant's voice outside of his suit and turned his head. He saw him plus a four-man fireteam moving out of the main door of the tower and approach the barricade. Jack turned his upper body to see him more clearly.

"It's Wictred, Sergeant. He's fighting the machines."

Sergeant Stone moved closer and stood up tall to look out over the improvised defenses. From his position, he had a clear view of the fight and also presented an easy target to the Animosh.

"That crazy son of a bitch!" he said, without any sense of amusement.

He turned his attention to the marines sitting at the barricades.

"Drones have picked up a dozen transport vehicles inbound, plus air support. Get your asses inside and prepare to defend that tower."

He pointed behind him at the tall structure with its small door, massively thick walls, and dozens of small windows. Jack looked at them, noting how they were at least three meters from the ground and spaced widely apart. They could have been no larger than his head, perhaps even smaller.

It's the perfect fort, or prison, he thought to himself.

"Move it, marines, go, go, go!"

In seconds, the whole of his squad was breaking from the cover and making their way inside. One man stood out in a light gray version of the PDS armor and was speaking with the Helion rebels at the barricades. He then returned to the tower, along with all but four of the rebels. Jack was the last of the marines to leave. He stayed in position, checking through his sight at Wictred's battle. One machine was a piece of junk on the ground; the second fought on without its weapons and just one arm. The third had backed away and lifted its thermal cannon.

It's going to shoot them both!

Jack was convinced of it, and if it fired at that range, there was a good chance Wictred would be struck in the back of the head. Jack activated the high-power mode on his L52 and took careful aim. Only the armed machine was stationary, and he had the perfect target. With a single pull, the three magnetized rounds slammed into the weapon itself, triggering an explosion that blew the weapon apart and tore chunks off the front of the combat drone. It took just seconds for Wictred to finish the remaining machines off. He looked back in the direction of the barricades. Nobody but Jack was waiting for him.

"Wictred, get back here, now!" cried out his friend.

Wictred needed no further encouragement and staggered back to the line, leaving the ruined machines behind. As he covered the open ground, Jack could see the damage to his armor. A burn mark on his chest marked the point where the first thermal round had struck, and there were dozens of smaller dents and signs of damage from his waist upward. One of the guns had been bent in half on his arm, yet he moved as if leaving a training field. When he reached the barricade, the Animosh called out, and as one, they broke from their cover and surged toward the now abandoned defenses.

"Come on!" Jack shouted.

He jumped up, loosed off a burst at the Animosh, and ran for the small door at the base of the tower. L52 shots rang out above him as marines on the upper levels of the tower rained down fire on the attackers. The door opened as he reached it, and Sergeant Stone himself manhandled him in. Wictred was close behind and crashed through the doorway, his armored body only just fitting inside, tearing a chunk of masonry from the wall as he did so.

"Watch out!" called out a voice from the dark interior. Jack did as he was told, just as the robotic Rams charged inside; first the supply unit and then the armored combat unit. They moved inside like a pair of metal animals, and Private Jenkell slammed the door shut behind them. Two more marines pushed a heavy storage unit made of metal against.

"I told you two to get back inside," the Sergeant said sternly. "Now get on the line. We need to hold this place!"

Jack nodded and moved away, not before spotting a

glimmer of a smile on the man's face. It wasn't much and vanished as quickly as it had appeared. Wictred joined Jack at the base of the interior, and he could now see the inside of the building. It was barren, much as he had expected. There were no sculptures or great artworks there, just bare stone and a number of wall-mounted computer units that no longer functioned. He moved to the nearest window before realizing he could never actually reach it.

"Uh, Jack, maybe this might help?"

He looked at Wictred, struggling to hide a laugh as the giant dragged a metal desk over to the outer wall. The tower was empty, and there were arched access points to the walls on two sides, with the third pointing inside to the main building. There were no doors; only large, featureless arches that would be easy get through.

"This place makes our barracks look like a five star hotel," he muttered, climbing atop the desk.

"Watch that mouth, Private!" barked Sergeant Stone.

Jack hadn't even realized the man was still so near. He had the uncanny ability to be able to move around without making a sound. Unlike the rest of the marines, he had his helmet's visor open to show his face in all its bitter glory.

"I want a squad at the windows. The rest of you prepare secondary defenses at these points."

He indicated toward the three arches that led to the other parts of the precinct. The intelligence agent appeared at one of the arches, along with a group of five

Zathee rebels and two synthetics. Several of the marines turned their attention away from the windows to look at them before Sergeant Stone shouted back.

"You heard me the first time, marines! Get your eyeballs on the target. These are local boys, nothing more."

He then walked along the interior of the tower, right along the outer wall so that he could inspect the defenses. He stopped at every window and made sure the marines were in the correct positions.

"Remember, if they see you, they will kill you. Keep your heads down and prepare yourselves."

Jack was now high enough to look outside and risked a quick glance. As the drone had shown, the Animosh had secured the street, and further vehicles were arriving some distance away. As he moved his head, the overlay showed where the detected enemy was even if they were obstructed from his view. As he watched them, something occurred to him.

"Sergeant Stone, why do they want this place so badly? We got the officials out, didn't we?"

The Sergeant moved past him to the next marine before answering.

"Good point, marine. Don't forget, they don't know they all made it. There is a much more important reason though."

"Location," said Wictred, remembering the briefing.

"Exactly," said Stone. "Whoever controls this point will

command access into the rest of the city. The precinct is the center of their line, and they were fools to not have a larger garrison."

Sergeant Stone spoke to the intelligence officer who approached with his group of Helions. They exchanged a few words before the officer spoke to the others.

"The Helions overran all the buildings in this area as the uprising began. They thought it would be over quickly, but the Animosh regrouped and retook the key buildings in less than a day."

He rotated and pointed with both hands at the interior of the precinct. The place looked as though it had been abandoned for more than the few days it had actually had been. Jack suspected the Helions would have looted the place, but it wasn't easy to tell. He'd never been in such a place.

"The only reason we are here now is that these survivors of the Helion government were trapped here. The Zathee and some of the other Helions stayed with them and waited for help...that's where we come in."

"Why these Helions? Aren't they all enemies of the Zathee?" asked Jack.

The officer shook his head as he repeated Jack's words to the Helions. It was in that moment Jack recognized the face of the synthetic Helion. It was the one that had helped them in the fight many months earlier.

What was his name? he thought, yet no matter how hard

he tried, he couldn't remember.

"Vadi?" Wictred called out, and in a flash Jack recalled his final conversation with the synthetic. He hadn't know the name of the two that helped in the battle on the tower, yet Vadi had been the only one to live and had dragged Jack into one of the Hammerheads. The scars on his face were the giveaway, a mark he had received when Helion security forces had struck at him in the battle. The synthetic lurched out from behind the heavily armed Zathee rebels and smashed his fist down onto Wictred's chest before looking up to Jack. He smiled, revealing a mouth much like Wictred and full of damaged, misshapen teeth.

"Jack Mora!" he growled with obvious pleasure.

It wasn't exactly his name, but Jack reached down to shake his hand nonetheless. The synthetic and Wictred could easily have been distant cousins, if it hadn't been for the lighter build and form of Vadi.

"How are you?" asked Jack, almost too politely.

Vadi continued to grin, and it was clear he had no idea what Jack was saying. The intelligence officer appeared agitated when another Helion ran in shouting. They spoke for just a few seconds before he started to speak in his radio. He finally looked to Sergeant Stone.

"Sergeant, reports from the local Zathee. The Animosh are moving underground and have captured the residential block there. They've cut off our only ground link with units from the 17th."

He pointed to his left, but none of them could see much inside the thick walls of the precinct. Captain Carter was clearly apprised of the same information, as his voice interrupted their conversation from within every single marine's helmet.

"Captain Carter here. We have a problem. Animosh commandos have captured the nearby residential block and are reinforcing the area with armored units. They have missiles on the roof."

Jack shook his head; he knew exactly what that meant.

"Great," muttered Wictred, "we're on our own now."

Each looked to their windows while Sergeant Stone organized the bulk of the Helions and the remaining marines with the barricading of the interior of the precinct. He kept a single squad of twelve marines just through the archway and inside the main building of the precinct as a reserve.

"We can hold this place. I want every man, woman, and child on the firing line. Keep the Animosh busy. Our backup won't be here for some time," he said calmly.

Captain Carter's voice finally returned.

"Phase Two of this operation is already underway. We must hold until relieved, Carter out."

The tall form of Private Callahan caught Jack's attention as he waved feverishly at his window. There were a dozen of them in the same situation, including Wictred who had managed to drag more furniture to the wall to reach a window of his own.

* * *

General Daniels looked at the tactical map with a growing feeling on unease. None of the reinforcements had landed yet, and the icons of the ground battle showed the number of enemy forces was increasing by the minute. There were different colors to represent the Alliance forces, Helion security forces, and the rebels. He hadn't appreciated quite how insignificant his own forces were in terms of numbers until he saw them on the map. The city was of a misnomer, and rebels surrounded the central government region on all sides.

Will they hold? he thought.

Numbers were one thing, but a Zathee civilian with no combat skills or military weapons couldn't be expected to hold against a concerted attack. Reports near the precinct already showed the rebels had been easily brushed aside, and more forces were arriving to help the surrounded Helions and their dreaded Animosh. In theory, the capital should have fallen days earlier, but the Animosh were steadily retaking lost ground.

What happens when they meet with Gun's forces? He'll be chomping at the bit to take them on.

Captain Hardy entered the open plan room from the CIC.

"General. Admiral Lewis reports that several small fleets are approaching; they are civilian ships under the flag of the Khreenk Federation. "

General Daniels knew the fear of Admiral Lewis only too well. He could see the man in the CIC opposite, and he appeared to have his hands full managing his fleet of ships around Helios. It was a lot of space, and his resources were limited. Daniels seriously doubted the Alliance could stop a concerted approach by any of the other factions.

"I see, are they a problem?"

Captain Hardy shrugged.

"Unknown, General. Admiral Lewis suggests you deploy earlier rather than later, just in case."

The man returned to the CIC, and Daniels turned his attention back to his small war room. Apart from the central tactical display, there were dozens of screens around them that showed direct tactical feeds from company commanders on the ground. He watched the other three senior commanders as they busied themselves with the management of their units.

This is going well, perhaps too well.

In the past, they might have been on the surface, but this was a new way of commanding the battle. They could do all of their work from this one place, deep inside the heavily armored hull of the Alliance's flagship. General Daniels had seen his fair share of action, and he had absolute confidence in the officers on the ground. He'd been a young marine officer once, and he'd sparred and then fought alongside Spartan in the Uprising. He now commanded three battalions of marines in the first major land operation on alien soil in history. Its significance for now was lost on all of them as they had the lives of marines to look after, and none of them took this lightly. Not least the lives of the civilians they had promised to protect.

"They are bringing in unexpected numbers of reinforcements. Intel screwed up big-time on this. My recon units have intercepted groups moving underground," said Lieutenant Colonel Koerner.

The others looked at the points he'd marked on the map.

"Praetor Grani was the head of the Animosh in the central districts. The Zathee say he and his commanders are now in charge. They've taken control of the capital buildings, including the council, and all of note in the hundred kilometer-wide sector."

He then planted his finger a third the way from the right of Praetor Grani's territory.

"This is the Animosh precinct and the attached transport hub. As of right now, they still control it. We believe it is how they are moving large numbers of supporters from the rebel districts. If we aren't quick, they'll have thousands more in position."

General Daniels wiped his brow but managed to stay

calm and collected.

"Understood. So we have the precinct, and we know the Animosh have it boxed in securely on three fronts. How about the eastern approach?"

Lieutenant Colonel Koerner shook his head.

"They had already cut off the eastern route with scouts when we arrived. Since then, they've brought in over a thousand more plus combat drones."

"It's worse than that," said Colonel Horst Brünner, commander of the 4th Battalion. His slightly chubby face betrayed a mixture of boredom and irritation at what was happening in the battle.

"By landing here," he pointed at the precinct, "you have left a salient that we will have to respond to. I can guarantee that Praetor Grani will be mounting every anti-air weapon he can find to stop us."

"Good!" growled Gun in reply.

Daniels could see the anger between Brünner and Gun, but he had neither the time nor the inclination to get involved just yet. Instead, he pointed at the precinct.

"This is my plan...and I choose to leave the recon units exposed in this place for a very good reason."

The officers were now silent, but Daniels could see Gun was smiling.

Why is it that of all the officers I have, the violent brute is the one that understands?

He waited but no one had anything to say. It was odd,

as the plan was a textbook operation, one that he was sure almost any Alliance officer would attempt to pull off. Finally, Gun pointed at the frontline his own forces had established along the eastern approach to the capital buildings. It was a broad front; far more than just the marines would be able to control.

"My forces have linked up with rebel troops and are building up numbers here, here, and here."

He pointed to three key areas that were equally spaced apart, with only one on the same path as the precinct, yet it was more than twenty kilometres away from it.

"My marines have provided limited tactical support. So far, the Animosh have seen only a small portion of our forces."

Daniels could see that Gun understood. He watched and left Gun to continue explaining.

"By controlling this one strongpoint in the center of the enemy, you are drawing their forces from the fighting with the rebels. If they want to capture it, they will need their best forces away from the front."

"Exactly," said General Daniels. "As soon as the relief mission begins, I will give the signal to our agents on the surface. The Zathee have been deliberately withdrawing to build up numbers for the final push."

Again, the other two commanders looked surprised at this news.

"A ruse?" asked Lieutenant Colonel Koerner. "You are

happy for the rebels to give up so much ground, and so quickly?"

Daniels looked out at the naval officers in the adjoining CIC before looking back at the tactical map. It was all in real-time and offered a degree of control he doubted any general had ever had in the past. It was almost like playing some kind of abstract video game.

Except in this game, I can get people killed, a lot of people.

"The ground is irrelevant to us and to the Zathee rebels. All that matters is who is controlling this city and planet within the month. If I have to lose ten square kilometres, well, fine. I need them weakened and concentrated in a place where our own forces can do their work."

Now Lieutenant Colonel Koerner seemed to grasp it.

"So, we send in armor to the precinct and then engage their best forces right in the heart of their home ground?"

Daniels nodded.

"Exactly. The rebels will stand no chance against the Animosh, and they will fare even worse against their machines. No, this means the rebels can strike hard, knowing that we will take care of the hard core of their forces."

"What about the rumors of mercenaries?" asked Colonel Brünner.

General Daniels noticed how the man kept this kind of information until it was of benefit. He wondered what else the man might be keeping to himself during this operation.

This man is a heartless, selfish bastard. I'll have to deal with him when this is over.

"I've heard nothing other than the suggestion by intelligence that our escorts have intercepted two small ships on the way back from the Khreenk Federation. They have been turned back."

Colonel Brünner pointed to the CIC of the ship.

"So there is a chance there could be more of them as we speak, trying to run our blockade of the planet?"

This man is starting to bore me.

"None of this is relevant right now."

He returned to the map and pointed to Gun.

"What's the status of the landing grounds, are they ready yet?" he asked.

Gun nodded quickly.

"Yes, my marines have taken all but one of the objectives. Fighter cover kept their interceptors of the Maulers, and every one of them landed without casualties. The last is a fortified strong point. It has been surrounded while we secure the three landing grounds. They are in our hands, and the local Zathee are expanding them for us for larger transports."

Daniels seemed pleased at this news, but once more Colonel Brünner interrupted.

"So you left an enemy bastion in the middle of your line?"

"Colonel, enough!" snapped General Daniels, his patience now exhausted.

"The priority is to secure a frontline to pin the remaining security forces into battle with the rebels. This bastion as you call it is a distraction, nothing more. Colonel Gun is correct in his assessment. The landing zones are the priority. Until we bring in the armor, we will be stuck with over two thousand marines with no heavy equipment, transport, or protection."

Colonel Brünner winced at this retort. It was clear he wasn't used to being spoken to in this way, and Daniels knew full well this man and his political connections would make his life difficult after this operation.

Ah, well, now I know how Spartan felt.

He took a long, exasperated breath before returning to the map.

"Now, let's get our armor on that planet. It's time the Animosh were introduced to our Bulldogs. I suspect they will not want to play."

Gun and Colonel Koerner both grinned at this, but Colonel Brünner was evidently furious at being spoken down to. Daniels spotted his face and shook his head in irritation.

"Let's hit them, and hit them hard!"

CHAPTER EIGHT

The Bulldog was one of several urgent purchases for the Alliance Marine Corps in the interwar years. With the Confederate Army disbanded, it would come down to just one service to ready for all eventualities. Lack of ground-based mobility was a big issue in the Uprising and resulted in the Corps fighting too many static battles where they should have been able to redeploy in a matter of hours. These new vehicles were modular and adaptable to a variety of situations. The eight-wheeled Bulldog was equally at home as a troop transport or a light support vehicle when equipped with turrets and additional weaponry.

Equipment of the Alliance Marine Corps

The sheer quantity of orbital traffic around Helios was a sight to behold. There were the hundreds of transports and passenger liners, and tens of thousands of even smaller vessels that were used to move between the orbital stations or the planet's many moons. Warships of the Narau Navy moved in small groups as they checked potential gunrunners to Helios, but there was little chance they would be able to identify such a vessel in time to intercept it. One group of ships stood out more than any other as it circled in high orbit. It was the 4th Heavy Strike Group; the most advanced task force of Alliance ships ever assembled. This powerful formation included eleven Crusader class universal warships, such as the now famous ANS Crusader, ANS Victory and ANS Serenity, as well as the vaunted Conqueror class Battlecruiser, ANS Conqueror. These were not the only Alliance ships in Helios space, but they were the only capital ships this close to the Helion homeworld.

Rear Admiral Lewis watched the planet from his seat in the CIC during a rare moment of calm. All around him buzzed activity from the Navy crewmen, but for now they had their own tasks to take care of, and none of these particular duties required direct intervention by Admiral Lewis. The crew's diverse tasks included managing the ships, coordinating the fleet's fighter cover while also assisting General Daniels with the ongoing operation on the ground. He leaned back slightly and breathed slowly, enjoying the moment of respite.

"Admiral!" cried out Lieutenant Rola Ryante, the ship's tactical officer. She was in her early thirties, tall, and rather manly in appearance.

"What is?" he replied in an almost bored tone. There was little excitement to break the monotony of running a blockade, and the most exciting thing to have happened so far was watching the many Hammerheads, Lightnings, and Maulers as they dropped down to the surface.

"We have incoming ships from the ninth moon. They have only just activated their engines. It is a stealth course, and they are making for an orbital course with Helios. The Narau ships are too far away to intercept."

"Stealth course, why?"

"They aren't civilian ships, Admiral. I'm detecting unusual weapon configurations."

Lieutenant Ryante almost seemed confused as she examined the details coming in from each of the ships. A stealth course was simply that the ships were operating on limited power and coasting, rather than using their engines. It wasn't easy detecting such traffic unless you knew exactly where and when to look. Luckily for these ships, there were many pieces of debris, dormant stations, and thousands of vessels, tugs, and cargo modules to hide them from active scanners.

"Put them on the main screen, Lieutenant."

The image from one of the long-range optical mounts showed a force of at least twenty vessels of various configurations. They were spread out over a modest area of space and moving fast. Several were quite clearly bulk cargo ships, but they were all fitted and equipped for combat. Some carried layered armor but all seemed modified for war in one fashion or another. What really stuck out the most was the ship in the middle of the formation.

"That's a Khreenk warship," said Lieutenant Ryante.

The vessel's size was difficult to gauge in space, but the ship's computers had already performed a number of calculations, and it was clear the ship was closer in size to Conqueror Alliance ships than anything else. Admiral Lewis shook his head angrily before pointing to his communications officer.

"Get me Admiral Lanthua of the Narau fleet, now!"

He paused and then added, "Hail that ship as well. I need to speak with her captain."

Lieutenant Ryante had already run detailed analysis of the approaching ships and put all the data she had accumulated so far on the main screen. It included everything from size and mass to approach vectors, velocity, and power configuration.

Admiral Lewis looked at the number with surprise.

"You're certain of this? This fleet of ships is heading directly to Helios, at that speed?"

She nodded, as the face of Admiral Lanthua, the Khreenk commander of Narau forces in this part of space appeared. He was the very same Admiral that had been attacked by the Biomech forces in Anicinàbe territory.

The alien spoke, and Admiral Lewis was forced to wait a few seconds for the translators to do their work. He noted the form of Alliance liaison officer, Captain Tory Campbell to his side.

"Admiral Lewis, how may I assist you? I understand you have concerns with this force of vessels?"

"Concerns? My officers tell me this is an armed fleet, and they are making for low orbit around Helios. Who are they, and what do they want?"

Again there was the short pause.

"These ships are one of the private operations in Helios. They are licensed to travel and to provide security services to companies. Their ships were cleared on the moon before leaving."

Lieutenant Ryante shook her head.

"According to the reference database the T'Kari gave us, that ship is an obsolete Khreenk battleship. Apparently, the class is around seventy years old, and they were all marked as scrapped."

Admiral Lewis looked back at the alien who had heard the same information. He waited, but the commander of the Narau forces said nothing. It was evident the Khreenk Admiral had no intention of giving up any information of significance. In that moment, Admiral Lewis' opinions of the Narau were confirmed.

They're just a force for politics and show. They have neither the skill nor the will to fight any real enemy. Anderson was right. We need to drive events here, not the other way around.

"Well, can you explain why you are letting an uncharted Khreenk warship and the rest of the ships head to the warzone? The Narau are supposed to be here to prevent escalation of this crisis."

The alien's face changed slightly, and he wondered if he could see a hint of amusement.

"Khreenk warship? My database flag this ship as an obsolete state vessel, sold for scrap, and now used as a transport. It is no Khreenk warship, I promise you."

Promises, what the hell do you know about them?

He thought of the three Alliance ships serving with this Khreenk Admiral and felt a glimmer of concern for them. There was nothing he could do though, not yet, but he would need to make contingency plans. The Helions had already managed to nearly destroy one Alliance ship in the terrorist incident against ANS Conqueror.

"These ships are on no civilian mission. I suspect they are smuggling arms, supplies, and potentially mercenaries."

Again there was the translator delay, and it gave him time to look at the ship disposition. It was easy to see how they had been arrayed to look like a merchant convoy, yet the low electronic emissions and limited radiation from their hulls suggested they had taken great risks in keeping their vessels cold and hard to detect. He wouldn't be surprised if they had even sustained casualties, due to the extreme nature of their journey.

"I have orders from Khreenk homeworld...to...let these ships pass."

Admiral Lewis stood up and banged his fist down on the console to his right. Half the officers in the CIC turned to see what the commotion was about.

"You are in direct violation of the Narau agreement. You do not operate on the side of the Khreenk. Your duty is to all the worlds that provide a tithe for the fleet. Now, I suggest you do your job, and stop those ships before they escalate the situation on the ground. Equipment of war could be used against the legitimate Helion government."

The alien stood calmly as the circuits did they job. After a couple of seconds, he bared a broken tooth before speaking.

"Legitimate? I am sorry, Admiral. The Khreenk do not recognize the rebels as the state government. Justitium Lyssk is the official leader of Helios, and during these troubles, we will provide whatever assistance is requested by his government."

There was a tiny delay as one of his comrades spoke with him.

"The Narau Fleet will of course assist in any way we can to keep hostile forces and equipment away from the crisis on Helios."

Admiral Lewis did his best to keep a straight face and turned to his executive officer, Commander Lisa Sonels. She was in her early forties, short and with graying short cropped hair. Her face was marked along her chin where she'd been badly burned in a skirmish the year before out on the Rim, deep in Alliance territory.

"Get me the fleet on the horn. I want them ready to intercept this rogue fleet. They should be ready for combat operations."

He said it slowly and loudly enough that most of the officers in the CIC could hear him, as well as Admiral Lanthua. The alien's expression changed to a peculiar mixture of anger and pleasure, one that he hadn't seen before.

"These ships have full authority from the Khreenk Federation to travel through this sector. My government will not allow you or any other person to interfere with their legal progress."

Admiral Lewis was now starting to lose his patience.

"Legal?"

"Yes, I have received important and classified information from the homeworld concerning these ships. There is no need to go any further."

The grin on Admiral Lewis' face suggested otherwise.

"I have a dozen warships enforcing a blockade here that disagrees."

Lanthua snarled at the insult.

"I do not take kindly to threats, Admiral. I have over sixty ships in my fleet, including a dozen Khreenk Federation cruisers."

He paused before lowering his tone, as though trying to be conciliatory.

"Listen to me, please. The flotilla is a private enterprise, chartered by a Khreenk businessman to supply humanitarian aid to Helions. It has been paid for in good faith for non-military reasons."

He leaned in a little closer so that his head enlarged on the screen.

"I am powerless to act on your behalf. The Narau are here to protect from external threats. The Khreenk are friends of the Helions. We have been since before your people learned to travel in space. I suggest you and your dozen ships stay out of the way. A confrontation between my fleet and your little gathering would be…problematic for your…Alliance."

The video feed cut off abruptly and should have left Admiral Lewis fuming. Instead, he was actually calm. The Narau fleet was indeed large, but it was fractious. He seriously doubted any of the other Powers would be happy with allowing their ships to be used by a Khreenk Admiral to his own ends. The tactical assessment back on the Admiral Jarvis Naval Station had given a low threat score to all of the aliens' vessels, with the exception of the Klithi. Even as they had been talking, he had been examining the detailed information on the Khreenk fleet. Though total numbers were secret, the Alliance had run into several of their ships over the last months and had even seen a small number in action. Admiral Lewis had grave doubts these ships could match a Crusader class warship, let alone his new flagship. He nodded privately, imagining for the briefest of moments what a clash between the Alliance and Khreenk might be before brushing it aside.

Victory or not, I don't think Anderson, or High Command for that matter, would be particularly impressed if I started a war with these people.

He turned his head to face his communications officer.

"Get this information back to Admiral Anderson and fast. Can you reach Captain Hampel? His ship is part of the Narau fleet."

"I'll see what I can do, Admiral."

He looked back at the formation of ships and the numbers alongside them. If Lieutenant Ryante were correct, this fleet of ships would be in orbit over Helios within seven hours. If, and it was a big if, they were bringing military forces, then the plan that had been so carefully laid out would fall apart. The marines, though well equipped and trained, would never be able to end the conflict in the decisive manner imagined. The only reason they'd intervened in the beginning was to put a stop to the crisis. He forced himself to stay calm, but it was almost impossible.

How the hell did that group of ships travel for a day and a half without anybody noticing? This Khreenk Admiral must be colluding with them.

A video link of Captain Hampel as well as the other two Alliance Captains appeared. They were the official representatives of the Alliance in the combined Narau fleet in this part of space and the survivors of the deadly Biomech attack in Anicinàbe space.

"Gentlemen, I take it you have seen the scans of this new fleet?"

Captain Hampel, the temporary commander of the small group of escorts nodded.

"We brought it to the attention of Admiral Lanthua twenty minutes ago, but he said it was legitimate traffic operating with the protection of the Khreenk Federation. My engineers have been assembling an assessment of their capabilities. I assume this is not the case?"

Admiral Lewis was forced to bite his tongue before answering.

"I want all three of your ships ready for a rapid extraction from the Narau fleet. There is a strong possibility the Khreenk are letting ships slip through the blockade and down to the surface."

Captain Hampel did not seem particularly surprised at this suggestion.

"I see. ANS Mantic and Narwhal intercepted a single Khreenk transport yesterday, but Admiral Lanthua overruled us and sent them on their way. Instead, we were ordered to board a civilian transport that contained nothing but Helion locals. They must have been tipped off because when we arrived they had an armed party waiting for us."

"What happened with the Khreenk ship?"

Captain Hampel blinked slowly in frustration.

"The last information from our scanners showed the transport entered the Helios atmosphere. I thought nothing of it at the time, just another procedure that is unfamiliar to us. If we argued with every decision made by Admiral Lanthua, he would have booted us out days ago. After all, the Narau ships have been stopping and checking hundreds of ships."

"I see. Well, get your people ready. I suspect we will need you to rejoin the fleet at a moment's notice, and Admiral Lanthua and his forces will not be happy when this happens, I can assure you."

"Understood, Admiral, just give us the signal, and we'll return to the fold. Our posting to this fleet has proven less than inspiring."

As the image vanished, Admiral Lewis was convinced he could almost make out a degree of relief on the face of Captain Hampel. It couldn't be easy operating under the command of an alien Admiral, but it was the price they'd been forced to pay if the Alliance wanted to play in the Narau club.

Just be thankful that Captain Campbell had the wit to save the fleet in the Anicinàbe sector.

Lieutenant Ryante had already added the rest of the

ships' captains to the tactical network, and images for each ship showed up on his display. He tapped the button on his console, putting him in direct contact with the captains of the other eleven ships in the fleet. With his hand, he sketched out the shape of the fleet that he wanted. It was a very wide dispersal and would be perfect for offering mutual gun support, as well as plenty of space for the smaller vessels and fighters.

"This is Admiral Lewis. There is a potential threat to this force. All ships are to prepare for battle. I want fighter escorts and bombers loaded and ready. Medics on standby, and all weapons charged and ready to go. We will discuss specifics shortly; in the meantime, get your ships in order for ship-to-ship action, and keep an eye on every single object in the sky. As of right now, you will consider all ships a threat."

He sent the course changes, fleet layout, and rules of engagement to each of them in seconds. It was efficient and required no wasted personnel in the loop. Each captain acknowledged the orders before signing off. The final mention of ship-to-ship action would galvanize them like no other. Many of the captains had seen battle, but it was a rarity for an officer to have ever served aboard a warship in an actual fleet engagement. He'd been on board CCS Crusader in the Great Uprising where she had fought a classic battle of broadsides using kinetic railguns. It had gone on for a long time, many hours in fact, and with massive casualties on both sides. It was a decision he would not come to lightly. The face of Admiral Anderson finally appeared on the emergency channel to the Naval Station in T'Kari space.

"I've seen the information sent over by your tactical officer; this is worrying, very worrying. You might be surprised to find it is exactly what we expected to happen, though. Chairman of the Joint Chiefs, General Rivers has already suggested to me that the military government on Helios might look outside for support. Even so, if this flotilla is in fact a mercenary force, it will be more overt than I would have expected. It could destabilize the entire situation for us, and that is something we cannot afford."

Admiral Lewis looked at the data while wiping his brow. His position was a difficult one. The Alliance had already moved troops down to assist the civilian population, but on the understanding that it would allow the Zathee to end the military takeover of the planet and the reprisals against civilian areas. The arrival of mercenaries would cause a seismic shift on the planet.

"The Khreenk have a long history, it would seem, of providing equipment and military services for those who will pay."

A series of images from Alliance files appeared around him, each outlining important information from the T'Kari and Alliance archives. Admiral Lewis noticed one describing an incident with a moon dispute between the

Khreenk and T'Kari. It showed that a Khreenk trader had supplied arms and even mercenaries to fight on behalf of the T'Kari. Admiral Lewis shook his head at this piece of information. He looked to the next room where the marine officers were busy conducting the ground operations. They had their hands full already in trying to provide support to the Zathee. The arrival of mercenaries was something General Daniels would not be happy about.

"My orders for this sector are clear, Admiral," said Anderson.

Admiral Lewis knew immediately that he had something significant to say.

"Helios cannot fall under the control of a military dictatorship with a population waiting to revolt. The planet must be stabilized, and a representative system of government returned to power. The President has been in discussion with the Joint Chiefs for the last three days about this. There was to be an announcement in a week, but your report is going to accelerate the process. You're the first to know."

Here is comes, he inhaled slowly, waiting for the ticking time bomb.

"This comes right from the top; it follows negotiations with the Helion government in exile, specifically the Helion called Naglou, one of the officials your forces helped rescue has been sending us daily messages. Now that he is under our protection, we've been able to firm up an agreement, one that will see them support Naglou and his council of representatives."

He nodded as he reached the last part.

"That's right; we're throwing in our lot with them, the whole deal, military, economic, and political. Helios and the Alliance are forming a permanent bond as allies."

He wasn't so much surprised at the idea of support, but the alliance with them during this crisis was unexpected.

By throwing the entire weight of the Alliance military onto one side, it risks provoking the other Powers. I just hope they won't take advantage of that.

"We are making an official announcement to the other Powers in the next six hours that Helios is under the protection of the Alliance. We will assist the legal government to restore authority on the planet and their colonies. As of now, the Centauri-Helion treaty grants us authority to use all and any means to keep the planet secure."

Admiral Lewis' brow became a furrow as he listened to the last part. Finally, Anderson finished speaking, and he was able to ask his most pressing of questions.

"Your rules of engagement are to revert to Alliance territorial rules. All of Helios space under the terms of the treaty is to have its sovereignty protected by Helios and the Alliance."

Anderson smiled in that wicked way that immediately gave away his intentions.

You planned this from the start, didn't you? That's why I have my ships and a marine regiment in Helion space.

* * *

"Artillery, get down!"

The sound was almost as loud as the gunfire from the rebels who manned the majority of the outer defenses of the precinct. The voice of the marine in the next section of the precinct was loud enough that he could have been heard over the sound of the battle, but there was of course no need for him to do so, his voice carried over the data network used by every one of them in this part of the battle.

Here we go again, Jack thought.

First one round came down outside the building and then another. Two seconds later the first barrage struck like heavy rain. It was the one weapon truly feared by the marines; the indiscriminate and indirect artillery fire that could kill a man without them even knowing it was coming. No matter where you took cover, there was always a chance one of the shells would tear through the roof or a wall. The calm voice of their Captain spoke to them in their helmets.

"Animosh forces have surrounded us. The good news is the 17th have landed and linked up with the rebels. Even as we fight here, Colonel Koerner is bringing in reinforcements on the ground captured by the 17th. We have marines in the transport hub, and they are still fighting in there."

Jack winced as a dozen more rounds crashed into the precinct. Half of them exploded uselessly outside, but the rest slammed into the walls and towers. A hole appeared off to the left that was large enough for two men to fit through. Another shell landed nearby that shook the walls and widened the hole even more.

"Defend the breach," snarled Sergeant Stone.

Within a few seconds, a trio of Animosh fighters burst in through the breach. Quite what they expected to achieve was anybody's guess. A dozen rounds from the defending marines killed the first two. The third was hit in the arm, and he staggered back outside, leaving behind the bodies of his dead comrades.

"They aren't exactly Biomech shock troops, are they?" laughed Wictred from the middle of the tower's ground level. He'd jumped down from his window to help secure the breach, but the gunfire had been more than enough.

"Watch the street, they are getting closer," said Sergeant Stone.

Jack returned his attention to his small window and followed the dark shapes of the Animosh. They were well equipped, trained, and even extremely disciplined, but Jack could see what Wictred meant. They were not used to dealing with a motivated foe, and marines were certainly that. The Animosh were more like the police security units on Alliance worlds. They might be very professional, but they were not expected to take casualties. The line of shields reappeared, and three groups of the Animosh were advancing one step at a time to the improvised barricades, now abandoned by the rebels. A warning tone beeped in his helmet, and his attention was drawn to the aerial overlay provided by the drones.

What's going on?

At first he couldn't see what the drones had spotted, and then as he zoomed out on his tactical map, he could see it. Colored shapes showed the convoys of Animosh vehicles as they thread their way across the multi-level highways and roads in the city. Almost all of them were making their way to the precinct. Another color showed even more movement, but he couldn't see anything from the aerial view, just the artificial marker added by the computer targeting system of the drones.

"Good work, marines. We're doing our job," said Captain Carter over the audio channel, "Over fifty percent of the Animosh forces have withdrawn from their operations against the rebels and are coming this way. Keep at it."

Then Jack spotted the movement outside. His line of sight was blocked, and it was only through the digital grid that his helmet could show him the outlines of the enemy. He counted over twenty of the paramilitaries and four more of those dreaded machines.

I thought they had less than a hundred to begin with?

"Sergeant, we've got hostiles. They're coming this way!" he said, keeping his eye on them.

"Good eyes, I see 'em!" said the Sergeant as he examined the data on his own helmet overlay.

"Okay, marines, you know what to do."

A few had already opened fire but now the rest joined in, filling the street with a deadly hail of fire. Two of the machines used cover like the earlier attackers, but two more advanced forward, each raising a thick plate about the size of a man in front of them. Jack recalled the images of ancient mantlets being used in medieval battles on Earth. He took aim and fired a high-power blast. The triple-round slammed into the armor, and the machine shuddered; yet it failed to penetrate.

Not good!

Jack looked over his shoulder.

"Sarge, we've got trouble. They're outside the tower!"

None of this came as much of a surprise to the seasoned marine. He had already brought his reserves to form a double line of marines. The front rank knelt, and the second closed up behind them. The end result was a formation resembled a Napoleonic regiment armed with muskets. Wictred stood to their right with his arm pointing at the outer wall and the gun loaded and ready.

"Wait till they are inside," he said slowly.

Next to the other marines, Wictred looked almost superhuman. Even so, it was a modest number of marines, and the sound of gunfire outside was getting louder. Half a dozen more marines from the Second Platoon ran into the tower, along with another corporal. They fanned out inside the tower and caught the attention of Sergeant Stone. Before he could speak, one of the Helion combat drones crashed through the thick stone wall. Dust and broken stone fell around it, and then it was inside the tower. Behind it came a group of Animosh fighters. The drone opened fire at close range, and one marine was cut down before even seeing what was going on.

"Bring it down!" shouted Wictred.

As one the marines opened fire, but the piece of siege equipment in the first machine's arms deflected the fire. It moved on to expose the breach, allowing more inside. The second drone climbed through and aimed its main weapon. The heavy automatic gunfire ripped into the interior of the tower. Luckily, the marines were primarily on the outer wall itself and were spared the worst of the gunfire. Private Callahan, however, ended up in its sights and was forced to jump from his position on top of a broken table, barely in time to avoid being struck by the burst. Without saying a word, Wictred jumped forward to the machine and grabbed the armored shield. As the two beasts wrestled, the marines spread out, putting round after round into the newly arrived enemy. Excited by the moment, a pair of the rebels broke from cover and ran at the second machine, along with Vadi.

"No!" cried Jack.

It was too late, and the machine's arms hacked the two rebels down before it took aim at Vadi. But unlike his comrades, he had seen battle before and was aware of the strength, speed, and accuracy of these combat drones. He ducked around it, jumped to the side, and then pulled past its arc of fire. The machine's sensors tracked him, and it twisted around to shoot, exposing its back to the marines. Jack couldn't tell if this was deliberate or simply a fortuitous moment.

This had better work!

He didn't hesitate and took careful aim with his L52. The machine was moving, but because of Vadi had stopped its forward movement. It twisted about on its waist pivot point, trying to strike the synthetic Helion. Jack didn't know the machine's construction particularly well, but it was fair to assume the exposed power unit, cabling, and joints on the lighter armored rear were its most vulnerable parts. He sent a single high-power shot directly into the control stem. The blast struck below its armored helm and sent the magnetized projectiles into the heart of the machine. The impact was followed by a blue flash, and it dropped to its haunches, to all intents dead to the world; a lifeless metal statue with thin trails of smoke hissing out from the cracks in its back.

"Good shooting, Private!" Sergeant Stone congratulated

him.

Wictred still hung onto the front of the combat drone to keep the machine with him. The struggle between the raw muscle of the armor-clad Wictred and the machine servos of the combat drone appeared to be evenly matched. A trickle of Animosh fighters ran in through the breach, but a single deadly volley from the new marines scattered them. They quickly retreated through the breach, leaving a number of dead and wounded. All that remained was Wictred and the shield-carrying machine.

"Stop playing with that thing and finish it!" barked Sergeant Stone.

The struggle wasn't easy, and both were heavily marked from repeated impacts of metal on metal. Jack took aim once more, but the movement of the two stopped him. There was no chance of him firing if he might strike his friend. Sergeant Stone was having none of this though, and he ran out from the protective line of marines and to the side of the combat drone. It detected him and tried to strike with its left arm. He lurched back and fired three shots with his carbine into its thick armor.

"Watch out!" cried Wictred, upon spotting the arm moving back for the Sergeant.

The man moved quickly but not quickly enough. The metal arm struck his armor and sent him staggering. Sensing victory, the machine leaned to the left and took aim with the arm-mounted weapon. Wictred saw it and released the drone's shield to grab at it. It was a fleeting moment, but Jack still couldn't get the shot.

"Stay back!" called out a female voice.

Then there was a great clanging sound, and a triple hole appeared just below the machine's chest. It staggered back and fell to one knee. Wictred and the Sergeant dropped back, and all hell broke loose. Dozens of carbine and rifles opened up on the unfortunate machine, and in seconds it was nothing but a smoking ruin. A small group of marines arrived, this time marked out with the red helmets of Captain Carter's personal guard.

"Good work, marines," he said, surveying the ruined machine and the many Animosh bodies, "Your Lieutenant has been injured trying to take the transport hub, and all my people are busy defending against a push on the left flank."

He looked to Sergeant Stone.

"I'll handle the defense from here. Your people are the closest. I need you to get across the street out there."

He pointed to the breach in the tower.

"In less than three minutes, they will have more troops here, and the hub will be cut off. Take this squad and four Rams to reinforce the platoon at the hub. Once inside, you'll be on your own. The good news is that it is only vulnerable on the two sides facing us. There's nothing but solid rock on the other two. After you're in, I can have my boys put down fire from the upper levels."

He pointed above his head.

"I have heavy weapons on top. Give me the word when you're ready, and we'll clear the street for you. Just remember, you need to stop the flow of underground traffic in there. I'll keep reinforcements off your back up here."

Sergeant Stone saluted smartly.

"Sir."

Carter was gone as quickly as he had arrived, but one of his junior officers stayed behind to assist with the defenses. Sergeant Stone wiped off some of the dust from his chest armor as he scanned the dust filled tower.

"You heard the man. We have a hub that needs securing. We take it, and we stop the Animosh from moving troops and supplies underground to fight the rebels. Get on the line!"

He moved past the collapsed machines, simultaneously checking the schematics for the hub. Directly beneath it were two major links for six road and rail lines. The other marines from his platoon were already filing into the damaged tower. He glanced out through the breach. He wanted to check on the Lieutenant but that was for later, right now he had a job to do. He threw a quick glance at his unit and turned back to the breach.

"Check your weapons, marines."

Outside were a dozen burning vehicles and countless bodies. Tracer fired arced back and forth from both sides of the street. Off to the left was the large dome shape of the transport hub, and around it were even more burning vehicles. He looked over his shoulder to check the rest of the marines were with him. Wictred and Jack were closest, with the others right behind them. More marines sent over by Carter were already taking their recently vacated positions on the wall.

"Okay, we get across the street and fast. When we're inside, I want a secure perimeter. The rest of us will join up with those on the lower level. We're taking this place and giving the rebels the chance they need to finish this. You got that?"

The marines cried out in unison.

"Good. Now, let's do this!"

CHAPTER NINE

Carthago is still considered to be one of the great melting posts of the Centauri Alliance. A place valued on the quality of its military recruits but also hated for its violence, crime, and political infighting; billions of citizens, many of whom were exiles generations ago after the Great War. Poverty and discrimination were problems that started well before that violent war, however, and it would take the great scouring that came with the exposure to the Orion Nebula that would force the people of Carthago to unite in ways never seen before.

The Old World meets the Newer World

Lieutenant Colonel Diego Koerner and Colonel Gun watched the final wave of Maulers and Hammerheads streak down from the Alliance warship. The Hammerheads were tiny in comparison to the large landing craft, yet both left almost identical trails as they descended through the rich atmosphere of Helios. The craft were the cutting edge in new equipment for the Marine Corps, and although the orbital assault was similar to the actions of the Uprising, the craft themselves represented a paradigm shift for the Corps. Between these two craft, entire companies of marines with the full support of wheeled Bulldogs, armored Vanguards, and Jötnar could be landed directly into a combat zone. Both marine officers were now wearing their combat armor, with Gun in the JAS heavy armor unit and Colonel Koerner in the standard issue PDS armor. Only Colonel Brünner of the 4th Battalion continued to wear his dress uniform; his scowl remained as he watched the other two.

"Is that all of them?" Gun asked.

Colonel Koerner almost grimaced as he answered.

"Yes, even the support troops are on their way now. We are fully committed to the ground operation."

He'd counted out each and every wave of craft leaving for the frontline, mentally checking them off as they broke from formation. The last batch was taking down supplies and equipment for those already fighting on the ground, but even they flew with a large escort of fighters. Admiral Lewis was clearly taking no chances, and both of them were grateful for that.

"That's not entirely true," said Colonel Brünner, "My entire battalion is still shipboard. I have as much combat power with my heavy units. I still feel they should be deployed with the rest of the regiment."

Gun glanced at him but said nothing. He was starting to get a little bored with this particular officer, and the fact he had access to so many of his countrymen was proving hard to bear.

"You don't have much time," General Lewis said, "You need to join them."

Both marines turned back to the tactical display where the General waited. They were all still in the tactical room, along with General Daniels while dozens of video feeds continued to bring in the latest information from the ground. A small number of junior officers moved about, managing the myriad of details required to coordinate such a major action on the ground. The situation had changed substantially as more troops had been landed and sent into battle.

"Colonel Koerner, your forces are in position?"

"Affirmative," he replied, finally dragging his eyes away from the massive display that recreated the effect of a glass window looking out into space. They were much further away from Helios than when they'd started the combat drop, and he was feeling increasingly isolated from his marines.

"Colonel Gun has secured strong forward positions and in record time."

Gun nodded politely at this compliment.

"Our first wave of Maulers landed ahead of schedule

and dropped in support of the Infantry Carrier Bulldogs. They are already on the frontline and preparing for the operation. We've experienced minimal disruptions on the landing and have prepared the three marine columns with full support, exactly as planned. They will be ready to leave in less than thirty minutes."

"Good...good," said General Daniels.

He was curious to see how the newly formed Bulldog units would perform. The initial models had been simple eight-wheeled armored transports, but due to its early successes, the model had been expanded into a full family that included the standard Bulldog Infantry Carrier as well as the Command Vehicle and Mobile Gun System, each providing specialized services to the Marine Corps. Though they had all been used to varying degrees, this was the first time such a large number had been in action. He turned his attention to Gun.

"Admiral Lewis is moving the fleet out to block these ships. I will need you on the ground earlier than planned. The Admiral has altered course. Give it another twenty minutes, and we'll be too far out for landing craft. He can't give me any more time than that, unless we're happy to keep a single ship in orbit over Helios. A bad idea, in my opinion."

He then turned his attention to Colonel Koerner who looked as if he was overheating while listening to his words. Both officers were keen to get off the ship, and even as he finished speaking to Gun, it was clear the two wanted to move.

"Same for you, too, Colonel. I need you with your marines."

"We have a Mauler ready to go with escort," he answered, "My guards unit is on standby."

"Very well. As explained in the briefing, you will share command of this operation, with Gun taking overall control of the general campaign on Helios. Colonel Koerner, your mission is to demonstrate along a wide corridor all the way to the Animosh precinct, just as planned."

Colonel Koerner nodded quickly, as though he was impatient to hear the rest.

"Now, make it clear and obvious that you intend on striking right into the heart of their territory. If we do this right, it will strip their forces away from the rebels along the wide front."

He rubbed his jaw for a moment and then pointed at the diagram on the display.

"You both know the plan as well as I do, but there is one thing above all to remember. This has to be a win for the rebels, not for us. A poor victory for them is better than a perfect victory for us. When this is over, we need the civilians to see us as their friends, not occupiers."

Gun lowered his head slightly in acknowledgement. The only person radiating any great emotion was Colonel Brünner. He looked at his two equals before moving his glare to General Daniels.

"And quite what am I supposed to do with my reserve forces if the fleet is moving out of orbit? In a few more minutes, we'll be trapped on the ships. In my opinion, splitting our forces isn't a sensible plan."

General Daniels pointed to the screen where the formation of ships had closed the distance to Helios by almost fifty percent from when they had first been spotted.

"Colonel, they are only two hours away from the orbit of Helios. We will provide the Admiral with boarding contingents if and when he needs them. I want you to ensure every ship has at least one experienced combat platoon in reserve to assist the marines already on board. The remaining forces will stay on standby for boarding operations."

He was sure he spotted a grin from Gun, but when he turned his attention on the old warrior, he could see nothing but his calm and dispassionate face.

Gun, you can be a real pain in the ass sometimes!

He looked back to the disgruntled Colonel Brünner who spluttered out his complaint before he could explain any further.

"My forces are the best equipped in the fleet. I have over two thousand Jötnar and Vanguards."

"Exactly, just what I need if this gets rough. There's nothing better in shipboard combat than a platoon of Jötnar at your back."

He moved his eyes to Gun.

"Isn't that so?"

Gun's lip lifted up into a snarl, but Daniels knew it was a smile, even if Colonel Brünner had no idea.

"In front, side, or behind, my Jötnar will always get the job done."

Colonel Brünner shook his head in disgust and spat on the floor. Gun could take much but not this. He reached over and stopped with his hand directly in front of his neck.

"Watch your mouth, Colonel. My brethren don't take kindly to insults."

He walked closer, his massive frame dwarfing the Colonel. Admiral Lewis tensed slightly as Gun approached the man. The possibility of some kind of violent confrontation was the last thing he needed. It would also require him to come down on them hard. It would be better all round if they could resolve it without him having to get involved either privately or officially. Gun pressed his face up close to Colonel Brünner so that there were just centimeters between them.

"And neither do I," he said with a tone he hadn't heard in a very long time.

Colonel Brünner stared at the monstrous form of Gun and looked for a second as though he might say something. Instead, he looked away and toward Admiral Lewis.

"We have work to do." He then stepped away from

Gun; the situation seemingly defused.

* * *

The Alliance Heavy Strike Group moved away from the glow of Helios and onto its direct intercept course with the Khreenk convoy. The first of its kind, this group of ships had been assembled after countless simulations and tests in a wide variety of battle situations. The great battles of Proxima and Kerberos, to name just two, had included massive numbers of ships yet had often proven indecisive. The new philosophy was to create fully independent and self-reliant groups of starships that could travel, fight, and survive in smaller groups. In millions of simulations, the twelve-ship force had been able to fight a Great Uprising era fleet of thirty plus ships and come out equally, or better. An entire regiment could be carried between the ships, with enough space for additional platoons of marines on each of the vessels.

This is it, Admiral Lewis thought.

The commanders from the 17th and 8th Marine Battalions had already left the fleet for the surface of Helios, and General Daniels was in contact with them as they helped with the ground operation below. He'd looked at the fleet disposition probably twenty times and still felt he'd missed something. The dozen ships were spread out in a wide box formation, with the veteran ships ANS Crusader and

ANS Victory taking up the vanguard. In the center of the box sat the great bulk of ANS Conqueror and two-dozen Lightning Fighters that ran escort patterns around the formation. The remaining eight ships were spaced well apart in a wide pattern around the center. There were no rotating sections on these vessels, and the only holdover to the wars of the past were the venerable fighter wings, some of which were over forty years old.

"Lieutenant Ryante, give me a full assessment of the tactical battle space."

The ship's tactical officer had already run hundreds of scenarios based on the detected ships in this part of space. Unfortunately, it was almost impossible to predict all the outcomes, due to the vast number of civilian and military vessels around the crowded space of Helios.

"We have over seven hundred vessels, orbital platforms, and containers in combat radius, Admiral. The Narau fleet is split into three groups; two near the planet and one intercepting transports. We are now just over halfway toward the target forces. There are no other signs of hostile vessels or potential threats."

"Good."

He looked at the disposition of the Narau forces for a moment. He wasn't completely happy with what he had heard so far from their Khreenk Admiral, but the Narau were a mixture of different peoples with an interest in maintaining the status quo. The worst he expected from them was inaction, nothing more. All they seemed to have achieved so far was to waste substantial resources for relatively modest gains.

"Very well. Maintain a watch on the planet; I don't want any more surprises."

Lieutenant Ryante nodded quickly.

"Affirmative, Admiral."

She looked back at her display and was dismayed to see a series of alerts flash up, but none were more concerning than electronic information picked up by their own passive sensors.

"The lead ship is scanning us. It's a deep scan. They are concentrating on our engine, power, and weapon units."

She pressed two buttons and scanned more data before almost choking.

"I've never seen anything like this; they are trying to break into our secure network."

The XO didn't even wait for more information from the tactical officer. She reached for the intercom and hit the fleet open channel. Admiral Lewis nodded toward her and looked back at the data.

"This is the XO. We are under electronic warfare attack. Switch to communications pattern Omega Three."

She looked back at the Admiral.

"This is serious; I'd classify the ship as a certain threat. An attack on our digital infrastructure is just as deadly as an attack with kinetic weapons."

Admiral Lewis watched the mainscreen with interest. The old Khreenk battleship was the first he'd ever seen at such close range. The rumors were correct. Their vessels were ugly, and this one was no exception. It was heavily plated with armor, and the scanners had detected multiple layers around key parts of the ship.

"I don't like this, not at all."

The XO seemed eager to get the ship into battle, but even now Admiral Lewis was hesitant to hurl themselves at the ships.

"No, we can keep them at bay. The Omega Three protocols will keep them out, at least for now. Let them try. In the meantime, I want our systems kept passive," he said, with surprising calmness.

The Khreenk vessel had so far ignored all hails from ANS Conqueror. The trajectory laid out by Lieutenant Ryante showed that the fleet was definitely making for a Helion orbit. The larger of the transports had already started to burn their reverse thrusters to prepare for a direct entry into the planet's atmosphere.

"Gun ports!" cried out the Lieutenant.

Admiral Lewis watched as a number of red diamonds appeared along the shape of the Khreenk battleship. Unlike the Alliance ships, the bulk of their weapons were fitted along the flanks. The Crusader class vessels' primary armament was fitted to fire directly from the bow of the ships. Admiral Lewis nodded to Commander Sonels.

"It's time, do it!"

The executive officer pulled the intercom unit from its mount and placed it around her mouth, much like a twentieth century telephone. They had planned this part of the operation nearly an hour earlier, but the momentous announcement she was about to make turned her throat dry. She looked at the Admiral and saw nothing but calmness. She knew exactly what had to be done and took a single deep breath.

"This the is XO. All ships prepare for battle!"

All twelve ships were connected via the active communications grid, and her order rippled through the fleet in nanoseconds. The crew of each vessel was already waiting at battlestations, but this final order set events in motion to turn the ships from ready for battle to actively ready. It seemed a minor difference, but the change in active systems on the fleet disposition diagram on her secondary screen suggested otherwise.

"Admiral, all ships report active. Electronic warfare systems are online, weapons charged, and point defense systems activated."

The last part was a critical moment. Once activated, the small automated-turrets fitted to every ship would have clearance to open fire on any unidentified vessel within a certain range. They were fast-tracking turrets and could hit targets as small as missiles and even destroy heavy fighters.

"Good work. And our weapons, are they ready?"

"Aye, Admiral. Capacitors for the particle beam emitters are fully charged and ready for use. The same for the rest of the heavies."

It was something of a misnomer to describe some of the ships as heavies. The particle beam emitters were the most advanced weapon fitted to Alliance warships and had been modified from captured equipment taken from the enemy in the Uprising. Half of the Crusader class ships were from the second tranche or later, and this meant they were slightly larger; it was this increase in bulk that gave them their name, rather than a designation of combat power.

"The rest of the fleet reports gun ports are open and weapon systems loaded and ready for battle, Admiral."

The so-called heavies were improved vessels that were equipped with the same weapons. They were easily able to strike a target with a concentrated beam that could release over a gigajoule of kinetic energy at near the speed of light. Modifications in the last year had upgraded the weapons to focus the energy on a smaller point in space and with an increased output of more than sixty percent. The other half of the Crusader class was made up of the first generation models and lacked the powerplants and internal space to operate these advanced weapons. They were still equipped with the modern gravity generators as used on all Crusader class ships, a technology that marked them out as a ship design leagues ahead of anything used before.

"Admiral?" asked Lieutenant Ryante, "The scans from Serenity and Crusader are detecting EM pulse projectiles charging. They may be readying them for use against us."

The mention of the EM pulse projectiles sent his mind spinning. There had been a number of weapon assessments made ever since contact had been made with the T'Kari. The most common weapons used by all the major powers were simple projectile launchers of some kind. Simple, easy to power and most important of all, they were incredibly hard to defend against if they were able to strike.

"How many?"

Lieutenant Ryante moved her left hand and dragged the weapon signature overlay to the main screen. Only one ship, the aged Khreenk battleship was marked out for this weapon. What surprised her the most was the number of weapons. She scanned from left to right, counting each in turn, as well as the gun port and individual weapon systems.

"Is that right? They have twenty of them, each charged and loaded."

"Yes, Admiral, cross-scans indicate the battleship is fitted with at least thirty launch tubes port and aft."

That was the last straw for him. None of the approaching ships had answered his hails, and now they were preparing heavy weapons for a possible attack against the fleet.

"What about life signs?"

Lieutenant Ryante checked one screen and then another. It seemed to be taking much longer than he would have expected. The scanners on board all Alliance ships were capable of detecting a wide variety of electrical and biological readings. Now that they were close enough, there was every reason they should be able to tell rough dispositions aboard each of the vessels. Finally, she turned around and shook her head.

"Uh, this is odd, Admiral. There is just one, a very faint life sign in the center of the battleship."

"What?" he said, a little more aggressively than he intended.

"It's true. The readings from Crusader confirm it. Each of those ships is carrying no more than a single person on board."

He considered her words, but already he could visualize something that sent shudders of near panic through his body.

A single life sign, and no crew! Where have we seen this before?

He looked down at his personal monitor and accessed the Alliance naval records. He didn't get far before Commander Sonels pointed at the opposing fleet.

"Admiral, you have to look at this."

He was so busy looking at the files that he almost didn't hear the sound of his XO. It was only when a junior officer cried out in surprise, he finally lifted his eyes and looked at the screen. The image had been magnified, and it showed the rear of the formation and a group of three warships.

"No...it can't be," he said with a mixture of confusion and horror.

The ships were nothing like the Khreenk, or anything in the Orion Sector for that matter. They were smaller than the Crusader class Alliance ships, yet multiple bands ran down their hulls for the rotating crew sections.

"They are Confederate heavy cruisers..." he said under his breath.

Lieutenant Ryante was already loading the silhouettes and configuration data into her system to check. It was fast, but the images were not perfect, and the system was forced to enhance each of the images while cutting them up into blocks for analysis. Images of ships from the records flashed past, but even the powerful analysis tools of ANS Conqueror couldn't match the speed of the Admiral. Unlike them, he recognized the shape from memory.

"They're the lost ships from the 7th."

Both Lieutenant Ryante and Commander Sonels looked at him.

"The 7th?" asked Ryante.

Commander Sonels, on the other hand, appeared to be familiar with the name.

"Yes, it makes sense...well, kind of."

She glanced at the information presented by the ship's

computer system. It had already identified the hulls of most of the ships and was now checking their configuration and weapons layout for names, models, and specification. He looked at the Lieutenant to answer her question, but all those present absorbed the information.

"The fleet was one of the largest formations of ships travelling between Alpha Centauri and Proxima Centauri at the start of the last War. Back then, there were no Rifts, not that we knew of anyway. A journey between Alpha Centauri and Proxima Centauri would take about nine months, give or take. The 7th was traveling on this route when they were sabotaged by the use of AI Hubs, and the Zealots attacked. Only a small group under Rear Admiral Churchill escaped."

Admiral Lewis nodded slowly.

"Exactly. The surviving ships played a major part in the last years of the War. Many went missing after the initial attack though."

Lieutenant Ryante was already adding the information together with the tracking data on the ships. She had plotted a weapon range and danger radius for each of them while the others spoke. She looked to the Admiral and nodded to the ships on the display.

"It would appear then that these ships are a mixture of derelicts taken from different worlds, presumably fitted out with AI Hub control units and forced to work for somebody…or something else."

The image of the ships seemed to have given them all something to think about. Most were surprised at the sight of the Alien ships, but it was the newly discovered Confederate warships that kept older officer's attention.

"Yes," answered Admiral Lewis finally, "the question is…when, and why?"

He looked down at the file on the 7th Fleet. It was an old datafile, one that hadn't been accessed in a number of years. The list of missing or destroyed ships reminded him of the responsibility he now faced by sending an Alliance fleet into a direct confrontation with an unknown enemy. It was a long time since his service as an officer in the War, and he'd be damned if he would lose a single life, let alone a single ship now.

"Are you certain of the life signs?" he asked.

It was a question he knew the answer to already, but before he could proceed, he had to be one hundred percent sure of what he faced. As he considered the approaching ships, the realization occurred to him that they might not actually be troop-carrying vessels at all.

"Yes, Admiral, just the faint signs from what I'm assuming are the AI Hubs.

If they're not carrying troops though, what are they for?

The feeling deep inside his stomach filled him with dread.

It's a diversion! These ships aren't carrying troops. They are expendable warships being used to draw us away from the planet.

"XO, how quickly can we return to Helios?"

Commander Sonels checked the orbital trajectories of the two fleets.

"We're already on an intercept course. If we change tack now, we'll reach Helios no sooner than that fleet."

Admiral Lewis shook his head.

"No, that's not what worries me. I think this is a diversion."

The XO was silent for a moment and looked unconvinced.

"Admiral, there's an emergency signal coming from ANS Spearfish. It's Captain Hampel."

"Put him on screen."

The image of the small ship's commander took them all by surprise. He looked sweaty, and there was a cut running down the left side of his face.

"What is it, Captain?"

"We've been betrayed, Admiral. The Narau, they are landing…"

The image turned black, and the sound cut off abruptly.

Lieutenant Ryante moved her tactical formation details to the right side of the main screen. It showed the positions of the Narau forces, the Khreenk battleship and its escorts, and finally their own ships.

"Admiral, the Narau ships have split up."

"What's happening?"

None of the officers knew what to say.

"Get me Admiral Lanthua!" he growled angrily.

The communications officer tried to reach the alien commander to no avail. Though most of the officers were busy managing their stations, a quiet lull fell throughout the CIC as the Admiral looked at the situation he was in.

I knew they would go for it. So, Anderson's information from Alliance Intelligence was right. The Khreenk are in league with the leaders of the military coup.

He almost rubbed his hands with anticipation until the realization it could mean open confrontation with an entire alien empire. Even so, this had been one of the potential outcomes, and he was still uncertain the Khreenk would chance anything more than smuggling. He looked to his crew with a newfound confidence.

"So, we're halfway to this unknown fleet, and the Narau are breaking up with some of their ships heading for Helios, is that right?"

Lieutenant Ryante nodded at him.

"Yes, Admiral. It appears the Khreenk ships are moving to high orbit over the planet. Either they are planning on a blockade of their own, or they are..."

"Planning to land ground troops on the surface?" finished Admiral Lewis.

Lieutenant Ryante grimaced in acknowledgement.

Bastards! So they really do think they can put forces on the surface. Would they dare put up a fight against our troops?

He looked to his executive officer waiting at his right-hand side.

"If we turn back, they will still have time to land a good number of craft, plus, we will leave this fleet at our back. We either take on one fleet, or we split our forces."

Admiral Lewis had already worked this out, and he was starting to wish he'd simply kept his fleet in orbit around Helios. It had been stupid to pull back when there were so many unknown variables. He beckoned for General Daniels to enter the CIC from the adjoining room. The Marine officer finished whatever he was doing and left his own small group of officers to join the Admiral. Admiral Lewis pointed to the main screen.

"It's worse than I expected."

The General grimaced.

"It usually is."

"My ships have been drawn out, and part of the Khreenk contingent of the Narau is heading for an orbital position. I suspect they intend to drop mercenaries to the surface to support the forces of Justitium Lyssk and the Animosh."

Daniels examined the information carefully. Though of equal seniority to the Admiral, he had seen much more combat that the Naval officer during the Uprising. He could instantly see their situation, as well as the predicament it put him and his men in.

"Admiral, my marines can hold, for now. My advice is for..."

One of the junior officers assisting the helmsmen cried out. Both senior officers looked at him and then moved their eyes to track the shapes on the main screen.

"Admiral, the fleet has altered its approach vector and is launching fighters."

"The target?" he replied, already knowing the answer.

"Us, Admiral. They are powering up their weapons. My sensors indicate they are a mixture of combat drones and autonomous fighters."

"You're sure?"

"Yes, Admiral, they are unmanned and heading this way."

The entire situation was now playing out exactly as he had expected. The hidden fleet had lured him away from the planet, and just when he thought it might be a good idea to change course, they threatened him.

Quite clever, really. By attacking with unmarked ships, and with no crew, the Khreenk can pretend it was nothing to do with them. But what if that is true?

That last thought unsettled him slightly. The potential for error was great.

"That settles it then."

He beckoned to General Daniels and his XO.

"This is going to get messy and fast. Get word to your people on the ground. Either they hold up and wait till we can assist, or they go for broke. I'm sending three ships back to assist with the bulk of the 4th Marine Heavy

Battalion under Colonel Horst Brünner."

"But they won't make it back in time," stated the XO.

"Normally, I would agree with you, that is assuming they follow the normal rules. I'm giving a full override to Commodore Andon Leson. The ships will proceed at 1.5G on a reverse course."

The raised eyebrows from the XO did little to deter him.

"They can handle it for a few hours. I suspect Gun's kin will probably enjoy it."

He then looked to General Daniels.

"I suggest you take a shuttle and board ANS Crusader. She will be your command ship until I can get back to you."

He looked at the data his tactical officer had sent over.

"Yes, that is good. The Khreenk ships will have ninety minutes before you reach them. If they are deploying ground forces, we have full authority to fire on them."

General Daniels looked surprised.

"Against the Khreenk? Wouldn't that be an act of war?"

Admiral Lewis appeared to calm a little while answering this question.

"Not at all. We are allied with the Helions now, and their assistance has been requested. An attack by mercenaries is an attack on their sovereign soil. We are in fact now obligated to act."

Daniels wondered if the Admiral had done this on

purpose to force the hand of the Khreenk.

"Very well. I will transfer my staff to ANS Crusader. Good luck, Admiral, you are going to have an interesting encounter out there."

He looked at the screen once more and sighed as he examined the vast bulk of the Khreenk battleship. It was an impressive looking vessel, heavily armored, and armed to the teeth, according to the figures running along both sides of the main screen. He turned and marched back to his small group of officers. Admiral Lewis called to his communications officer.

"Get me Anderson on the horn and fast. This is going to get messy, very messy!"

CHAPTER TEN

What was the leadership behind Echidna during the Uprising? The War was over and the Alliance spreading its light from world to world, yet few understood what had actually happened. The Zealots were a holdover from the days of the Great War and the many religious persecutions. The military leaders of the Echidna Union seemed to share one thing in common, a desire for advancement no matter what weapons were used. There were even rumors that the icons themselves were payment for the technology of the Biomechs, a contract that only a handful of people would ever known about.
Holy Icons

Spartan inched around the corner of the passageway so that he could check out the next bend. The slow pulsing of the red warning lights had been running for more than ten minutes, and yet there was still no sign of any level of security.

"Where the hell are the guards?" asked Khan.

Spartan threw him a sideways glance, raising a hand to tell him to stay silent. He looked back around the corner and watched the shape of one more Biomech machine. As before, this looked like one of the senior machines, like the ones that had captured and tortured Khan. He felt a pain in his left hand but tried to ignore it; the hand was now long gone. He rested the T'Kari rifle on his broken arm and took careful aim. This machine was almost totally stripped of any color, because of disinterest or perhaps age. Even so, it was as big as Khan and moved on two massive legs. They seemed oversized compared to the smaller torso. In front and behind marched a dozen T'Kari, each in fully enclosed armored suits and rifles at their shoulders. Their feet made an odd sucking sound as the magboots attached and detached in rhythm on the floor.

"We have company," Spartan whispered to his friend.

One of the T'Kari stepped forward rather than using the lack of gravity to move effortlessly. Spartan tried to reach out, but the female had already stepped out from the cover and into the passageway facing the approaching machine. Spartan took aim with his borrowed rifle, but Khan pushed down on the barrel. Spartan looked at him and his shaking head.

"No, she must have a plan."

He looked back and watched carefully. He could now

make out the shape of the Biomech with greater certainty. The legs were substantial, yet he noticed there was no discernible head. The torso was egg-shaped, and six or more spindly arms hung down loosely around the body.

"What is it?" asked Khan.

Spartan looked at the thing, but he could honestly find nothing useful to Khan. The female T'Kari walked halfway toward the party before lifting her hand and saying something in the T'Kari language. Those around the Biomech looked confused and then started arguing with her. The machine took a single step forward before the female T'Kari turned around and pointed in the direction of Spartan. One of them must have spotted something because they spoke quickly and excitedly. The machine twisted and faced in the same direction, with two arms pointing out toward and right at him.

"The bastards, they've betrayed us!" growled Khan.

Without magboots, their mobility was limited. Even so, Spartan moved out from cover and took direct aim at the machine.

If I can kill one of their masters, maybe they'll go a little lighter on us? he thought optimistically.

Before he was able to shoot, the group of T'Kari turned on the machine, and three opened fire with their rifles. The others attacked it with whatever tools or weapons they could find. An arm was torn off, and a T'Kari spun out into the passageway with blood spurting from a deep gash to the neck.

"Nice!" roared Khan, and with a kick he floated off toward the machine.

Spartan took aim, but in the bloody melee there was no opportunity to open fire. He was forced to close the distance like Khan, but by the time they had arrived, another T'Kari lay dead and the machine was smashed to ruin. Spartan stopped in front of the female who had once more opened her helm to reveal her face. She looked at him and then to her people. Her words streamed out, but Spartan very quickly recognized his name.

"Uh, Spartan, how does she know who you are?"

He shrugged in reply.

"How the hell would I know?"

Khan tapped his shoulder, and he looked back to see the group of ten T'Kari plus the two they had already found. The female nodded to him, and then in a shocking move, all twelve lowered themselves to a single knee, as if he was some kind of savior.

"I think they like you," laughed Khan suspiciously.

"Yeah, weird, right?"

He sensed they might be able to help though, if properly motivated. More sounds from behind them in the next passageway encouraged him to make a decision, and fast.

"Follow me!"

Spartan pulled himself out of the corridor and into yet another wide passageway. By his count, this was the seventh storage area inside the station. It seemed like Spartan and Khan had been on the station for days, yet he suspected it was an hour, probably a great deal less. The more he thought about it, the more he suspected it was closer to thirty minutes. They reached the end and came to a crossroads. The female T'Kari pointed to the right-hand entrance for them all to go through.

"Where do you think it goes?" asked Khan.

Spartan raised an eyebrow.

"Really? Come on, let's see what she has to show us."

They went down the much smaller passageway, a hexagonal shaft with observation windows on two sides. As they moved along, it gave them a wide view of different parts of the space platform they were inside. From the shape of the structures, the Rift generator plants, and number of moored vessels, it was clearly something much more than just a control station. They had already spotted at least a dozen massive hangars. As they pushed on, Spartan wondered what else might be aboard this place, other than storage rooms filled with tubes that contained creatures and machines of many configurations. The female T'Kari beckoned to one of the larger doors. As he approached, it automatically opened. He pulled himself inside, and Khan watched him go in before moving to follow. There was something about this particular section that stopped Spartan in his tracks.

"Just look at this place," he said quietly.

Khan moved in right behind him and moved his head slowly, taking in the detail. He counted hundreds of cylinders, and that was just in the one room, each of them stacked five high. He counted at least five more rows of the same. Spartan stayed with the two T'Kari, but his curiosity forced him to move closer. It took only a few seconds to reach the nearest of the pod type devices. Tubes ran above and below the unit, and different colored fluids ran continually.

Khan leaned forward until his face touched the dull transparent plastic. His reflection appeared far worse than he would ever have imagined. The face looking back at him was pale and tired. He was surprised at his transformation during his captivity.

"Man, do I look bad!" He stared at the pod.

"What is it?"

Khan looked back to Spartan and shook his head bitterly.

"It's Biomechs again, just like me."

Spartan wasn't as shocked as Khan. He had seen this technology on several occasions before. Leaving the two T'Kari, he pushed off from the ground and drifted toward the first pod. Khan grabbed him and pulled him close to the misted transparent front. The face inside was definitely a synthetic and close, if not identical, to those created in the middle of the Uprising. The female T'Kari pointed at the pod and then to Khan. He shook his head, but it wasn't at all clear if they understood what he was trying to communicate.

"No, I am free. These are Biomechs warriors."

The female spoke with her comrade and then moved back to her group, her boots making that odd sucking sound. Khan turned his attention to Spartan who was turning his head to get the scope of the place.

"This place is a storage site, like a forward base of operations."

Khan nodded in agreement.

"For where though?"

Spartan raised an eyebrow at his question.

"Remember the Rift this place is right next to? My guess is they are waiting here to send these troops into battle against a station or colony. "

"Ours?"

Spartan moved his head from side to side.

"Maybe. Remember how many Biomechs were unleashed in the Uprising. We wondered how the Zealots managed to get so many, so fast. What if the Biomechs had given them a force to start with, and then the tech to create more?"

"Why though? If they have the troops, they could manage on their own."

Spartan wasn't quite sure what the answer was to that particular question. All he knew was that no matter where he traveled, he seemed to come across machines and Biomechanical creatures that had been built for one purpose, the total destruction of an area. Then it dawned on him. He pulled Khan closer to his face.

"They aren't looking to conquer. How much territory did the Biomechs themselves ever take in the War? The creatures were just tools, weapons for their war. I have an idea."

"Really," muttered Khan. He had no idea where Spartan was going with this line of thought.

"I think these Biomechs aren't as powerful as you might think. They want people, races, and empires at war. They want struggle and weakness."

"But why?"

Spartan had been thinking on this problem long and hard. There were many things to consider when it came to the wars against the Zealots and their masters. The more he discovered, the more complicated the entire thing became.

"You remember the machines on the ship; they were ancient creatures, cocooned inside advanced machine bodies. If you were thousands of years old, wouldn't you want to stay that way?"

Khan said nothing and returned his gaze to the dead face of the thing inside the pod. It saddened him to see what amounted to as a cousin inside these chambers. His kin might be reproducing naturally now, but they would never forget their roots; one based on blood, deception, and science. Spartan watched him and glanced at the waiting T'Kari before continuing.

"They do not have the numbers, so they use others to keep themselves safe. They send this technology against all of us to keep any of us from turning our attention from our own troubles and back onto them."

Khan thought about it. It wasn't something that had really occurred to him, but the more he considered it, the more it made sense.

"Interesting, so they wait behind their Biomech warriors and ships, and send agents throughout worlds to start wars and spread destruction while their own worlds stay fat and safe."

Khan turned around to face Spartan. His face had changed to bitter anger.

"Remember our interrogation, Khan? I don't at all, but I do recall part of what they passed on about their world. They are powerful, and they see themselves like gods. But they are ancient, and there are no more of them."

"The leader, the one who opened up his armor?"

Spartan smiled grimly.

"Yeah, their bodies inside are broken and old. The massive one that tried to arrive on Hyperion was probably one of their commanders. Their robotic bodies get bigger and more powerful I suspect to match their position."

Khan's lip curled up again.

"Then I say we get home, build up a fleet, bring fire to

their worlds, and end this once and for all, unless we want the cycle to go on forever."

Spartan nodded slowly in his direction.

"My thoughts exactly, old friend."

Spartan hadn't actually considered the cycle idea, but it did make sense. He began to wonder what might have happened if the Confederacy hadn't won in the Great Uprising. Would something else have then attempted to tear whatever was left apart?

Like sending us out to Orion to find new people to struggle against?

That made him feel a little uneasy. The Biomechs, the Zealots, and their myriad of enslaved supporters created an enemy that was difficult, if not impossible to identify, let alone to fight.

"Typhon and the others, they must have been indoctrinated to operate as intermediaries between the Biomechs and those fighting on the side of Echidna."

"Yeah, notice how this whole Echidna thing just seems to be a way of getting people to treat a machine creature as something like a god. Why didn't we see that, Spartan?"

There was a short pause while the two considered that point. In the end, Spartan rubbed his forehead and smiled.

"We will persuade our military and the T'Kari, plus anybody else we can find, to work together. It is time to stop them, permanently."

Khan heard something at the doorway and leaned

over. It was the two aliens moving closer to speak quietly together.

"What about them?"

Spartan considered for a moment.

"Well, so far I've only seen the occasional machine on this station. It could be almost entirely automated. There are quite a few T'Kari, so they must be slaves, like the ones we came across on the Raider ships. I say we get them all off this station and back to T'Kari space with us. They might have useful information if we're going to turn on the Biomechs."

"Did you see the T'Kari ships docked on the lower coupling?"

Spartan nodded.

"Yeah, you can just about make them out back there, through the side observation ports. Why? What are you thinking?"

Khan's lip turned up with pleasure.

"I think we should get our friends out to one of them. They understand the tech. If we can get on board, we must be able to steal one."

Spartan seemed happy at the idea, but he was aware of the potential for disaster with this plan. The Biomechs could have easily disabled the ships or simply placed a few guards to protect them.

Well, it's not like we have many options, is it?

He pointed at the pods around them. They seemed

insignificant in size, compared to the hundreds and hundreds of the devices.

"What about all of this?"

Spartan suspected his friend would want to free them, but it wasn't going to be likely. Each of the Biomechs would have been programmed over a period of months, possibly even years as they were prepared for their missions. The process of integrating Biomechs into the Alliance had proven almost impossible, and the majority continued to fight even once their programming had been purged. It had been different for Khan and the others, as a traitor had altered their coding at an early stage for his own nefarious reasons.

We would need access to this place for months if we wanted to turn them.

Spartan tried to work out how he could break this news to his friend, but Khan already appeared resigned to their fate and had an idea of his own.

"We steal a ship and blow this place."

For a second, Spartan thought his friend was joking, but there was nothing but determination on his face.

"Yes, it's about time they felt a little of our wrath. Come on!"

They both headed the T'Kari group but would have stopped if they'd seen their expressions beforehand. The female had already moved out to the doorway and was watching the shape of a vast spacecraft approaching the station through the nearest of the three observation ports. In space, the Biomech warship had seemed large, but at this range seemed positively massive.

"Uh, Spartan, this could be a problem."

Spartan coughed, a cold feeling now gnawing at his stomach.

"No…this isn't a problem. This is an opportunity. Follow me, I have an idea."

The battered shape of Spartan whisked off down the passageway as he pushed and pulled his way at surprising speed. Khan followed right behind, and the T'Kari moved as quickly as their magboots would allow. They spent almost ten minutes working their way through the innards of the station, pausing only to check with the female T'Kari on directions. Finally, they reached a wide blast door with symbols running around its frame.

"This is the place," said Spartan.

Khan looked concerned.

"The docking ring for the ships? What if they have guards?"

He clenched his fists around the chunk of metal he was still holding to use as a club. Spartan noticed the movement first through the thin circular observation window cut into the blast door. He moved closer and tried to work out what was happening, but then it became clear.

"A rotating section. The ring must be spinning around the axis of the station. The smaller ships are docked directly onto the ring. That's weird."

Khan lifted his right shoulder in a slight shrug.

"Compared to that thing out there, the T'Kari ships look like shuttles. We do the same thing with landers on the platforms around Hyperion."

Spartan looked down at the rifle he'd taken from the T'Kari. It was longer than any rifle he'd used before and looked in poor condition. Corrosion showed on the metalwork, and it was heavily worn and marked along the barrel and receiver. Khan spotted him looking down at the weapon.

"Yeah, I don't think their gear gets much in the way of practice."

Spartan grimaced and looked back to the tiny window. He could make out the ring walkway and the dozen or so airlocks that led off to the ship docking ports. He cradled the weapon and looked over to Khan and the waiting T'Kari. One of the aliens pointed at the ship, making a gesture with his hands of a ship taking off. Spartan assumed that was what the T'Kari was trying to say anyway.

"You ready?"

Khan nodded, and Spartan could only assume the others would follow.

"Right, let's go!"

He struck the door seal button, and it hissed open, revealing the walkway that moved past them to the right. It was like a massive treadmill, and he used the grab rail to move out to it before placing his feet on the ground.

Weird!

Khan did the same and was quickly followed by the others. In seconds, the entire group was on board the massive rotating ring that reminded him of the habitation rings of other stations. It was wide, easily big enough for ten warriors of Khan's size to stand abreast. Trolleys with equipment dotted the sides, and storage racks were filled with spares and supplies.

"Spartan!"

He turned. Khan was pointing at the T'Kari. The entire group had broken into a run and was heading for one of the airlock sections to the right of the ring. Spartan tracked their movement with his head before reaching a pair of flashing red lights. The airlock door opened; at the same time two more that flanked it opened up. Out rushed five T'Kari, each clad in black armor and with their weapons raised. Two dropped to one knee while the others stayed upright, but all pointed their rifles at the escapees.

Typical!

Spartan took aim with his rifle and waited. The argument seemed to go on forever before the female T'Kari stepped between them. One of the black armored figures opened fire. The blue pulse of energy burned a hole the size of a man's fist in her chest, and she staggered back, falling into the waiting arms of her comrades. The argument turned to a firefight, and two more T'Kari fell before the black figures moved out unscathed, taking up positions behind the trolleys.

"We need to sort this out, and fast!" shouted Spartan.

Khan was already halfway there with his metal club raised when the black armor clad figures spotted him. Another door opened at the other end, revealing the form of two more of the Biomech soldiers. One walked on four legs, the other looked much like the serpent monster Echidna. They were covered in black metal plates, and red dots glowed where their eyes should be. The four-legged one was Khan's size while the other stood at a height of nearly half as tall again. The taller called out in a machine-like tone.

"Screw this!" muttered Spartan and without thinking opened fire. His shot hammered into the armor of the serpent-like machine's chest, burning a hole into it. It was nowhere near enough to stop one of these machines. Another dozen black-armored T'Kari surged out of the gap and formed up in front of the Biomech machines as a living shield.

"They're insane." He looked to Khan. He'd reached the firefight between the two groups of T'Kari. Like some ancient demon, he swung his metal club and with each strike downed one of them, even as their gunfire burned into his thick flesh.

We need to get out of here!

He ran as quickly as he could after the rest, ever nervous

that off to his side was the group of reinforcements, as well as the two Biomech machines.

They aren't taking me prisoner, not again.

He reached Khan. He was bleeding from a dozen wounds. The surviving T'Kari fanned out around the now sealed doorway and trained their guns on the approaching machines and their black servants. Khan spat blood on the floor and looked to Spartan.

"What now?"

He pointed at the sealed door that led out into the airlock chamber and to the waiting T'Kari destroyer size ship.

"We get through that door and out of here."

"How?"

Spartan lifted his rifle and took aim.

"Just like the old days, my friend. We keep shooting until we win!"

Khan was a bleeding mess, but it was impossible for him to hide the massive grin showing on his face. He lifted his metal club and brought it down repeatedly on the door. Spartan blasted it with his rifle. A handful of the T'Kari watched in astonishment as a small hole appeared. One said something loudly, and then three of them were joining their fire to Spartan's.

* * *

The interior of the transportation hub was in a much worse state than Jack could ever have imagined. He assumed most of this had occurred when the rebels had initially overrun the site in the first few hours of the revolution. As they crept through in two lines, he noticed the charred remains of a civilian. There was no sign of any weapon near them, but the deep wound in the alien's back suggested they'd been killed while fleeing, or cut down in a deadly crossfire. Sergeant Stone stopped and lifted his fist. All the marines behind him dropped down. Even the four Rams following the unit stopped and waited like four-legged statues.

Where are they?

They had been inside the structure for nearly a minute, and apart from bodies, they'd not run into a single one of the enemy. A metal flap on the side of one of the Rams lifted up, and another of the hexrotor drones buzzed off ahead of them. Outside it was silent, but in the quiet confines of the structure, its angry buzzing sound was easy to hear, even without the sound amplification of the PDS Alpha armor. Gunfire ripped behind them as the heavy weapons of the rest of the unit hit around the streets, keeping away any reinforcements above ground.

"Keep moving," announced the Sergeant after what felt like a massive delay.

They each lifted up from the ground and moved on. Wictred looked like a giant inside the confines of the hub. They progressed into a wide-open circular area that ran under the vast dome. The helmet overlay showed the lines of tunnels and roads beneath their feet as well as the position of the other marines.

"Okay, people. The lowest levels are secure. There's one tunnel here that needs to be blocked. Animosh forces control it, and they are bringing in more troops to overrun this place."

He looked at the two files of marines.

"We don't have time to play. The drones count over a hundred Animosh and at least three combat drones down here."

Jack tried to slow his breathing. No matter how hard he tried, the image of the machine ripping and hacking into the bodies of friend and foe alike filled him with dread. He thought of Vadi, the synthetic warrior who was fighting so valiantly with the marines at the precinct.

Get a grip, you idiot. You have work to do.

"The entrance is two hundred meters that way. Fix bayonets and get ready. We're going to rush this place and stop them cold, understood?"

The marines nodded in the affirmative. They were outnumbered five to one, and according to the information coming in from the drones, the Animosh and their machines were spread out both in the tunnel and also on the levels and platforms around it. They were clearly in the process of consolidating their position, prior to bringing in more troops.

"Right, follow me!" cried Sergeant Stone.

He ran off ahead of the marines, and without even considering the consequences, the marines chased after him. They held their rifles and carbines low and ready, with their bayonets fixed. It almost felt like being out on yet another run to Jack. They moved fast, and the air regulator was pushed hard to keep a solid supply of oxygen to his lungs. The armor felt heavy around his legs, but he pushed on. Then he spotted two Animosh scouts waiting at the end of the path. The Sergeant ran past them as though they weren't there, and the following marines shot them with subsonic silenced rounds from their carbines.

Poor bastards, Jack thought, as he ran past the bodies.

Wictred moved past him and threw himself at a weapons mount that was only half assembled. It was based around a large platform and fitted out with a pair of large caliber guns. He smashed it from its mount and kicked the single worker who was still trying to fix the mounting. His metal boot crashed into his victim's head. He looked at the weapon as the other marines surged past. With a single pull, he ripped out the gun from its mount and cradled it in his arms. Jack stopped and looked at his friend who was already checking the unit. He turned his head and grinned widely at Jack.

"You have to get the biggest gun, don't you?" he laughed.

Wictred nodded and rested the unit on his left arm.

"Why not?"

More marines ran past, and Jack waved at Wictred.

"Come on, you fool. We have to keep moving."

Everything seemed to slow down to Jack as they worked their way down the path and toward the platform and entrance to the tunnel. It took nearly a minute for the two to work their way back to the front of the squad. By the time they were near the Sergeant, they were past the last bend and moving down to the platform. Flood lamps shone down from both sides and cast a vivid yellow hue on the ground. Flickering light rippled around when a dozen Animosh spotted their approach. Their crates of weapons and supplies offered limited protection as they rushed through the middle of the surprised Animosh. Five were busy unloading gear, and Wictred and Jack crashed into them with their guns blazing and stabbing wildly with their small arms.

"Die!" roared Wictred. He pulled the trigger on the gun mount he was still carrying like some valuable prize. The weapon shuddered, and his body shook as the great gouts of flame cut two Animosh to shredded chunks of blood and armor.

"Keep moving!" shouted Sergeant Stone with a hint of amusement.

Stone brushed past and covered another thirty meters to the platform. Some of the marines returned fire, but most of them chased after their Sergeant. The tunnel ran along the platform, much like the old-fashioned railways still used on Alliance colonies. Three large vehicles waited on the track with tons of supplies sitting on them. Sergeant Stone leapt from the edge onto the first one, landing on its flat bed at the rear. Four of the guards tried to stop him, but he embedded his bayonet deep into the first's chest and then ripped his pistol from his thigh, firing at the rest.

"Duck!" Jack cried, landing next to the Sergeant.

Without checking, the Sergeant ducked down as a blade swung over his head. Jack cut the enemy down with carbine fire, as a door opened on the vehicle. More Animosh streamed out, but Wictred arrived and blocked their path like a metal giant. He struck down two with the gun; the others panicked and tried to run. The powerful weapon seemed to terrify them with its close ranged brutality. Some were cut down as they fled. It roared like a tank's secondary weapons. The small number of survivors threw down their weapons and surrendered on the spot. It was over before it really began.

"Okay, marines, lock the prisoners in one of these cars. Stack their weapons and establish a perimeter. I want combat Rams in the tunnel at both ends, and two to stay here to guard the platform. Everybody else will follow me into the tunnel. It's time we drove these bastards back!"

CHAPTER ELEVEN

Unmanned Autonomous Vehicles were encountered in large numbers over the skies of Helios during the Zathee Insurrection. With limited access to conventional military forces, the new government under the control of the dictator Justitium Lyssk was forced to bring into service all possible combat units. Robotic security robots, reconnaissance aircraft, and the four city squadrons of robotic fighters were pressed into service. The Alliance's only robotic fighters were space-based, so once more it fell to human pilots to take on machines in the yellow skies of Helios.

Robots in Space

The battle for the government buildings of Helios had turned into a full-scale riot, with civilians and state security units battling over every square meter of ground. Vehicles burned in the streets, and individual struggles were

261

decided in buildings large and small. For every Alliance marine or vehicle, there were a hundred or more civilians. They were ill disciplined, poorly equipped, and yet they continued the final big push. As Gun strode through the heart of the battle, he could feel it in his body, the mood of the majority; each desperate to end something few had spoken of until a week or two earlier. Gun understood more than most how it felt to be under another's yoke.

We'll end this, today!

Around him waited a large group of marines, including a pair of Vanguards. While the others continued with their pre-allocated tasks, he had handpicked his own guard unit when he landed. There was a mixture of ranks; all of them enlisted men and women, apart from the extremely young Lieutenant David Read. The man had taken over command of this ad-hoc group for the duration of the battle. He was taller and substantially stronger looking than any of the others. A quick check on his file as they marched to their objective had shown Gun that Lieutenant Read was a sportsman back in college.

Just the kind of man the Corps likes to recruit, he thought, throwing a glance at the man.

The officer was directing the guard unit into a safe formation; a vanguard of four marines and the rest in small groups at the sides of the street, and one kept close to him at all times. It seemed excessive to Gun, but he wasn't going to argue. If nothing else, it meant he always had a body of marines to send into combat on a whim.

"Sniper!" Private Larned shouted.

Three shots rang out, and the inbuilt defensive measures inside Gun's armor tagged the incoming fire, and then used a mixture of radar range finding and acoustic matching to locate and track the source of the gunfire. A small flashing red diamond appeared on his overlay, showing the proposed position of the shooter. He looked in its direction and spotted two more flashes. The marines returned fire but not before Private Larned took a thermal charge in the visor. It shattered his helmet and killed him instantly.

"Bring him down!" he roared in anger.

It wasn't necessary, of course. There were hundreds of marines moving through the cover of the abandoned capital. Drones were en route to the target, and he watched with satisfaction as a single missile fired from a hunter-killer hexrotor eliminated the sniper.

"Target's KIA,'" said Lieutenant Read.

Gun nodded and pointed forward with his right hand.

"Keep moving forward. We have work to do."

They continued on and only a short distance behind the skirmish screen of marines from 4th Company. In the middle of the street moved two of the Bulldog Mobile Gun vehicles. Each was equipped with the latest model 60mm railgun, a much larger and heavier version of the L48 weapons used by the marines and Vanguards in the past. Railguns were difficult to use on a smaller scale, but miniaturization had seen a major leap since the end of the Uprising. The technology was now at a stage where a single weapon and its accelerator unit could be contained inside a Bulldog vehicle. It wasn't perfect, but when the two vehicles tore apart an Animosh armored vehicle with a single volley, Gun could barely conceal his pleasure.

"What do you think of them?" asked Lieutenant Read.

Gun answered without moving his head even a millimeter.

"They have a lot of problems, limited ammunition, overheating, and very few in production so far. Even so, just look at that!"

He extended his right arm out toward the column of smoke rising up from the ruined Animosh vehicle.

"What would I give to have one of those guns strapped on my arm!"

Lieutenant Read did his best to hide his smile. The marines were professionals, but none of them seemed to relish the opportunity for combat and blood like Gun and his people. Gun wasn't the first of the Jötnar the young Lieutenant had met, but he was the first he'd seen in battle, and it had been a revelation.

"Captain Jackson reporting. We've secured the lower street levels. Animosh security forces are withdrawing back across the sector bridges. Do we have permission to blow them before they get back to safety?"

Gun wanted to say yes so badly. By launching surgical strikes like this, they could end the battle in hours. The Animosh had numbers and defensive positions, but they couldn't handle the firepower, skill, and the sheer brutality of the marines.

"Negative, we have our orders from the General. The Zathee have to win this, not us. We open the door. They have to do the rest."

"Understood. In that case, watch yourself, Colonel. Some of their forces are falling back in your direction. Rumors have it the Helion Guard is in the area too. Looks like the rumors were true."

A formation of Thunderbolt Fighters screamed overhead and unleashed a barrage of laser-guided missiles at a group of Animosh armored vehicles. They had vanished behind the peaks of the tall tower blocks, and they exploded in a bright orange explosion. More fighters rushed past, engaging in a massive dogfight with dozens of Helion drone fighters. Trails from missiles mixed with their own vapor trails left curled lines in every direction.

Just like old times, Gun thought and took another step forward in the street.

He was on one of the many raised walkways running at multiple levels in that part of the city. A single marine Bulldog troop carrier had crashed into a barricade and lost three wheels. Even so, the top-mounted gun unit continued to track and fire on the defenders further down the roadway.

"Helion Guard, who the hell are they?"

He remembered hearing something about them in one of the many briefings, but nothing solid came to mind. As he thought about it, the computer sprung to life. He had been talking to himself, but the onboard computer fitted to the JAS assumed it was a question directed at the system. It checked all available reports and status indicators before collating them and running them through its analysis engine.

"The Helion Guard is reported to be an elite battalion of a nine-hundred female Helions, each handpicked from the finest genetic stock of the main Helion cultures. Each of the cultures provides an annual tithe of people, and they are never seen or heard from again."

So, no Zathee. Makes sense.

"According to the public record, they are known informally by the Zathee as the Night Hunters, due to them never seen and remove threats silently and without casualties."

Gun smiled at the last part.

Really, no casualties? Well, we shall see about that.

Scores of marines fanned out around him and rushed from cover to cover, putting down an accurate and deadly rain of bullets. Hidden behind a concrete block came two fighters, both carrying bomb harnesses and rifles. He spotted them out of the corner of his eye and extended his right arm to point at them. One of the Vanguards behind him tracked the target and blasted them with the suit's built-in weapons. They were cut apart before they could respond.

That was my target, he smiled.

Unlike the Vanguards, the JAS armor was optimized for close combat. The Jötnar were hardly known for their stealth tactics and marksmanship, but when it came to direct assault, there was nothing better; not even the Vanguard platoons could match the speed, strength, and sheer tenacity of a unit of the humanoid Jötnar. He checked his systems for what must have been the tenth time before spotting the status indicator for the armor-mounted weapon.

You idiot!

There were two models currently in production, but he had chosen the one fitted with serrated blades on each arm and a single shoulder mounted weapon unit. He had forgotten the thing was even there, being as he'd always carried his weapons in his hands or on his arm. By placing the unit directly onto his torso, it freed up his limbs for full movement. He twisted his head but could only just make out part of its shape. Having such a powerful weapon attached to him reminded him of Prometheus, and the weapon they had fitted to him to kill humans. Back then it had been nothing more than a Gatling gun strapped to his arm. Times had changed, but in other ways they were still the same for him.

Bastards!

He remembered those he'd killed on the fiery world of Prometheus. He didn't regret the killing, but his hatred for those who forced him to do it had never abated. He looked back at the hundreds of civilians waiting well behind the marines and in cover. Many more were following up along the smaller walkways and passageways littering that part of the city. He looked back to the outer defenses. Heavy weapons and snipers were positioned high up, and on the lowest level a number of barricades and concrete blocks had been erected to hold back the rebels.

We'll create an opening for you, and you'll have your chance.

Gun was happy to fight, and most of the time even the cause didn't matter to him. But one thing he didn't like was being used for somebody else's gain. The crimes he'd been forced to commit on Prometheus were a constant reminder of what he wanted to stop. He glanced at the overlay, spotted the weapon activation, and flicked the switch, all by using just his eyes. It was fast and surprised even him.

"Weapon system armed and active," said the computer.

Five Vanguards strode past him in their large exo-armored suits. To the uninitiated they might look similar, but they couldn't be more different. Gun wore a modified armored suit, whereas the Vanguards used heavily modified combat engineering units that had been fitted out with enclosed crew sections, thicker armor, and additional weapons. Spartan had pushed hard for their introduction, and his hard work was coming to fruition. Bullets and thermal rounds bounced off their thick hide as they moved ahead, the marines following them. They made a whirring sound as their servomotors and hydraulic units moved them at a surprising speed. He even spotted some Jötnar wearing armor much like his own. They were working alongside a similar size group of Vanguards, and smashing their way through a pair of heavily defended barricades.

"Watch out!" cried a nearby marine.

Five combat drones came from the ruins of a repair station just ahead of them. They were fast and their weapons leveled. It wasn't unusual to run into these combat robots, but the effect they had on the rebel civilians was devastating. At least thirty of them turned and ran. The machines gunned them down, closing the gap to Gun and his line of marines.

"Take cover!" called out the Lieutenant. The marines scattered. The first rounds struck about them, and they were forced to throw themselves down to avoid the gunfire. Gun signaled to the remaining three Vanguards in his own force and stepped ahead of the marines in plain sight of the machines.

"They are not man enough to fight us; cowards. They hide behind their machine toys!"

His words caught some of the marines by surprise. There were already hundreds of robotic Rams supporting the ground troops, and small numbers of robotic fighters also in use by some escort ships in the fleet. Gun had a particular hatred of them though, especially those used against them. As far as Gun was concerned, there was nothing more cowardly than having a machine do the fighting for you. He pointed both of his armored fists at the machines.

"Destroy them!"

Round after round struck his armor, and at least two smashed through the plating on his left leg. He ignored it and took aim with the shoulder-mounted weapon. It was a heavily modified L56 Mark III and fitted on a fully rotating gimbal. It was essentially a larger scale version of the L52 carbine, but with five short barrels and two separate ammunition feeds that ran into a pair of large boxes on his back. It was only being fitted to a small number of vehicles, as well as some Vanguards and other units. He tracked from left to right, tagging each target. The gun followed the direction and opened fire in its maximum firepower mode. Like the carbine, it loaded, charged, and launched the magnetic projectiles simultaneously at the target. Up to nearly two hundred meters, the rounds were so close they struck as if one massive round. After that, they started to spread like a hypersonic shotgun. Every second it sent a powerful blast; putting a massive smile on

Gun's face.

"Keep moving forward!" he growled, upon spotting his marines taking cover. One jumped up without checking and took a round into his helmet. If it had been the old PDS armor, the man would have had his head torn right off. Instead, the PDS Alpha armor had the reinforced gorget around the throat. It was this that took the impact and sent the man sprawling. One of his comrades dragged him to safety; the others climbed over the cover and pushed on.

Good, that's better.

Gun continued forward, quickly checking his overlay to ensure the rest of his units were doing the same. He now had over fourteen hundred marines, Vanguards, and Jötnar on the ground and moving in small forces to push the Animosh back. Even so, his entire battalion was only large enough to cover five percent of the ground around the triangle. It was falling on the rebels to do the bulk of the work.

"Colonel!" cried out Corporal 'Killswitch' Durham, a middle-aged marine with an L52 across his chest. Gun recognized the distinctive paint scheme on his back. He'd failed one of his scenarios by accidentally hitting the cargo bay vent release. If it had been a real mission, the entire squad would have died.

One of the surviving drones made it through the gunfire and brought its heavy metal arm down to crush Gun. The

Corporal jumped in the way and opened fire. Although his rounds struck the machine, they proved ineffective; unlike the machine's attack that cut the man clean in half. Blood sprayed over the front of Gun's armor and over his face.

"Try this then!" Gun snapped.

He reached out and grabbed the heavy combat drone with both arms. His left fist with its serrated blade jammed into its arm. He proceeded to lift it until the machine was nearly a meter from the ground. It flailed out, but he simply laughed and looked right in the center of its body. With a massive roar, the shoulder-mounted L56 fired a powerful round directly into it. The impact threw the drone back five meters, and it crashed to the ground with smoke belching from its ruined carcass.

"I love this!" he growled, to the surprise and amusement of the marines around him.

The drones were smashed, and the defending Animosh broke and fled back to the safety of the tall walls and structures of the outer defenses of the Triangle.

"The sentries in Sector Seven are withdrawing," he said over the radio to his liaison officer with the Zathee. He didn't need to say anymore though; from the protection of the debris came a great wave of rebels. They surged past Gun and the marines, over the barricades, and into the outer defenses protecting the area known as the Triangle.

Good, now it's time for Koerner to do his part.

He sent a request to the Colonel, at the same time

checking the aerial feed from a pair of hexrotor drones that were buzzing over the city like predatory birds. The streets and raised overpasses were a mess; crash-landed vehicles and improvised barricades stretched out on hundreds of different points. His frontline marine units were now heavily intermixed with the huge numbers of civilians that had come out into the streets. Through it all though, it was simple to track his forces and maintain control over them, even if to the untrained eye it looked like an uncoordinated mess.

Gun reckoned only a tiny number of them had any useful military experience, but they were eager to end what must have been a long and bitter repression. He identified the rest of his units and updated their new objectives. He wanted the marines to keep hitting the defenses hard. As breaches were made, he would give the signal and let the Zathee continue onward. No matter how messy the situation was, Gun hadn't been happier in months, perhaps years. Fitted out with the latest JAS armor, he felt like a metal god as he advanced with the marines through the upper levels of the city.

"Gun, my forces are ready to strike out for the precinct," Colonel Koerner said over the communications channel.

"Good work, that's ahead of schedule. Keep me posted on your progress."

"I will. How is the assault on the capital?"

Gun did his best to hide a grin of pleasure.

"These Zathee rebels will not hold back. My drones show the Animosh security forces have fallen back to this fortified position, a killing ground the scouts are calling the Triangle."

"That's the pyramid section north of the government buildings, right?"

Gun nodded, not that the man could see him. His own position was roughly a kilometer from the southern end of the Triangle, and already they were finding progress slow. Ideally, he would bring in artillery, mortars, and airstrikes, but General Daniels had refused his request. The battle had to be won by the Zathee and with minimal damage to the city.

"Yes, it is the size of ten city blocks and six levels high. There are landing platforms, anti-aircraft mounts, and reinforced positions at every point. The Zathee reached it an hour ago and were forced back with heavy casualties."

"Numbers?"

Gun checked the overlay on his visor, something that he never really had much access to in the past. It showed the tactical disposition of all Alliance units in the area, as were tagged enemy units.

"It looks like half of the Animosh have withdrawn to the Triangle, along with most of their leadership. Maybe fifteen thousand plus combat drones and heavy weapons. Twice as many are trying to withdraw underground from their remaining bases. If they make it there, they will be impossible to move."

"I see. And the transport hub?"

There was a short pause.

"Our marines are still fighting to secure it. Listen; even if it is captured, they will have the number to overrun the place within the hour. You have to reinforce Captain Carter, or this will turn from a short revolution to a full-scale civil war. We cannot afford a stalemate."

"Gun, I will demonstrate in and around the precinct with everything I have. I promise you that within the hour the precinct and the hub will be in Alliance hands."

Gun nodded to himself.

"Good luck, Colonel. I'll continue the encirclement of the Triangle; nobody is getting out of there."

* * *

The interior of the T'Kari ship was almost identical to the one he and Khan had been trapped aboard during their incident so long ago, though he suspected it might be a fair bit smaller. Spartan couldn't even remember how long ago it was, other than that it felt like a lifetime. The T'Kari had split into two groups, one staying with Khan and Spartan, and the others heading further along the docking ring toward another of the ships.

"You reckon they can start this thing?" asked Khan.

The door hissed shut behind them, and one of the

shorter T'Kari beckoned for them to enter the passageway to the left.

"I know. This goes to your control room," he replied, knowing the alien wouldn't understand him, "Just get your ass moving. I'm not going back!"

They moved at a brisk pace, and one of the T'Kari almost stumbled trying to keep up with Khan. It was the image of the newly arrived reinforcements at the station that did it for all of them, and the image was still fresh in their thoughts. Once they'd made it aboard the ship, a large number of guards, including at least eight Biomechs machines, had rushed into the docking ring. The thought of those powerful things gave Spartan all the motivation he needed to keep his aching legs moving. It took them less than three minutes to reach the front of the vessel where two of the aliens were already sitting down and running through a number of system checks. A third opened his helmet to reveal an old, haggard looking face. He started to speak and then waited. Spartan looked to Khan and back at the alien.

"What? I don't understand you."

The alien continued to speak, and Spartan sighed, turning back to his friend.

"Great, let's just hope they do the right thing."

This part of the ship was equipped with seating and computer systems for at least twenty T'Kari, far more than the mere handful they had to offer. On the outside it had looked very similar to the Raider ships, but now they were inside, Spartan could see there were many differences.

"What kind of ship do you think this is?"

Khan looked at the displays and controls and then to the other ships at the docking ring.

"Look at the hull. These ships have been modified, and recently."

Spartan looked at the sleek shape of the T'Kari ships, each of which seemed slightly different. They were very alike the civilian transports used by the T'Kari, but these ones were damaged, some with scorch marks that ran halfway along their hulls. Plates had been fitted on the outside, and there were dozens of simple weapon mounts fitted in odd places.

"I'd say these were seized in battle, and the Biomechs must have been modifying them for something. Based on the number of guns, they're making them into gunships of some kind."

On cue, a number of displays flashed up, and the front of the room changed to look like transparent glass. To the left was the umbilical connector between the ship and the station. Right in front, and still in space, was the Biomech warship. Off to the right was the Rift. Spartan pointed to it.

"We need to go that way!" he said, half expecting one of them to understand.

One of the T'Kari pulled up a detailed starmap model

and beckoned for Spartan to approach. He did so and looked at the images; none of it looked particularly recognizable. There were clusters of stars as well as scrolling lists of images. Many flashed by, but it was a pale blue orb that caught his eye. He pointed, but it was gone before he could raise his arm. The ship shook and then detached from the umbilical. Alarms sounded, and no sooner had they broken free of the station than a dozen small turrets start shooting at them. Only the ships maneuvering thrusters were operational at this distance. Spartan reached up to the display and dragged back the images until finding the blue orb. It had much in common with the rich world of Terra Nova, but there was something different about this one. The landmasses were not familiar, yet he was certain he'd seen the image many times in the past.

"Earth," he said under his breath.

The world was still part of the Alliance. After all, Earth was the birthplace of humanity, but it was a shadow now, as was the entire old Solar System. Over centuries, the planets and moons had been stripped of their surviving populations, many of whom had moved to the new colonies in Alpha Centauri. Even so, the last stories he'd read said there were still billions of people living there in the shielded worlds of Mars, Earth, and the numerous colonized moons. The development of the Spacebridges, or Rifts as they were now known, had allowed instantaneous travel back to the old worlds, and many thought this would start a new period of development of these long mistreated and plundered worlds. Khan looked at the blue orb.

"Are you sure?"

Spartan raised a whimsical looking eyebrow before tapping the T'Kari on the shoulder. As the alien turned around, he pointed at the object.

"That one. Take us there."

The alien looked at it for a brief moment and then back to his comrades. He spoke quickly and loudly as each started up their systems. The entire shipped seemed to buzz with energy as it pulled away from the station, still taking considerable gunfire.

"He wants something," said Khan.

Spartan didn't understand. He could see that of the three of the aliens on the ship, the taller one was pointing to a seat and computer system further back. There was a bank of six seats, each identical and fitted with screens and controls. The odd thing was that they didn't match anything else inside the ship, even the color was wrong.

"What does he want?"

Khan laughed.

"I wonder about you sometimes, Spartan. Those have been added, and if you look at the other ships, what has been changed about them?"

"Guns," he answered, almost reverently.

"Yeah, if I didn't know any better, I'd say the alien

wants you to control the weapons."

Spartan headed for it and sat down. There were controls, a targeting array, and a live video feed from cameras somewhere on the ship. He reached out, and his hand's movement was detected. The feed moved, as did the target reticule.

"Spartan, it's a gun system, you fool. Just point and shoot!"

The system continued to rotate until an image of the docking ring and the group of small ships moored alongside filled his screen. The ship shuddered as more and more fire struck them. He put the reticule on one of the turrets.

"What now?"

Khan brought his fist down on the system's screen, and a quadruple burst of gunfire rippled out to the ring. Dozens of holes were torn through the outer skin, and he was sure he could spot bodies floating out from the breaches.

"Nice, keep at it, Spartan," he said as though suddenly he was in charge. Even so, Spartan continued to select targets for the computer while the scores of small weapon mounts on the ship exchanged fire with the station.

"I don't get it. These are just point defense systems. Why don't they use their big guns?"

He pointed to a pair of massive turrets that was equipped with guns as big as the primary weapons on a Confederate barge back in the last war. It appeared to be the station's primary weapon system, yet it didn't fire. In fact, as he selected more targets, he noticed the thing didn't even move.

"Why do you think? If they blow us up, they risk damaging the station."

"Of course, and if the station goes, so will the ships connect to it, the Biomechs on board...and that damned Rift."

"What about them, though?" asked Khan, pointing out to the second of the ships that had broken free.

"Yeah, looks like they made it off the station, too."

"Not for long, look. The hangar doors are opening on the top level."

Spartan looked at them and could just make out the shapes of dozens of fighter drones lined up inside. They were the same designs as those launched by the Biomech ship that had chased them there to start with. As the door lifted up, they could see something much more worrying.

"Uh, Spartan, look!"

There were four much larger vessels. They were bigger than a fighter, perhaps three times larger and thin in the middle. A dozen Biomech eight-legged machines fitted themselves onto special mounts that ran along both sides of the craft. Four engines, one at each corner, provided the propulsion.

"Dammit. If we moved to the Rift, they'll destroy us

with gunnery, and if we stay here, the Biomechs will land those machines on our hull and board us."

Khan nodded.

"And even if we avoid the guns, the fighters will get us by the time we reach the Rift."

Khan moved to the next computer station and ripped away the seat. It was far too small for him and best moved aside so that he could reach the controls. He brought up a targeting reticule and aimed it at the hangar. As he selected it, he could see the shape of two turrets along the nose of their ship tracking to the right in the direction he was pointing.

"Have some of this!"

With a tap, both turrets opened fire. They were simple weapons that fired kinetic rounds. Just meters before striking, a single defense turret unleashed an invisible blast that disintegrated the rounds. Khan crashed the base of his fist into the system.

"Particle weapons!"

Spartan continued to track objects and open fire as their ship moved from the station. They were only a hundred meters away, yet he felt better already. The shape of fighters and the dreaded combat machine transports moved slowly, each staying in range of the particle emitters around the hangar. Spartan recognized the shape. They were identical to those fitted to the Echidna warships in the Uprising, a technology that had almost won them the

War. As he took aim, a great shape blocked his view.

"What the hell is that?" he shouted.

Khan watched in surprise while the T'Kari changed the view to a wide-angle lens. The second T'Kari ship was now free, but instead of chasing after their own ship, they had taken up a position in front of the main guns of the station. The yellow arcs from a hundred gun turrets on the station, the Biomech ship, and the T'Kari warship filled the area of space with shards of superheated metal.

"What are they doing?" asked Khan.

The T'Kari were arguing, but the taller one struck the female and then shouted for the last time. The female pulled out a weapon and aimed it at the leader. There was a pause and then a flash, as the female put a single round into the leader's head. He stumbled and fell, leaving a growing pool of blood about him. The female T'Kari looked at Spartan, bowed her head gently, and then struck a button. The ship vibrated, and they were accelerating away at high speed. Khan leaned in closer to his friend.

"Those poor fools are buying us time to escape."

Spartan nodded grimly.

"Yeah, and that guy wanted to stay back and help them."

He looked at the body of the dead T'Kari and the slick pool of blood that continued to expand around him. Though he felt sorry for the alien, he couldn't disguise the fact they might actually make it to the Rift now. Khan spotted the gloom on his face.

"What is it?" he asked.

He turned to the left and watched whatever Spartan was looking at.

"The Rift."

CHAPTER TWELVE

The Jötnar Battalion had been expected to return to the military at some point in the near future. Political agreements between the government on Terra Nova and the Jötnar changed things considerably. Now the Jötnar were granted equal citizenship, which meant access to both the Navy and the Marine Corps. Their strength would be felt on Helios where once more the Jötnar would prove their worth in the fire of battle.

The 1st Jötnar Battalion

Jack leaned close to the side of the tunnel and strained his eyes to see as far as possible. The computer told him the bend was over a kilometer away, yet in the dark, slightly damp interior he could hardly tell. Dozens more marines waited like him, each with their weapons trained down the tunnel. Even as they waited, more marines arrived and brought with them the mobile defense units. Two ran past him with a Ram and an officer behind them.

"Get back!" called out the officer.

The two marines pulled open the sides of the Ram and removed boxes that were about the size of a man's head. The first of them went ahead of Jack and placed the unit on the ground. He could now see the shape. It was rectangular and enclosed inside a semi-transparent mesh housing.

"About right?" asked the officer.

Wictred waited in the middle of the tunnel and simply nodded in agreement. He was preoccupied, listening to the sounds of the approaching enemy forces that were getting louder and louder. The officer tagged the ground by using the engineer's interface inside his helmet. It was a simple device but incredibly useful, adding markers on the ground that could only be seen by other marines in the tunnel. The two marines positioned six of the devices and rushed back into the tunnel, away from Jack.

"Well, what now?" he asked Wictred.

Wictred snorted in reply at him.

"Watch."

His friend knelt down and tapped the rear of one of the units. The frame hissed and then expanded to a meter in each direction in just a few seconds. From inside, a tiny transparent bag inflated, filling the framework to create a sealed box.

"Uh, what are we supposed to do with that?"

Wictred tapped the other units and they did the same, much to his friend's annoyance. Unlike Jack, Wictred had been to the engineering briefing in the last week. He'd seen the demonstration of several new pieces of equipment, and these were the newest piece of tech in the Marine Corps.

"Just watch...give it a few seconds."

Jack waited patiently and almost gave up when he spotted a narrow flash at the base of the unit. A gray mist hissed out and filled the transparent bag. It made a high pressure groan and then stopped.

"Well?"

Wictred kicked at the gray shape, yet it refused to move. Jack moved to it but kept his head down, just in case. He tapped it, noting the sound and weight felt like concrete. It was dense but not as hard as stone, more like damp cement or even sand.

"Portable Barricade Units...you know, PBUs!" said Wictred. He tapped the top of the third unit as it filled with the gray mist. "Maybe attend the lecture next time. Each engineering platoon is getting kitted up with this stuff."

Jack watched as the defensive wall built itself before his eyes. As well as being a meter tall, they also fitted together, creating a solid defensive position from which to fight behind.

"Wait," Wictred said.

Jack looked up to his friend.

"What is it?"

He held up his hand to remind Jack to stay quiet. It only took a few seconds before Wictred looked back to Jack and the other marines in the tunnel. Sergeant Stone was jogging along its length and stopped next to Wictred.

"You heard?"

Wictred raised his head slowly.

"Yes, Sergeant."

Stone surveyed the defenses and seemed satisfied.

"Good, the engineers are establishing a reserve weapons store two hundred meters back. Rams have placed sentry markers and mines further into the tunnel. The Animosh are coming."

Private Frewyn stared into the tunnel.

"This way? How many?"

Sergeant Stone nearly smirked before answering.

"Son, you have a tactical overlay, why don't you start using it?"

That reminded Jack, and he switched to the larger scale overview. He almost choked when he spotted the swarms of flagged enemy troops converging on their position. He might have panicked, had it not been for the calm voice of his Sergeant speaking.

"Colonel Gun and the 17th have engaged the Animosh from every direction. They have broken their outer defenses, and rebels are pursing them. Drones show them falling back in massive numbers. The precinct and this transport hub are right in the center of their route back to their secondary defensive line."

"So if they want to get back, they will have to get through here?" asked Jack.

Stone nodded.

"Exactly. In less than two minutes, the entire east flank of the Animosh will try to break through three tunnels here. Our job is to hold this one, the lowest."

He turned, looking into the wide tunnel.

"And the largest."

He paused for a few seconds as if expecting something to happen. Finally, he spoke to the marines.

"Right. We have a job to do. Our friends in the precinct will stop any Animosh getting inside the hub from above. All we have to do is stop several thousand Animosh and their machines from getting through the shafts."

Another squad of engineer marines jogged past, along with four Rams. They stopped short of the mines and proceeded to deploy the Rams. From where Jack waited behind the new defenses, he could see the Rams lowering themselves to the ground, creating a number of defensive turrets. As they started to run back, the flags on Jack's helmet overlay flashed.

"Here they come, boys. Keep your heads down!" Sergeant Stone shouted.

Jack kept low and surveyed their position. The tunnel

was actually four separate tunnels and merged into a large arched hall big enough to house a military warship. Each tunnel was wide enough to drive three or even four Bulldogs abreast. The marines had constructed two defensive lines with the PBUs, and the engineering squad was busy constructing a third back near the platform. He couldn't make out the details other than that the wall was already two meters high and filled half the width of the platform. He counted two platoons of marines in position and waiting behind the two front lines, with the gaps mixed with Rams and other defenses. The lines were not complete, but they should be enough. Even so, he counted less than ninety marines against several thousand Animosh and their support units. The engineers were certainly capable of helping, but right now had their hands busy improving the third line, and he doubted another dozen marines would turn the tide, one way or the other.

"Hostiles, nine hundred meters!" shouted another marine.

Jack looked deep into the tunnel and watched the red outlines move closer and closer. The wall mounted sentry drones had already spotted the approaching enemy forces and sent the details to the waiting marines.

"Jack, why don't we just blow the tunnel?" asked Private Callahan.

"Who knows? Maybe they don't want us to cause any more damage."

Wictred heard them talking. He was walking along the line a short distance away from Sergeant Stone.

"We're not down here to kill them all. We're here to stop them moving their forces. The longer we can keep them busy, the better."

Jack was surprised at his friend's grasp of what needed to be done. He was right, of course. They were behind the frontline, yet this one place was used to move Animosh forces safely to a hundred different positions. If they destroyed the tunnels, they would just have to find an alternative. By letting them feel they had a chance, they could be contained, and that would give the Helions their best chance at finishing the job.

"Makes sense. We're here to pin their troops down so the rebels can end this. The 17th have surrounded them and are making breaches in their defenses. We are a thorn in their side. If they want to plug the gaps in their defenses, they will need to deal with us."

"Really? I don't think so," said Private Riku, "More likely we don't have the time or gear to do it. Have you seen the walls of this place?"

Jack looked off to his right and at the smooth wall. He'd assumed it was solid rock but on closer inspection could see it was some form of metallic substance.

"What is it?" he asked quietly.

Sergeant Stone appeared behind the group.

"Keep your eye on the tunnel, marines. We ain't paid

here for gawping. You will let them get close and then hit the bastards hard."

He pointed in the direction he wanted them to look.

"Look what we have here."

A six-wheeled vehicle with Animosh markings raced down the middle tunnel. The Helions' vehicles shared some similarities with those of the Alliance, but they tended to be smaller and were designed for urban pacification rather than general combat. The front was a sealed unit with a slab front and small vision slits, the perfect design for use in street riots. As it came closer, three more vehicles appeared behind it. They were all moving dangerously fast. White flashes danced about the turret mount fitted above the crew areas.

"Keep down!" Wictred called out.

He was just in time, for as the marines ducked, the burst of gunfire ripped into the PBUs. These were thermal rounds, the type of ammunition favored by the Animosh. The gunfire was wild and erratic, and with the vehicles bumping about, it was almost impossible for them to target any particular individual. They must have spotted the marine defensive line but nothing seemed to slow them down.

The charges? Why haven't they gone off? Jack wondered.

"Take aim!" Sergeant Stone ordered.

Every marine rested a rifle or carbine on the defensive walls and took aim at the approaching vehicles. They didn't need to be told to select the high-power modes; it was simply a matter of training. They waited, and the vehicles came closer and closer. By the time they were within four hundred meters the shapes of hundreds of Helions was just about visible. They were like a horde of wild animals, running or jogging after the armored vehicles. Jack looked back at the final wall the engineers were working on. He could see only four marines were guarding it; and behind that was the platform, the transport hub, and the rest of the tunnels.

This is insane. They'll run through us in seconds!

Wictred must have noticed his friend's nerves. He dropped down next to him even though half of his body was still exposed. There was something about Jack that had changed. It wasn't cowardice; he'd seen enough of that before. It seemed more like Jack had dropped his hotheaded arrogance of youth, something he'd always quite liked about the young man. Before, Jack would have leapt into battle without thought, just like him. Now Jack was becoming more calculating, as if he suspected life was in fact far more dangerous than before.

"You ready, Jack. This is gonna get messy, and we need guns on the line!"

Jack glanced at him and felt flushed with anger.

"Don't worry about me, Wictred, I know what I'm doing."

He spotted Sergeant Stone's arm in the air and then it

dropped, a simple yet effective signal for the entire unit.

"Fire!"

On the Sergeant's order, the entire front defense line opened fire. A full platoon, over forty marines, filled the tunnel with magnetized rounds from their carbines and six explosive shells from each squad's support L48 rifles. The front of the nearest vehicle vanished in a cloud of torn metal and glass. It quickly twisted and tipped as the driver tried to avoid the gunfire. It slid down the left tunnel on its left-hand side, its wheels still spinning wildly before coming to a grinding halt. The others managed to swerve to avoid the wreck and hurtled even closer before being stuck by more explosive rounds. In less than thirty seconds, the tunnel started to fill with noxious smoke fumes from the vehicles. Sergeant Stone walked along the line; upright and ignoring the stray rounds coming in from the approaching Animosh.

"Not bad, marines, not bad at..."

He flipped out his sidearm like a handgun from the old West and gunned down two Helions that rushed out from the smoke. They both fell face down to the ground. What shocked the marines nearest the killing more was that these were not Animosh, they were unarmored Helions carrying rifles.

"Who the hell are they?" Wictred shouted.

"Command thought as much. Justitium Lyssk must be getting desperate. He's drafting in militia from the Irkerk,

Yuulen, and the Sh'Dori. They have numbers, that is all."

"Sergeant!" called Private Jana Jenkell, the unit's medic.

The marines turned their attention to the smoke just as the first wave burst out. Jack's first view of them was of two combat drones and nearly fifty Helion militia. They looked hysterical as they ran with their guns firing. He took aim, but the advancing machines took all of his attention.

"Keep up your fire!" continued Sergeant Stone. He waited calmly and took aim with his pistol. Jack flicked the switch and proceeded to strafe the line with automatic gunfire. Puffs of blood marked those he hit, and countless figures fell to the ground. More and more continued forward, and even when the Ram gun turrets fired, they kept moving along. Two marines jumped up and ran back from the frontline, only to be hit in the back by thermal weapons.

"Animosh!" Wictred hissed.

Behind the civilians came a tide of the cloaked warriors. They seemed as keen to shoot their own militia as they were shooting at the marines. They used as much cover as they could find but refused to throw themselves onto the guns of the marines. Sergeant Stone ducked to the side as one tried to hit with accurate rifle fire.

"Animals, they're driving the civilians along like cattle."

Sergeant Stone's face turned when he realized what was happening. He spoke into his intercom over the platoon channel.

"Lieutenant, we have diversionary troops pouring in down here. Their main force is somewhere else."

Another marine was hit, and then an explosive charge tore a hole in the first barricade. Two combat drones pushed into the gap, blasting away at the marines a few meters away. Privates Sanford and Giblin were cut down; the others either fell back to the second line or tried to hold off the machines.

"This isn't right!" muttered the Sergeant.

He moved backward, firing his pistols as he went. He checked once more with the rest of the marine commanders as he moved.

No reply from the Lt.

"Marines, fall back!" he shouted.

The battered platoon moved back with only three marines and Wictred remaining to fight off the machines. Helion civilians quickly leapt over the broken defenses, only to be shot down by those waiting on the second. Jack was already moving back from the machines. He wanted to stay but thoughts of the things ripping his friends apart sent panic through his limbs. He took aim, but one of the marines jumped in front and was crushed as a third machine climbed through. They were not like the Biomechs' weapons of war. They were slower and more like mobile weapon emplacements. Even so, they were strong and able to deliver substantial gunfire.

"Jack, help me!" shouted Wictred.

Any doubts Jack might have had were discarded at the plea for help from his friend. He grabbed a grenade from the thigh mount and hurled it to the wall. As soon as it made contacted, it flashed white hot, instantly killing the three nearest. He moved his bodyweight forward, aiming his carbine at the horde of enemy pouring over their line. The L52 was a wicked weapon at this range, and he cleared the defenses so that Wictred and the others could break for cover. Even Wictred was forced to withdraw as the Animosh moved up and sheltered behind the broken defenses. More gunfire ripped into the tunnel, and the machines were finally knocked out. The surviving civilians scattered all directions, but the shapes of a hundred Animosh filled the cover behind the first defense line.

"What now, Sergeant?" Wictred asked from behind the next piece of cover.

Seven marines lay dead in front of them, and smoke had reduced visibility to less than fifty meters.

"Marines, fix bayonets!" growled the Sergeant.

There were no questions. Each did their work silently, and only then did Jack notice their lack of sound. They had beaten off the first wave, yet so many of the enemy remained a short distance away. A handful of grenades moved back and forth between both sides, which confirmed to Sergeant Stone that something had to change.

"I want that barricade retaken, are you with me?"

The marines in the second line shouted out

enthusiastically.

"Then follow me!"

The Sergeant was over the wall well before the others. Jack was sure he saw at least two rounds strike him, but on he went. Wictred was next, and then he found himself over the top and running back to the position they had recently abandoned. They surged past the wrecked machines and leapt over the outer wall to find themselves in amongst the Animosh. Whereas before the battle had been one of ranged firearms, now it turned into a bloodthirsty melee, with rifle butts and bayonets doing the hard work.

"This is insanity!" Jack said, but nobody heard him.

Wictred swung his fists and crushed anybody within reach. The Animosh desperately tried to fight them off. Jack stabbed the first Helion he saw, and then stumbled and landed on his back. He tried to move, but two more enemies stepped up to him, both aiming rifles. A great blast of air rushed overhead, and the two Helions vanished, to be replaced by the shapes of fresh marines. They surged past and two stopped to help him up.

"Who, what?" he said, confused.

"8th Marine Battalion. Looks like we got here just in time," laughed the first.

More of the marines rushed past, chasing down the retreating enemy forces. Jack glanced back and saw Stone leaning against Wictred, who was sitting down on the broken first barricade.

"Not bad, son," he said with his eyes squarely on Jack's face, "I said you had it in you."

He coughed and then lifted himself back to his feet.

"Okay, marines. Reload and get ready for the next wave. There are plenty more coming this way!"

Jack lifted his carbine, checked the clip, and then rested it on the broken defenses. Riku, Frewyn, and Jenkell all moved around him and did the same. Private Riku was the nearest, and she flashed him a smile that did more to show her facial scar than she might have wanted to. Even so, it filled Jack with a feeling of camaraderie that he really needed.

"You guys okay?"

"You kidding?" replied Private Riku, "I've been itching for some action for a while."

Jack was sure he could see a glint in her eye as she said it. He wondered if it was a clumsy attempt at a pass, and it distracted him for several seconds. He looked at her face, and although her scar was always noticeable, he couldn't hide the fact she was probably the most beautiful woman he'd ever seen. She spotted him looking and grinned.

"What? You like what you see?"

For what must have been the first time ever, Jack didn't know what to say. He opened his mouth to speak, but nothing came out. Private Riku nodded in the direction of the bodies and wrecked vehicles.

"Here they come. You ready?"

Jack took aim down his carbine and placed the reticule over the chest of a running Animosh fighter. He squeezed the trigger within a second of the rest of the platoon.

I am now.

* * *

Admiral Lewis paced the CIC of his flagship while he waited for the distance to close between the two fleets. Already his own forces were well within range of the approaching craft, yet so far not a single shot had been fired, and he was loath to be the first one to do so.

"Lieutenant Ryante, your thoughts?"

The young tactical officer didn't even have to think about it before she replied.

"Admiral. Our fighters have fired warning shots, and they are continuing on their course. In less than three minutes, they will be able to bring an exponential rate of gunfire on our forces. When we move past that window, it could go either way."

Yes, and we still have plenty of marines on board.

He looked at the officers on his bridge and back to the disposition of the remaining group of Alliance ships. He was tempted to contact Admiral Anderson again, but he didn't have the time.

You've already made one mistake today. Don't make another one.

"Very well. They've been given the chance. Let them

know we mean business. Target the battleship and give them a volley."

"Admiral."

Lieutenant Rola Ryante already had the lead ship in her sights. She tapped the final release button, and the ship hummed with power as the forward emitters unleashed incredible power. The particle beam was completely invisible in the vacuum of space, although the minute particles of dust around Helios allowed a small quantity of light to be reflected. At the speed of light, the powerful blast struck the battleship and exploded a section the size of a destroyer. Large chunks ripped off, yet it continued onward. Admiral Lewis almost called off the attack when scores of warning lights flashed through the CIC.

"Admiral, they are opening fire!" cried out Lieutenant Ryante.

"Very well."

He lifted the intercom and selected the channel to all the ships' captains. There were some orders that needed to be done personally and not by a computer.

"This is Admiral Lewis, engage the enemy fleet."

The opening phase of the battle was as short as it was bloody. The nine ships of the Alliance 4th Heavy Strike group used a mixture of particle beams and railguns to decimate the ships in the front of the enemy fleet. In the first five minutes, a third of the automated ships were burning hulks; the rest slowed their advance and interspersed themselves with the Alliance vessels. Rather than firing as individuals, they selected one target at a time, unleashing all their firepower into one place. The robotic fighters, on the other hand, ignored the capital ships, merely circling the Alliance fighters and drawing them into a cat and mouse game of space combat. The first ship to be hit was ANS Sentry. Hundred of shells and missiles rushed to her, but only a fraction made it past her battery of defense turrets.

"Is this all they have to offer us?" complained Admiral Lewis.

It wasn't that he wanted some great battle, but the destruction of a fleet as large as this made little sense. It would have taken considerable time to assemble such a force, as well as substantial resources.

"Admiral, the Confederate ships and the Khreenk battleship have changed course. They are on an intercept course with us."

"Stop them!"

She nodded and directed the primary weapons of four Alliance ships to the targets. Gunfire flashed from both sides, and now ANS Conqueror started to take damage. Even her massive batteries of defense turrets couldn't stop every impact.

"Gun ports open, they're launching nukes!"

Nuclear weapons were an old weapon for use in space. Though very powerful, they were nowhere near as useful as when used for terrestrial battle. In space there was no shockwave, and all ships were heavily shielded against radiation to protect their crews. Even so, a direct impact by a nuclear weapon could easily disable or destroy even the largest warship.

"New ships, range seven hundred kilometres!" called out the XO with a minor hint of surprise in her voice.

Admiral Lewis looked at the tactical screen and surprised to see the Alliance signature appear.

"It's Captain Hampel, Admiral. His ships are providing a defensive screen."

He smiled at this news. The small escorts were nothing compared to the massive capital ships, but their defensive weapons were the latest the Alliance had to offer. In tests they had been shown capable of destroying targets as small as a coin at incredible ranges. There were no formations now for this kind of battle. The ships from all sides were interspersed with the Alliance ships engaging the nearest threatening targets, as opposed to the automated fleet's system of selecting one ship at a time.

"All railguns load Sanlav rounds and bring them down."

The railguns had their benefits, and the older models of ships quickly turned to the special close ranged rounds developed early in the Uprising.

"What is the status of ANS Sentry?"

"She's sustained heavy damage. Her engines are offline. She can't take much more, Admiral," said the XO.

"What can we do to take the fire off her? Why did they target her?"

He looked at the displays. Sentry was the closest to the enemy battleship.

"She's the closest to their flagship!"

"Admiral?" asked the XO.

"Helm, set a collision course for their flagship. Maximum speed."

His orders shocked the crew. To them it must have looked as though he were mad, sending his own ship to destruction for such a modest chance of destroying an enemy ship. Even so, they carried out their orders, and they were soon heading toward the battleship. He had already sent the orders to the other ships to pull back and fire on the enemy at range. Almost immediately, the guns of the enemy fleet changed their targets and proceeded to fire upon the flagship.

Lieutenant Rola Ryante smiled inwardly.

"They are firing on whichever ship is closest to threatening their battleship. That is a pretty simple command system."

Admiral Lewis nodded quickly.

"Exactly. Their tactical systems are primitive at best. This fleet isn't here to destroy us. It is here to keep us busy while they do whatever it is they are doing. We will maintain a distance of ten kilometres. The rest of the fleet will select the smallest of their ships, one at a time. Keep firing until they are all burning."

"What about us, Admiral?"

His confidence had returned.

"Simple, I want us to present our beam to them. Captain Hampel and his escorts will form up on our opposite flank and assist with a defense screen. Every single gun will open up a flak corridor."

"And their ships?"

"Leave them to the fleet. We will take the punishment while they finish the fight."

The ships changed formation quickly, and in minutes the automated fleet concentrated its full power onto the single Battlecruiser. The occasional projectile struck into her flank, but incredibly after twenty minutes of continuous bombardment not a single nuclear missile had reached her. The 1st Battle of Helios ended with the complete destruction of the automated fleet for the cost of a single crippled Crusader class ship. By the time it was over, Admiral Lewis was sweating profusely. He looked over the casualty and damage reports. He counted less than fifty on his own ship, but it was the information coming back from ANS Sentry that almost made him vomit.

Two hundred and twelve dead, seventy-two wounded, and for what?

Because of his decision, hundreds of men and women were now dead or wounded. One of the newest Crusader class warships would need months of repair work, assuming it was even salvageable. He wiped his brown and ran his finger along the lines of data.

"Admiral, incoming message from the AJ Naval Station. It's Admiral Anderson," said the communications officer. He nodded slowly in reply.

"Put him on the main screen."

The face of the Admiral filled half of the main screen, and he was surprised to see the man was smiling at him. There was a delay while the signal worked its way from the Naval Station, through the Rift in T'Kari space, and then through Helios to his ship.

"Admiral Lewis, I have been monitoring the battle reports in the T'Kari Sector. You've done great work. Your Captains are to be commended. This is one of the most decisive battles in the Alliance's history."

Admiral Lewis wiped his brown again, wondering quite how many battles the Alliance had even fought in its short history.

"The ground operation is going well. Our troops have the Animosh and their commanders boxed in around the Triangle sector."

He took a short breath as if he was preparing for something bad.

"The T'Kari inform me they have intercepted communications between the Khreenk and the forces of Justitium Lyssk."

Now it was Admiral Lewis' turn to hold his breath as

he waited for the inevitable news.

"It looks like they are attempting a rescue of their High Command."

The face moved to the right, and a map of the Helios Sector appeared. To the left were the planet and the small group of ships under the command of the Khreenk Admiral. A short distance away sat the three ships led by ANS Crusader.

"Your ships are too late to stop them getting on the ground. I need you to blockade the planet. Do not let Justitium Lyssk and his commanders escape, or this war could go on indefinitely."

"Understood, Admiral. We're on the way."

CHAPTER THIRTEEN

The wild frontier of Alliance space was based in T'Karan, the area of space that was once the heart of the T'Kari Empire. With just a few small colonies of these advanced aliens remaining, they quickly turned to the Alliance for protection and became the first group of outsiders to join the growing empire. First there were just the humans that had originated on Earth. Then came the synthetics, creatures built for war with technology from an unseen race. The T'Kari were the third people to become part of the Alliance, but they would not be the last.

A Brief History of the Alliance

ANS Crusader and her two sister ships burned their engines at maximum power as they approached Helios. Directly in front of them waited the force of Khreenk ships, each of them sat in high-orbit like a group of fat slugs. The distance was less than a thousand kilometres when the shapes of two-dozen troop transports detached and made for the surface of the planet. Admiral Lewis watched the video feed from aboard ANS Conqueror.

"Admiral, can we open fire?" asked Commodore Andon Leson.

Admiral Lewis knew full well that destroying transports loaded with unknown numbers of Khreenk could be disastrous. According to Admiral Anderson there was a chance they might be on a rescue mission, but they could easily be mercenaries. Yet he had no idea who might be inside. It was just as likely they were simply prisoners. He just didn't know, and enough had died on his watch that day already.

"Have you been able to reach Admiral Lanthua?"

The Commodore looked back at him on the video communication channel. He shook his head.

"No, Admiral, he is refusing to answer our hails."

"Very well, your orders are to establish a close-proximity position and to deploy fighters. They are not to leave Helios, understood?"

"What if they try to leave?"

Admiral Lewis grinned.

"Then you will have to stop them, by any means necessary."

* * *

The last assault comprised over a hundred Helion militia that were forced to charge the guns of the marines, or face being shot by the Animosh security forces. Over a quarter of them tried to escape, but the Animosh were merciless. As the last civilian fell to the ground, Jack had to turn around and opened his visor. The stench of blood, smoke, and battle filled his nostrils, and he vomited behind their barricade. Wictred saw him and shouted over.

"Jack, you okay?"

He retched twice more before reaching for his water bottle and taking a swig. He spat on the floor and looked back to Wictred.

"Yeah, just great."

"Marines, this is it. They are falling back in large numbers. Push them back!" said Sergeant Stone calmly.

One by one the marines climbed out from whatever cover they were using and moved toward the place where the enemy had emerged. First they walked past or over the hundreds of bodies, then past the vehicles, and finally deep into the tunnel. The bight lights from their armor-mounted lamps lit the way and revealed the cost the civilians had played. Even that far back, there were bodies on both sides.

The civilians, they must have fought the Animosh, right here in this very tunnel. And we killed those that got away.

It took nearly twenty minutes for them to reach the higher level of the tunnel. There were fewer bodies there until they reached the loading area. This was the point where the surface tracks entered the tunnels. Scores of wrecked vehicles littered the place and bodies lay charred and burned to a crisp.

"Look!" called out Wictred.

Jack lifted his gaze to dark shapes in the sky. They were moving fast and off to the right. Vapor trails from scores of fighters and drones continued to fill the sky, but it was the dark shapes that seemed to interest the marine officers the most.

* * *

The numbers of civilians around the Triangle was growing. Gun's forces almost seemed redundant as he watched them climb through broken windows or over wrecked vehicles, overrunning previously contested enemy positions. It was just as well though; he looked at his own forces and was amazed by the amount of blood, dust, and dirt on their armor. Try as he might, he couldn't find a single unblemished marine. Lieutenant Read appeared, and he seemed even filthier than the rest.

"Colonel, out spotters have intel that the enemy has abandoned the transport hub. They are moving overland and easy prey to our air cover."

Gun smiled uncontrollably.

Good work, Colonel Koerner, your marines did their job. Now it's time to end this.

"Where are they going?"

"This is the strange thing, Colonel. They are moving to the docklands."

A series of at least twenty sonic booms echoed across the skyline, and above them emerged the black shapes of Khreenk troop transports.

"That's less than a kilometer away, behind those structures?"

He pointed at the towers off to the right.

"Yes, Colonel."

An urgent flash alert showed inside his visor. It was from the fleet. Before he checked it, he gave his orders to the rest of the marines in the area.

"Company commanders, keep up the pressure on the Triangle. All units within combat range of the docklands are to move there immediately. The Animosh are regrouping."

"Colonel!" called out a marine from the back of an open backed Bulldog. They were another of the variants used to transport small units of Jötnar and Vanguards. He climbed up, shouting orders to the rest of the marines. In less than a minute, the column of vehicles had broken away from the fighting. The remaining marines climbed over the debris littering the final defenses of the Triangle. Gun had a new objective, and as they accelerated toward the landing platforms in the docklands, he could see the dark shapes of the new troop transports heading in the same direction. He checked the aerial view of the docklands. This particular area was inside what had been the Animosh frontlines. His forces were spread thin, and he desperately needed numbers in position and fast. His eyes scanned quickly before he found the transport hub. It was only a short distance from the docks.

"Lieutenant, I need to speak with Captain Carter. I have a job for him."

* * *

Jack couldn't believe how happy he felt after climbing out of the underground hellhole. They were now two levels above ground and waiting at the side of an abandoned street. Most of his platoon was there plus marines from the other units that had so recently arrived to assist in the battle.

"What's happening?" he asked.

"Didn't you hear the Sergeant?" replied Private Frewyn.

Private Riku walked up and slapped him on the back.

"Jack, we have new orders."

She pointed one level up and just under a kilometer away. It was a raised platform with roadways running alongside it. Sitting on the platform was the dark shape of some alien transports.

"See that platform. Those are Khreenk transports.

Corporal Wictred says they are landing mercs."

"What?"

A group of eight Bulldogs approached. Half were the mobile gun units, the rest standard troop transports. Waiting hands helped pull the marines inside, but when it came to Jack's squad there wasn't space. Three more open-topped Bulldogs appeared with a number of Jötnar and Vanguards hanging onto them. Jack raised his arm. He found himself lifted inside by a familiar face.

"Jack?"

He looked into the grinning face of Gun.

"Gun? What are you doing here?"

Another helped Wictred inside, who then proceeded to smash his fist into Gun in what looked like a fight, but was the closest the Jötnar ever got to showing a normal level of feelings toward each other. He finally stopped and looked down at the two of them.

"You're in time for the end game."

Jack looked back. There were a large number of vehicles flying the unit pennants and markers of his own battalion. Gun must have assembled a mixture of units en route to attack the dockland area. Gun stood up and pointed ahead.

"Faster!"

The column of more than fifty Bulldogs continued at high speed. There was relatively little defensive fire, as they were well past the frontline and now inside what had been safe parts of territory controlled by Justitium Lyssk's forces. The highway became wide and split off into three main routes as they entered the outskirts of the docks. Jack looked at the dozens of mushroom shaped structures that pushed up high into the sky. Sitting upon the nearest six were the black transports and around them hundreds of soldiers clad in black armor. Even at this range, Jack could see them running for cover around the platforms.

"Attack!" he roared.

At this point the highway had essentially stopped, and the entire level was more like a massive flat runway, with the reinforced mushroom landing pads dotted about at intervals of two hundred meters. The Bulldogs spread out into a wide group, the mobile guns leading. They fired on the move and were quickly rewarded with a number of yellow explosions around the transports and the soldiers.

"Who are they?" Wictred asked.

Gun pointed at another ship that was moving to land on one of the platforms. He picked out the yellow runic symbols on the craft's flank.

"Khreenk ships. They must have paid them to turn this battle around."

He laughed as a shell exploded nearby and sent hot metal into the armored flank of the Bulldog. It shuddered slightly but continued on.

"It's too late for them; the rebels will have the capital within the hour."

That was when Jack saw the convoy.

"Look, to the left!"

Gun spotted them right away. It looked like a group of at least fifty vehicles of all different shapes and sizes, and they were heading right for the central landing platform. Atop the structure was another transport, but this one was even larger than the others, perhaps twice the size, probably capable of carrying two to three hundred warriors.

"It's Justitium Lyssk. He must be trying to escape."

Fifteen vehicles split off from the column and changed their course to intercept the advancing marines.

"They mean to stop us," Gun said, selecting an open channel to the other troops.

"All marines, we have to stop those transports from escaping. Bring them down!"

The black colored armored vehicles stopped two hundred meters from the central landing platform and then spun about to present their flanks. Armored shutters opened up, and hundreds of red armored warriors leapt out. Some climbed up on top of the vehicles. Others took cover behind them, but the majority spread out to use whatever cover they could find. By the time the marines were in range, they had established a cordon around the central platform. The marines might have been able to crash through them, but the black armored soldiers from the dozen transports already on the ground had to be dealt with first. Two Bulldogs were torn apart by the guns of the nearest waiting transport, and the rest scattered to avoid being hit. Gunfire hit them like rain, and within a few seconds three more of the Alliance vehicles were wrecked.

"Marines, dismount!" Gun ordered.

His personal Bulldog stopped and he jumped off, followed quickly by the other marines. There was ample cover with wrecked vehicles, crashed ships, and small buildings and control stations all around. They scattered to find cover; more and more gunfire tore into their positions. One round slammed into Gun's collar, and he spun around and fell to the ground. Wictred helped drag him to safety, but it was nothing more than a painful impact.

"What now?" he asked.

Gun looked out at the bloodbath around the platforms. His forces were outnumbered five to one, and the vehicles of Justitium Lyssk were already disgorging their precious cargo to the waiting transport. Gun wanted to order a full frontal charge but knew in his heart it would just get them all killed. He looked at his tactical map on his visor.

Yes, that will work.

"Colonel Gun. I need air strikes in this sector," he said to the nearest controller.

There were already dozens of fighters busily engaged in the battle overhead. In just a few seconds two flights of Lightning Fighters broke off and screamed past to strafe the ground target. As they closed, the gun turrets on the transports opened fire with terrifying effectiveness. Three fighters exploded as they blasted past. He called again, but a message interrupted him from high orbit.

"Colonel, this is Commodore Andon Leson. I have orders to stop these Khreenk transports leaving Helios. What is your status? Can you stop them?"

He leaned out from cover but like the rest of his forces, he was pinned down by superior firepower. He bit his lip so hard in frustration that blood trickled down the left side.

"Negative, they have a strong defensive cordon; I need more marines and air cover to finish this."

"What the hell!" muttered Jack, looking up.

Gun followed the direction of his gaze. A large dark shape had entered the atmosphere and was streaming toward the surface. Flames and smoke bellowed around it to give the effect of some great comet. Even as he watched, Gun's computer system was analyzing the ship and its trajectory.

That's not fair, he thought when the conclusion was presented. The ship was heading directly for the docks. The shape and size showed it was something close to a destroyer class, and no matter how many missiles were fired at it by Alliance fighters it wasn't going to be stopped. He looked at Jack and then to Wictred, both of whom were covered in a mixture of blood and dust.

"We can't stay here," Jack said.

Wictred placed his hand on Gun's shoulder.

"He's right. That thing will hit like a nuke. We have to move, and fast!"

Gun looked back up and spotted the black smoke trail of a burning ship. It must have been the size of a destroyer and was heading to the ground at such a speed it would never be able to recover. The marines were pinned down by gunfire, but even this sound paled next to the rumble coming from the falling ship as missiles tore chunks from its armor.

"They aren't helping; it's just turning from one target into many," said Wictred glumly.

The rattle of heavy caliber gunfire from the Bulldogs started to take effect, and Jack leaned out to watch a dozen of the black armored warriors fall down from the heavy fire. Given time, it looked like they might prevail, even against the odds. He lifted his carbine and took aim. A gentle squeeze, and he put another on his back, a smoldering hole in the soldier's chest armor.

Who the hell are they? he wondered.

Missiles rushed toward the ship from a gaggle of circling Alliance fighters, but it was already wrecked and out of control. Alarms flashed inside his head, and for the first time Gun felt real fear, not for himself but for his marines. He wanted Justitium Lyssk caught, but not by losing everybody around him. He looked at Jack, his friend's only son, and knew if he didn't act fast they would pay the price. The computer was still monitoring the falling ship, and it gave an estimate of just over a minute till impact.

"Marine units, fall back, immediately!"

He stood up tall, ignoring the incoming fire and roared loudly.

"Get back, now!"

It wasn't easy moving back but certainly safer than trying to engage the black armored mercenaries or the vast number of warriors around the landing platforms. The surviving marines clambered aboard those Bulldogs still working, and the rest simply ran as fast as they could. Jack and Wictred ran alongside Gun as the sound of the falling ship turned to a scream. He threw a quick glance over his shoulder and spotted the black ships lifting off from the ground and powering up their engines.

Bastards, they planned this!

Even the Alliance fighters were forced to rush from the scene, trying to get out of the danger area. A small number ignored their orders and continued to chase down the transports. Only one was brought down by the time the ship hit the docklands area.

"There!" Wictred pointed at a control tower.

The small number of Bulldogs swerved while trying to escape, and Jack, Wictred, Gun, and a dozen other marines ducked down along the lower frame of the tower. The impact was greater than any of them could have expected. Jack found himself lifted from the ground before he crashed to the floor. The impact knocked him out cold. A cloud of dust and shockwave smashed into the tower and around the rest of the marines.

* * *

Admiral Lewis stared at the Khreenk ships with an angry, almost bitter look on his face. The black transport ships that had escaped from the surface were already loaded inside. It was a standoff that he suspected could only end painfully. Several more vessels had joined the force to give Admiral Lanthua twenty-one ships, as opposed to the eleven functional ships of the Heavy Strike Group. Admiral Lewis had been forced to leave Captain Hampel's frigate squadron behind to guard ANS Sentry before she could be towed back to the Naval Station in T'Karan.

"So they send down one ship on a suicide mission as a cover to get Justitium Lyssk off-world. Ballsy," said Commander Lisa Sonels.

"Yeah, and it leaves us with a problem, a damned big one."

The communications officer turned around and nodded.

"Admiral Lewis, the commander of the Khreenk fleet wishes to speak with you."

General Daniels walked into the CIC and took up position on the flank of the Admiral. He spoke quietly so that nobody else might hear.

"The Zathee standard is flying over the capital. The revolution is over."

Admiral Lewis should have been happy, but the formation of warships facing him was of more concern to him than the planet right now. He twisted his head just a few millimeters.

"Good news, General. That is a good start."

He then looked to his communications officer.

"Put him on the main screen. I want you all to see this."

She nodded and pressed several buttons. As before, the image of the alien filled half of the mainscreen, with the rest showing a forward view from the fleet of Helios and the alien fleet sitting and waiting in high orbit.

"Admiral Lewis, it is good to see you again," said the alien through his translator, "I have orders to return my forces to Khreenk space."

Yeah, I don't think so.

Admiral Lewis shook his head angrily.

"Your people sent an automated fleet against my forces and caused untold casualties on Helios. You will stay here and face the legal system of the Helions themselves."

The alien did his best job to mimic the smile of a human.

"Ships coming from in from the Khreenk Rift!" shouted

Lieutenant Rola Ryante.

The large screen to the left of the main screen showed the tactical dispositions of forces around Helios. It zoomed out a little to show three of the nearest Rifts to the planet of Helios. Dozens of red diamonds marked out the ships.

"Forty-three capital ships, all Khreenk. They will be in range in twelve hours, Admiral."

He looked at the information and returned to the smiling face of Admiral Lanthua staring right back.

"These are the escorts for the Helion refugees my government has promised to help. We are setting a course for our Rift now."

The image cut without giving Admiral Lewis a chance to answer. Already the ships near Helios were powering up their engines and making their way away from the planet.

Sixty-four ships and the possibility of starting a war.

He looked at General Daniels who seemed tired and irritated as him.

"This fight is over, for now. You have to let them go."

He knew the General was right, but the thought of letting the dictator of Helios escape, along with an unknown number of his followers left a bitter taste in his mouth.

"I know," he said finally, with disgust in his voice.

General Daniels gazed at the fleet of ships as it moved away from Helios.

"We cannot risk open conflict with their ships. We have Helios secure. We can deal with this dictator if and when we see him again."

Admiral Lewis nodded in agreement, but he was less than convinced at the General's prognosis.

"What about the fleet we've already fought. Whose ships were they? If they were controlled by AI Hubs, then that mean somebody, probably the Khreenk, has contact with the Biomechs or their allies."

General Daniels didn't seem particularly surprised at this.

"Yes, I thought as much. I suspect they are receiving military or technological aid from the Biomechs. If that's true, then we need to prepare and not start a war, not today."

The two senior officers looked down at Helios from the mainscreen while the fleet of Khreenk warships moved away unmolested. Civilian traffic continued to move about as though nothing was happening.

"Signal from Colonel Gun. His forces are withdrawing to their forward bases. It's over down there."

Admiral Lewis sighed quietly. His chest had been pounding for what must have been hours, but at least the immediate crisis was over. He looked around the CIC and at his crew. All were busy, and ANS Conqueror had entered battle once more to come out relatively unscathed and with a single battle honor to her name. He tried to feel good about it, but the defeat of the unknown automated fleet left him feeling uneasy.

If we did so well, why do I feel like we've just been cheated?

* * *

Spartan grabbed onto his seat with his one good hand and clenched his teeth. They were only seconds away from the Rift, yet the gunfire coming from the pursuing Biomech warship was pounding them. Alarms seemed to be sounding from every single direction. Through the main window, he watched the station grow smaller and smaller. The second T'Kari ship was still there but was surrounded by continuous flashes of yellow.

"They are going to die, all of them, for us."

Khan watched, but he seemed less affected by what was happening around them. They were now seconds from the Rift when the blast occurred. Khan thumped Spartan and pointed at the display.

"Look, the station!"

He shouted at the nearest T'Kari.

"Magnify, now!"

The alien fumbled and tapped something. The image of the station enlarged to show the stricken T'Kari warship. Something was different. The burning remains of the ship were lying on the station as secondary explosions tore her hull apart.

"Those crazy bastards. They must have rammed the station!" said Khan, the admiration clear in his voice.

Their own ship shuddered and vibrated as more shells slammed into the hull. A small fire broke out at the front, but they all ignored it. The ship was now in the Rift, and it would be seconds before they emerged from the other side. As Spartan usually did, he held his breath as if he was under water. The tunnel was something of a misnomer. It was more a doorway. As they slipped through, they appeared somewhere else, a place that Spartan had never seen. He wasn't able to savor the moment because the Biomech warship was right behind them and entering the Rift.

"Spartan, we've got a problem...a big problem."

Then they were completely through and into a different sector. They covered several kilometers before the bow of the enemy ship appeared.

"Here they come," said Spartan softly.

The T'Kari moved through dozens of buttons and options, trying to keep their crippled warship as far away from their purser as possible. Then the Rift began to shudder. First it flickered like the crest of a wave as it shifted and moved about. Even the Biomech warship seemed to distort slightly, and then in the blink of an eye the Rift vanished, leaving the twisted remains of the front third of the Biomech ship drifting behind them. A single blue flash appeared from its center, and the remains tore themselves apart in a bright explosion. It looked like a growing ball of superheated plasma.

"Those crazy sons of bitches did it!" laughed Spartan, his relief clear in his face.

The image of their forward view moved slightly as the ship drifted out of control. At first they saw nothing, and then the great blue orb shifted in front of them. All five of them, even the T'Kari gazed at the shape with awe on their faces. Spartan wiped the sweat from his face and whispered to his friend.

"We're home."

He looked back at the blue planet, with its great oceans and large landmasses. He'd seen pictures of the world before, but he had never expected it to be quite as stunning as it was.

* * *

The lights faded slowly from black to daylight over a full minute. The windows from the medical facility looked out onto the city and provided a distraction for the many patients inside the building. Teresa opened her eyes slowly and looked about. She immediately noticed the monitoring equipment, machines, and cables attached to her body. She almost panicked but forced herself to stay calm. Her limbs felt weak, and for a second she feared she might be crippled. She lifted her hands in front of her face and sighed a breath of relief. The door opened, and in walked a doctor. He stopped at the end of her bed and looked at her.

"Major Morato, how are you feeling today?"

She wiped her eyes and tried to remember what had happened. She could see the images of the fighting on Helios, the blood, and her son. That was all.

"What happened?"

The doctor moved closer.

"You lost a lot of blood and suffered head trauma. You were in a coma until last week. Since then you've been moving in and out of consciousness."

A coma?

She almost panicked at the news.

"How long?"

The doctor sat down on the bed beside her.

"You've been here almost nine months now. We didn't expect you would wake up after the violence your body went through."

"Jack?"

The doctor smiled.

"Private Jack Morato? He's just fine. I spoke with him less than an hour ago. He is on his way back to Terra Nova, along with the casualties from his unit. Your other two children are also coming here. They will arrive within the week."

"What's happened to him?" she asked, worrying about

the mention of the casualties.

His face relaxed a little.

"Not him, sorry. He came through the ground combat completely unscathed. He's one of the Heroes of Helios. Our forces helped overthrow the Helion dictator. We are now allies of Helios."

Teresa looked at him and then out of the window to the towers and buildings of Terra Nova, the capital world of the Alliance. Although she felt weak, she forced herself to sit up, raising her gaze to the skies.

Now all I need is to find Spartan.